W[illegible]nd?

S[illegible]as passed before Hannah's brain r[illegible] what her eyes were seeing. Pushing through the door was Buster the alligator, his mouth full of wildflowers.

Like a bouquet, she thought wildly as Buster took a step toward her.

That was it. Hannah leaped onto the counter and scrambled over it, landing in a surprised Buck Shanahan's arms.

"Oh, my God," Hannah whispered.

"Shh," he said. He didn't put her down.

Moving slowly, Buster edged his huge body into the office. His gaze never left Hannah as he made a relatively quiet groan and dropped the flowers on the floor.

"I don't believe this," Buck whispered.

Then, slowly, with great reluctance, Buster backed his huge length out of the office. Outside, he offered another mating roar.

"Wow!" Buck said. "Buster just brought you a bouquet."

Hannah stared at him, seeking balance. "I'm underwhelmed."

Also by Sue Civil-Brown

The Prince Next Door
Breaking All the Rules
Next Stop, Paradise
Tempting Mr. Wright
Catching Kelly
Chasing Rainbow
Letting Loose
Carried Away

Sue Civil-Brown

Hurricane Hannah

ISBN 0-373-77114-2

HURRICANE HANNAH

This edition published by arrangement with Harlequin Books S.A.

www.HQNBooks.com

Printed in U.S.A.

No alligators were harmed in the writing of this book. No humans were harmed by alligators in the writing of this book.

Poker is not advocated as a way to settle disputes or make money, except on Treasure Island.

Flights to Treasure Island depart regularly. Return flights are unpredictable.

Buster will meet you at the airport. Bring a chicken.

To the survivors of Katrina,
from survivors of Charlie, Frances and Jean.
Our prayers are with you all.

Hurricane Hannah

CHAPTER ONE

HANNAH LAMONT DIDN'T have a whole lot of choices left, and she busied herself debating who she was going to skin alive: her mechanic, or the jerk who'd sold her this piece of junk claiming it was in A-one condition.

Because right now, she and the corporate jet she was ferrying were in serious trouble. Evening dimmed the sky, the clouds reddened with warning, the islands below looked too small and unpopulated, and her fuel was running low thanks to something that had blown about fifteen minutes ago. Her radio had quit, so she couldn't call for help or direction, and her hands gripped the yoke as if they were throttling someone.

She bought and sold used corporate jets for a living. Never before had she ferried one in this kind of condition. Paranoid thoughts of sabotage began to swirl around the back of her brain.

She couldn't imagine how Len, her mechanic, could have missed anything essential when he checked out this plane. She knew he'd spent four weeks bringing it up to snuff. And bringing these used jets up to snuff kept her in business. She took pride in delivering planes that were as good as new, even though they might have already been flown for a decade or more.

So what had gone wrong this time? Some kind of metal fatigue? Something that there was no way Len could possibly have noticed? Or just plain crazy bad luck?

But what the hell. She could always go out in a so-called blaze of glory.

Then she spied salvation. On an island that was mostly a volcanic cone, she saw not only signs of civilization, but, also, on a plateau, she made out an unmistakable airport. It was a small airport, and she could only hope she would have enough gas for the reverse thrust, because those landing strips looked awfully short.

But what choice did she have at this point? She couldn't even warn them she was coming in. She just had to go. Dipping down low, she circled in and said a quick prayer. This or nothing.

As she descended to one hundred feet and circled the field in the standard oval approach pattern, she passed over the heads of a gaggle of people who looked at her like she was crazy.

Well, she *was* crazy. If she hadn't been crazy she never would have taken over her dad's business in the first place. No, she'd have found some sane job in an office somewhere where she didn't have to put her life on the line on a routine basis. Because she couldn't escape the fact that flying the Caribbean skies was asking for trouble, what with countries that wouldn't let you land, smugglers who were trying to fly off the radar, commercial flights that thought they owned the airways and small, private planes piloted by people who shouldn't be allowed to get both feet off the ground at the same time.

And of course, always the risk of being mistaken for a drug runner herself. But her luck there had been pretty good, when all was said and done. She'd only been shot at once, and held at gunpoint twice. So far the local police had been fairly decent to her. Once they ran their drug dogs all over her plane, that was.

And in some airports, she was even left alone.

This flight to Aruba should have been a piece of cake. She hadn't even had to fly into the Bermuda Triangle, which always gave her the willies, wondering if *this* was the time some bubble of methane would decide to thaw and rise from the sea floor, thus depriving her plane of all lift.

But what should have been, wasn't, and as soon as her wheels touched the runway, she threw on the reverse thrust for all it was worth. At least that worked. The shields immediately dropped behind her engines, redirecting the push forward.

But still the end of the runway raced toward her too fast. This was an airport meant mostly for small planes, and older prop jobs, not jets that had to come in faster in order to maintain lift. She had the brakes on for all they were worth, the flaps were at full, and all her hopes hung on the fact that she was light, having lost almost all her fuel.

She heard her tires screaming, and expected to hear them blow. The runway wasn't smooth either, forcing her to jolt so hard her teeth banged together.

Oh, God! The runway disappeared almost right in front of her!

She wanted to close her eyes against her coming demise, when she realized that her plane was slowing so fast that her safety harness cut into her shoulders and lap like a knife.

Thank God!

Moments later, she and her plane came to a shuddering halt with only a few feet to spare.

For a long moment, she sat perfectly still, trying to catch her breath. Then the adrenaline turned to fury, and she wanted to kill someone. Now.

And anyone would do.

ON THE TARMAC below, Buck Shanahan's adrenaline was also surging. He peeked at his hole cards again, though he didn't need to. The two black Sevens were right where they'd been last time. Coupled with the

Seven of Hearts on the table and the two Jacks on the table, that gave him a full house—three Sevens and two Jacks—and a chance to even things with the man who sat across the table from him.

Bill Anstin had become Buck's nemesis. Treasure Island had been so perfect before Anstin moved here with his high-stakes dreams about turning the island into a major casino resort. Buck liked it just the way it was: sleepy, peaceful, an ideal place to hide from the world.

Each had a constituency. The old islanders, offspring of castoffs from neighboring islands and the earliest white settlers, tended to side with Buck. Anstin's backers were the new arrivals, most of them Wall Street wizards on the run from the SEC and their investors, looking for a place to hide and launder their ill-gotten gains.

As with every controversy on Treasure Island, it was litigated at the poker table, the "Court of the Green Felt." Buck versus Anstin, heads-up, no-limit Hold'Em, best two out of three games. Last week, at his casino, Anstin had hit a lucky flush to win the first match. This week they were playing on Buck's turf, at the island's small airport. And Buck was about to take him down and even the match.

When the jet came screaming in over the airport, Buck and Anstin and their audience instinctively ducked low and covered their ears. It passed right over their heads, the jet wash sending cards flying all over the tarmac, before the pilot circled back around and hit the runway with a screech of rubber and the roar of twin jet engines on full reverse thrust.

Craig, Buck's mechanic, stared wide-eyed at the plane as it screeched and roared farther down the runway. "What the hell?"

Buck stood up and bit on the end of his unlit cigar tight enough to make his jaw hurt. "Idiot. Flying jackass!" He watched, somewhere between fury and fear as the pilot of the jet struggled for control, the tail fishtailing a bit as if the reverse thrust weren't distributed evenly between the engines. In his heart of hearts he believed his runway wasn't long enough.

"Get the fire fighting equipment," he barked at Craig Thomas, and started trotting down the runway. "This is one pilot I want to save so I can strangle him."

The list of offenses was long. Not radioing ahead to request permission, not checking landing conditions, not being sure the runway was long enough…. Not to mention scaring the hell out of him. And—by far the worst of the violations—scattering Buck's winning cards.

The jet finally rolled to a stop, within twenty feet of the end of the runway. Behind him, Craig caught up in the golf cart that was their only fire engine. It wasn't like they were a major airport. Buck caught the rail and bounded up, standing on one foot as they drew close to the plane.

The engines were winding down. Then, with an awful choke, one of them just stopped. Moments later the other choked, too.

Buck heard that sound and felt his heart slam. Okay, so maybe he wouldn't kill the pilot. The guy had come in on fumes. But then his anger surged again. What the hell was he doing flying on fumes anyway?

What if he hadn't found Buck's airfield?

Worse yet, what if that jet had rolled off the runway and over the lip of the plateau?

And why couldn't he have waited until Buck finished the hand?

HANNAH LAMONT SAT at the controls, her hands still frozen on the yoke. Ahead of her, just a few feet from the end of the runway she had almost run out of, spread a beautiful view. All of it sharply downhill. All of its tropical glory shouting: "Death!"

She actually wasn't sure she was alive until she realized her hands hurt from gripping the yoke. Prying her right hand free, she reached for the throttles and pulled them back, shutting down the already silent engines.

Then she started shaking like a leaf in a hurricane.

Adrenaline, which had carried her this far, fled like a rat off a sinking ship, leaving her all too mortal and filled with aftershocks.

It wasn't that her life had never been on the line before. When you flew smaller aircraft, you often had a lot of near-misses. But this one was different somehow.

Different, she realized suddenly, because it never, ever, should have happened.

Anger sparked in her again, renewing the strength in her limbs. Unclasping her harness, she rose and stomped back behind the pilot's cabin and hit the button that opened the door and dropped the steps. The hydraulics, working like a charm, hissed as the door opened from the top and descended, turning the steps right-side up.

She was just about to step on the first one when a golf cart carrying two men raced up.

She didn't like the look of the guy who was standing on one foot and hanging onto the rail. He looked like an afternoon thunderstorm that had sprouted the stub of an unlit cigar. Handsome, yes, but angrier than an alligator that had missed dinner.

"What the hell," he shouted, "did you think you were doing?"

"Choosing life," she shouted back. "I suppose you'd have preferred I ditched it?"

"Radio," he said. "You have heard of the concept?"

By this time he was off the cart and standing at the foot of the stairs, glaring up at her.

"It went out on me. Half an hour ago. Then I started losing fuel."

"And you were idiotic enough to take this piece of crap into the air?"

That did it. The rats returned to the sinking ship and brought more adrenaline along with them. She stomped down the stairs, stopping on the bottom one so she could look this jerk in the eye.

"It wasn't a piece of crap when I left. You got a problem, take it up with my mechanic. I sure intend to."

Then she pushed past him and started striding back up the runway, going she knew not where, just needing to be away from this idiot until she had sorted through the last half-hour and decided just how she was going to kill Len, her mechanic.

"Where do you think you're going?" the guy demanded. "This is *my* airport and you can't leave this garbage on my runway."

She turned and faced him, hands on her hips. "Just how do you propose I move it? There's a leak in the fuel line somewhere, and there aren't enough fumes left to taxi her. Maybe, Mr. I-own-the-airport, you can tow it? I'll pay."

Buck watched her storm away, and the funny thing was, all he noticed was the beautiful red hair and the way her rear end swayed. A beautifully shaped rear end, cased snugly in her green flight suit.

"Dammit!" he swore.

"Come on, Buck," Craig said reasonably. "Let's get the trash off the runway before someone else tries to land. Then you can argue with her some more, 'cuz she sure as hell ain't going anywhere."

Buck was in no mood to listen to reason. He bit down so hard on the end of the unlit cigar that his teeth cut through it. Swearing, he spit the pieces out and glared toward the woman's retreating back as if she had caused it to happen.

Hell, she *had* caused it. If he weren't so damn mad at her.... And who the hell did she think she was anyway? The Queen of England?

"Come on, Buck," Craig said impatiently. "We gotta get this thing off the runway. It's a hazard."

Grunting, Buck hopped up on the golf cart and the two of them zoomed—well, as fast as they could in a golf cart, anyway—back toward the hangar.

She was a woman, he reminded himself sourly. A woman. God had put women on this earth to make life hell for men. They were trouble on two feet. Headache and heartache and every other kind of ache. He should have *known* there was a female at the yoke of that plane. It should have been obvious from the moment she zoomed over his head.

Craig spoke as they neared the hangar. The

woman pilot was approaching one very angry crowd. "Whatever you're thinking, Buck, just put it aside for now. This is business."

"Yeah. Like my cards weren't business?" Business. That's all it was. It wasn't as if he didn't have to deal with idiots on a regular basis. Just because she'd scared the bejesus out of him didn't make her a worse idiot than the rest.

But she had cost him a critical win. Now he'd have to play another match against Anstin to save the island, and he didn't like having all of that riding on his shoulders. Another match. He swore savagely.

He felt his breast pocket and realized he didn't have another cigar on him. Hell's bells. Glumly he folded his arms and decided he could grind his teeth for a while instead. He wasn't all that anxious to face that wasp again, and certainly not just for a cigar.

No, he'd rather take the whole thing on the chin at once.

HANNAH THOUGHT she had lost her mind, run over the edge of the cliff and landed in hell. H—E—Double-hockey-sticks, hell.

Because, as she approached the crowd that had been gathered around a small table, cards wafted on the breeze and people started yelling at her and each other.

"You idiot!" one man shouted. "He was gonna win!"

"I saw it," yelled another. "He had a full house."

"Yeah, right," said a woman. "Like I believe your lying mouth."

Then they all turned and glared at Hannah.

"You," said a short, stubby man with the face of a bulldog, "may have just cost us our island!"

Well, someone was insane, she thought. Not knowing what else to do, she fled into the office beside the hangar before they could gather a lynch mob.

THE OFFICE was tiny but it was surprisingly neat. Hannah found a coffeemaker with a pot on the hot plate that looked freshly brewed. She sniffed it warily and realized that not only was it fresh, it was Jamaican Blue Mountain coffee. Her favorite. She inspected one of the dozen ceramic mugs hanging on hooks from the wall, found it apparently clean, and poured herself a cup.

She sat on one of the plastic chairs before a window that gave her a view of the entire runway. Her blood was still boiling, and she could hardly wait to find a way to phone Len and tell him what she thought of him.

Then her hands started shaking violently. She had to put the mug down on a dusty table as shudders began to run through her. The adrenaline was letting up and reality was sinking in. She had come *that* close to dying. That close. Those engines had quit at the end of the runway. Too close.

Then the tug drove past the front window, and Mr. I-own-the-airport gave her a mocking salute. Anger flooded her again, saving her from her momentary weakness. It took a lot of effort not to flip him the bird in return.

That shocked her. She didn't do stuff like that. She didn't use those words or gestures. Maybe she was a little…crazy right now?

The anger had done her good, though. Her hands were no longer shaking, and she picked up her mug, determined to look as if she made emergency landings on a regular basis. As if not a single one of her feathers had been ruffled. She wouldn't give that idiot male the satisfaction of knowing that she had, for even a few seconds, been terrified out of her mind.

The coffee was *delicious.*

CHAPTER TWO

BUCK AND CRAIG MANAGED to coax the dead jet back down the runway and into the already crowded hangar without so much as scratching the paint. They greased the job with some colorful language, but, at last, the shiny but dead Learjet 36 was parked next to Buck's pride and joy: a fully refurbished, heavily pampered and polished DC-3 he used to ferry supplies to the island.

Unfortunately for Buck, the DC-3 didn't have quite the charm when viewed beside the sleek, self-important jet.

"She's a beaut, ain't she?" Craig remarked as he came to stand beside Buck.

"She can't fly, that's the kind of beaut she is."

"Aw, Buck, can the crap, will ya? The woman had no choice about landing. You heard those engines die. She's a damn good pilot for pulling it off in one piece."

That was the part Buck wasn't quite ready to acknowledge. He wanted to stay mad for a while, especially when his mind insisted on resurrecting the image of her bottom as she walked away. He didn't have room in his life for that kind of stuff. At least not the kind of stuff she was probably handing out with all the usual emotional strings as the price tag.

In fact, he'd moved to this godforsaken island to get away from all the Delilahs of the world. Last thing he needed was to get the hots for one who was not only beautiful, but a pilot, as well. Dangerous territory there.

"Let's close up," he said, refusing to respond directly to Craig. The daily afternoon thunderstorm was rolling in, and while he'd built this hangar to withstand almost anything, you never knew. But one thing was for sure, the reinforced steel doors had to be closed and barred for maximum security. He didn't care about much, but he cared about his planes.

Outside again, with the hangar securely buttoned down, he paused to take in the golden glow of the late evening, and the reflection of it on the arcs of cloud that were approaching. Tropical Storm Hannah was edging toward hurricane force, last he'd heard. There was still a chance she would miss the island, but that chance was shrinking steadily.

From his aerie, Buck saw that the cruise ships had already vanished from their moorings, sailing off to friendlier, safer climes. Anstin's casino, a series of huge tiki huts that sheltered the machines, tables and bars, was probably already moving everything into storage. The fishing town itself, of late containing more casino employees than fishermen, had started battening the hatches that morning.

But Hannah might pass them by. Even if she hit, the storm shouldn't be too bad.

Shaking his head, he realized he couldn't find an excuse to stand out here any longer. He was going to have to go into his office and work out the business details with the Valkyrie.

He still believed that Eve was the biggest joke God had ever played on mankind.

THERE SHE WAS, sitting on one of his plastic chairs, looking like she owned the universe, holding a cup of his finest Jamaican. Had he offered her coffee? He was sure he hadn't. But then, a redhead who looked like that was probably used to having the world at her feet, used to having her own way. *Delilah.*

He wiped his hand on his pants, just to make a point of it, then extended it. "Sticks, I'm Buck Shanahan," he said, adding nothing that might illuminate her.

"Hannah Lamont." She shook his hand a little too firmly, as if she were used to the world of men and the handshake. Maybe to make a point.

"So what the hell happened, Sticks?" he asked as he rounded the counter and opened his humidor, seeking further dental protection in the form of a cigar to chew on. It was better than grinding his teeth.

"I don't know. My mechanic signed off on that plane before I left. I was on my way to Aruba to drop her off for her new owner. All of a sudden I was leaking fuel like a hose. Then my radio went out. And while we're talking, my name is Hannah, not 'Sticks.'"

"Seems like you might need a new mechanic. And until I decide otherwise, you're 'Sticks,' because that's what I was holding, ready to even things up with that bastard Anstin, when you tore in here like a bat out of hell and killed the hand."

"Pocket Sevens?" she asked.

"Damn right. I made Sevens full of Jacks on the turn and was about to get all of his chips. Instead...."

She held a hand up. "I'm sorry I messed up your little game for something as silly as trying to survive."

"Little game?" He took a slow breath, willing himself not to tell her exactly what he thought of her. "That was no little game. It was a heads-up match to determine the future of this island! Or did you think those people you passed on the way in here were joking?"

"You're not serious," she said.

"I'm dead serious, Sticks. That's how we decide things around here. Only fair way to do it, and a damn sight fairer than U.S. elections lately. And it saves us from being overrun with lawyers." He let out a huff. "*Little game.* You know about as much about life as your mechanic knows about jet engines."

She didn't even smile. "He's certainly going to be dead once I get back to Houston."

He wanted to like her then. He really did. But he decided he didn't need the headache.

"We'll take a look at her," he heard himself volunteering, then wanted to kick his own butt.

"Thanks. My company will pay, of course."

"Of course." Then something struck him. "*Your* company?" She bristled a bit, as if expecting a comment about how it was rare to see a woman who owned an aircraft company. It would never have crossed his mind if she hadn't bristled. Now he needed to bite back the urge to tick her off.

"I own it." Her voice was sterner than it needed to be, a sort of tacit offer of a duel at dawn. "Lamont Aircraft. We buy and refurbish private planes."

"Looks like this one didn't get refurbished enough."

"Do tell." Her voice dripped with sarcasm.

He unwrapped his cigar and stuck it between his teeth, deciding it was safer to bite tobacco than bite her head off. God should never have invented women. Or if he had to, then maybe he should have made them more like men: uncomplicated.

And now he found himself feeling almost sorry for her mechanic. *Damn!* "How long you had that mechanic?"

"He's been with the company fifteen years."

"You don't look that old." He was almost delighted when he saw *her* grind her teeth.

"I'm old enough. It's my company. And I want to know what went wrong with that aircraft."

"We'll get to the bottom of it," he promised, which he shouldn't have done, but when Delilah was in the room, men were known to do stupid, stupid things. "Craig and I are pretty good mechanics."

Instead of saying something snappy, she merely said, "Thank you."

Well hell. Now she was going to get nice on him? No thank you!

He rolled his cigar to the other side of his mouth and clamped down on it. "It'll take a while, of course."

Her eyes widened. "How long?"

"Well, I don't exactly carry a parts store for Learjets. In fact, this'll be one of maybe three or four times I've worked on one."

"Oh, great."

He grinned, enjoying her discomfiture. "So I'll have to figure out what's wrong, then fly out to get parts. And I can't do that until after the storm passes."

"Storm?" She looked even more unhappy.

"Don't you pay attention to the weather reports?" That would be a mortal sin for any pilot.

She snapped. "Of course I do!"

"Then you can't have missed the fact that we have

a tropical storm headed our way. It might even be a hurricane by the time it gets here."

"I was flying around that," she said.

"Well, Hannah, get ready to meet Hannah, because you sure as hell flew right into her path."

"THAT WOMAN IS a piece of work," Buck told Craig as they stood staring up at the Learjet while waiting for the shop computer to download schematics of the plane.

"Yeah. All women are," Craig agreed. And he was married and had three kids.

"Why do you suppose that is?"

"I dunno. I just know we can't live without 'em."

"I'm working on it."

Craig snorted. "That woman volcanologist—Edna, isn't it?—she's got her snare set for you."

Buck looked at him, and Craig finally shrugged. "Okay. Have it your way, boss."

"Believe me, I intend to."

Craig rolled his eyes. Buck chewed a little harder on his unlit cigar and wondered why it was that men who were married wanted every other man on the planet to be married, as well. It was almost like some kind of brainwashing.

"That Mary Jo must've really been something."

For an instant, Buck froze. He couldn't believe Craig had mentioned that woman. His former wife in his former life. The woman who had screwed around with all the available navy guys while her husband, Buck, was at sea as a carrier pilot.

"I told you not to mention that name."

"Sorry, boss."

That would teach him to have one too many beers. A slip like that and he was hearing about it for the rest of his life. He glared at Craig who held up both his hands.

"Sorry," Craig said again.

"You better be." He returned his attention to the jet, thinking he wouldn't mind sitting in the left hand seat and taking her out for a spin. It had been a while since he'd flown anything that fast, and sometimes he still yearned for his fighter-jock days. The speed, the g-forces…they got into a man's blood.

He sighed and went over to the computer to see how far along they were on printing out the fuel-line schematics. Sheesh, the thing was as slow as molasses at the North Pole.

"It's the satellite uplink," Craig said knowingly.

"Yeah? Then fix it."

"Damn, boss, you don't want much!"

"Then tell me why the satellite uplink should be so slow." He rotated his unlit cigar to the other side of his mouth.

"Do I look like a psychic? Probably because of the approaching storm. Traffic is likely heavier than usual. I dunno. Maybe it's not the satellite uplink at all. Maybe it's the printer."

Buck was acting like an ass and he knew it. Admitting it didn't make him feel any better. But the truth was, it was getting late in the day, and the probability they would have those schematics in time to work on the plane today was highly unlikely.

And worse, his win against Anstin, his prime opportunity to save the island, had fluttered away in a blast of jet winds.

"Why don't you just go home?" he suggested. "Unless the storm hits, we'll start in the morning. And take the woman with you."

"To that motel? No way. I wouldn't put my worst enemy in that cockroach pit."

"Then what am I supposed to do with her?"

Craig shrugged. "She can sleep on her plane." He jerked his thumb toward it. "It looks posh enough for a sultan."

"Except a real sultan would be buying a new one."

"Quibble, quibble, quibble. You need to get laid, man. Then maybe you wouldn't have all that energy to waste on stupidity."

With that, Craig stalked out the side door, a man-sized door, that hadn't been locked up yet. Buck stood alone in his hangar with two large planes and a couple of small ones that belonged to island residents, and wondered why he put up with Craig.

Of course, Craig was a natural-born mechanic. That helped. In front of him, the computer still hummed, a bar showing that the download had progressed eleven percent. Beside it, the big printer was busy drawing schematics. How complicated could it be?

Complicated enough. A plane, any plane, was a complex beast, and the newer they were, the more that complexity had been magnified.

So he had two choices. One of them involved going back to his office and facing the redheaded Valkyrie. The other meant sleeping out here on a battered recliner in the small parts office.

He decided the Valkyrie presented the lesser of two evils. He'd shoo her off to sleep on her plane, then peace would prevail, at least until morning.

He opened the door to the outside, rather than the one farther to the rear that joined with his living quarters behind the front office. Whenever he could, he preferred to walk outdoors.

But this time he froze on the threshold. Red sunsets weren't unusual in the tropics, but this one blazed like fire, and it raged in the east, rather than the west, high in the sky because of the clouds of the approaching storm.

Magnificent. He soaked it up, filling his heart, mind and soul with the beauty. *That* was why he'd moved to this godforsaken island with its loony inhabitants and crazy casino. Because here he could live halfway up the side of a volcanic cone and be left pretty much alone while still running an adequate business.

Stepping out, he worked the mechanism that safely reinforced the door from the inside, then walked around to the front of the hangar to look west.

The sun was riding the rim of the Caribbean like an angry red eye. The water, usually a soothing Caribbean blue-green, was dappled in red and purple, and beginning to look choppy.

There was nothing in the world, he thought, like the sunset before a tropical storm.

Then, without warning, a different red filled his vision. It was silky, redder than red in the evening light, a fluffy cloud around a perfect face with challenging green eyes.

"Did you find out what was wrong?"

He might have sighed, except he didn't want to give her the satisfaction. Instead he clamped down on his cigar. "Nope."

"Why not? I thought you said you'd find out what was wrong?"

Now he bit down hard. "Actually," he said between his teeth, "I'm printing out the fuel line schematics right now. At the rate it's going, it'll probably take all night. You can thank the manufacturer for that."

Her eyes flashed. In that instant, they looked like lightning reflected off the stormy gray-green shallows of the Caribbean Sea. But then, as if something flicked a switch in her, the flare quieted.

She nodded acknowledgement to him. "Thanks."

To his surprise, it didn't look as if she had to force the word out. Temperamental but in control. Despite himself, he was piqued.

At that moment, Craig roared by on his way down to his home in town. His Jeep kicked up a little loose gravel as he went by, waving at them.

Hannah Lamont waved back, then returned her attention to Buck. "I'll sleep on the plane then."

"Sure. No problem." He pointed to the door. "Bar it when you get inside. No telling when that storm is going to hit."

She nodded, but this time a flicker of uncertainty crossed her face. "See you in the morning, then."

She started to brush past him, but then he had to deal with the fact that not only was he being a jerk, he was being a *rude* jerk. There were some courtesies he couldn't ignore even in an attempt to avoid Delilah. "You got anything to eat on that plane?"

"I was supposed to be in Aruba shortly."

Mentally kicking his own butt, he said, "Come on back to the office. If I have to make dinner for myself, I might as well cook for two."

"You cook?"

He wasn't sure if that was an intentional insult or just genuine surprise. So he opted for surprise. "Yes."

He rolled the cigar a little before adding, “Not all men are helpless without women.”

Her eyebrows arched. “I didn’t mean that. I *don’t* cook.”

No! He didn’t want to like her. No way. Instead of responding, he stalked past her toward the office and soothed himself with the reminder that she would vanish from his island the very instant he repaired her plane.

There was security and safety in that. A promise of the uncomplicated future he really wanted.

CHAPTER THREE

HANNAH WAVERED between wanting to strangle Buck Shanahan, and wanting to like him. He was as prickly as a pear cactus and seemed to have taken her in instant dislike. Other than ruining his poker hand (and she still did *not* believe that so many people could be insane enough to determine the fate of their island with a poker game) during her landing, she couldn't imagine why. Well, she *had* been a little… upset when she deplaned, but any person with a half-ounce of common sense would understand what she'd just been through. Adrenaline tended to make you that way.

Still, he fed her. He didn't invite her into the inner sanctum behind his office, nor did she especially want to go there, but when he emerged a half hour later he offered her cold potato salad, cold fried chicken and a healthy serving of steamed broccoli. All of it was savory. She gave him marks as a cook, if not as a mechanic or human being.

"That was wonderful," she said when she'd

sucked the last bit of meat off the bone. If it hadn't been rude, she'd have licked the plate, too.

"Thanks." He sounded gruff. Then he took their plates into the back, leaving her alone to look out at what was now getting to be a very dark night. She could see a portion of the earth's shadow on the highest clouds, an arc of darkness moving toward zenith now, the red winking out behind it.

She supposed she ought to go out to the plane before it got any darker, but she felt strangely reluctant to move. So instead, she helped herself to another cup of coffee, and settled back in the chair.

She expected Buck to remain in his hermitage, but to her surprise he returned and sat on the far side of the counter from her. She could just see his head above the countertop.

She decided to try being sociable. "How long have you had this airport?"

"About eight years."

"And before that?"

He looked at her. "Top Gun."

She sat up straighter. "Really?"

He scowled at her. "Why would I lie about that?"

"I can't believe you could give that up!"

That made him smile for the first time since she'd met him, and oh, what a smile it was. It transformed him completely.

"Eventually my back had enough of the g-forces. And I had enough of the Navy."

"But you must miss it."

"Yeah," he admitted reluctantly. "Once in a while."

"This must sometimes seem pretty tame."

He cocked a brow at her. "Not when people try to take my head off with their wings. It reminds me of that Samuel Johnson quote. 'Nothing concentrates the mind like the imminent prospect of being hanged.'"

She nodded, wondering if there was more to a man who could quote Samuel Johnson, but said only, "I wondered if I'd have to ditch her."

He shook his head. "Not a good thing, ditching. Planes tend to fall apart in all the wrong ways."

"So I've heard."

Silence fell between them for a few moments. Then she asked, "Where did I land, anyway? There are so many small islands out here, and while I have a general idea where I am, I'm not sure which lump of rock I'm sitting on."

He rotated his cigar to the other side of his mouth. "This lump is called Treasure Island."

"You're kidding."

"Nope. The first person known to have settled here was One Hand Hank Hanratty about eighty years ago. He was a fan of Robert Louis Stevenson, I hear." The cigar bobbed as he resettled it. "Rumor has it the alligator bit off his hand."

"The *alligator?*"

"Yeah. Apparently Hanratty brought him as a pet. Says something about the guy's character. Anyway, Buster, the gator, is still around. Hanratty isn't."

"Well, if he brought only one gator, I can understand why the thing bit off his hand. Buster must be lonely."

Buck shrugged. "He goes to Bridal Falls sometimes and scares the tourists when they're having a tropical wedding. Mostly he just keeps to himself. Nobody wants to get him a mate, though. This isn't his native habitat, and we don't want the place crawling with gators, either. It'd scare the tourists."

Hannah nodded. "What do tourists come here for?"

Apparently she'd asked exactly the right question, because Buck suddenly grew expansive. "Well, now, there are really cheap cruise lines. They like to pull into harbor here and let their passengers gamble at the casino. They market it as tropical charm, but what it really is is a bunch of big tiki huts with games, slots and a couple of bars. I guess it impresses people who come from way up north."

Hannah nodded, envisioning it. "It would have a certain kind of charm, I guess."

"If you've never been to Vegas or Reno, yeah. Anyway, they pull in for a day of gambling, and sometimes passengers will get married by the captain at Bridal Falls. I don't reckon anyone knows who was the first person to do that, but it's become a bit of tradition in these parts. Townfolk will attend to make it festive."

"That's nice."

"It's downright stupid, if you ask me."

She felt herself bristling at his attitude, but tamped it down. She needed this idiot to repair the plane. She also needed to use his radio or phone or *something* to let her buyer know she would be late. Although after this he might not want the jet at all. She smothered a sigh. "What about the mountain? It looks like a volcanic cone."

"It is."

"Active?"

"That's the story."

Gloom began to settle over her. Could it get any worse? "How active?"

"It shrugs from time to time. Been awhile since the last eruption, though. Maybe five hundred years."

"How often is it supposed to erupt?"

He suddenly grinned at her over the countertop. "Getting nervous, Sticks?"

"Absolutely not!" She had the worst urge to bean him with his cigar. Purposefully irritating, that was what he was. "Do you ever light that thing?"

He took the cigar from his mouth and studied it. "Why would I want to do something that stupid?"

"Then what is it doing in your mouth?"

He grinned again as he looked at her. "I have this oral fixation."

To her horror, she blushed beet red. Quickly she looked away, out the window, hoping the last bit of red light would hide the blush.

"I'm going to bed," she announced, rising quickly and putting her mug on the counter.

"Good idea," he agreed. "You want to get some sleep before the storm hits."

That froze her in her tracks. "Can we check the weather?"

"Sure. I've got a feed."

She was relieved to hear it. At least this godforsaken airport had moved that far into the twenty-first century.

He turned behind the counter and flipped a dial. Soon a mechanized voice was reading the forecast. Then he flipped another switch and a fax machine began to print out a weather map.

Interested, as all aviators were interested in the weather, Hannah forgot her embarrassment and leaned over the counter, listening and watching.

"Tropical Storm Hannah has developed wind speeds in excess of sixty-five miles per hour. The storm has stalled at its current location and appears to be strengthening, with the barometer steadily falling...."

"Hell," Buck said. Moments later he ripped the fax off the machine and stood up, putting it on the counter so they could both look at it. Their heads came close to knocking.

"Cripes," he said, "look at those isobars. It's tightening up."

"Do you have an earlier map?"

He turned and pulled a sheet of paper off a shelf. "Here, see?"

Indeed the lines that measured barometric pressure were drawing closer together, around a circle that could swiftly become the eye of a hurricane.

"It doesn't look good," she said reluctantly.

"No, it doesn't." He took the cigar from his mouth and tossed it in the trashcan. "If she'd just kept moving, we'd have had a tropical storm. No big deal except for the casino. But if she stalls out there long enough, she could become a real beast."

Hannah nodded and met his blue eyes. "I don't like this."

"Me neither. You might be here awhile, Sticks."

"Is this place safe?"

"I built it to be. I didn't want to lose everything every couple of years."

"Well," she said hopefully, "maybe even if it becomes a hurricane it won't go past Category One."

"We can hope." He sighed. "Come on, I'll walk you out to your plane. I forgot you don't know your way around."

The late evening was perfectly still, and growing

darker by the second. The land had not yet cooled below the temperature of the surrounding water, so nothing moved. Later there would be a breeze, but right now the night was quiet and balmy. The air, full of moisture, felt soft to the skin. Hannah thought prosaically that in a climate like this, there'd be no need for moisturizers.

Buck opened the door to the hangar, letting her pass through first. He'd left a light on near the computer, so the cavernous space wasn't completely dark. The printer was still humming, although the computer had gone into screensaver mode. Reaching out, he threw the switch that turned on the lights above Hannah's plane. Then he went to look at the progress on the schematics.

He moved the mouse, and the progress bar appeared. "Nineteen percent. This is unreal."

Hannah looked at the long stream of paper that was folding up on the floor. "No kidding. That's my fuel system?"

"One and the same. And that's less than twenty percent. We're going to have our work cut out for us unless we find something obvious."

"Well, it had to be some place the fuel could leak from fast. I didn't have a whole lot of time."

He nodded. "We'll find it. In the meantime…"

"Yeah, get some sleep. You'll wake me if things start to get worse?"

"Sure, why not? Worrying is a useful thing to do."

She scowled at him. "I don't want to worry. I want to enjoy the storm."

"Enjoy?" He looked at her like she was crazy. "You're kidding."

"I love storms. Always have. I'd like to be awake for this one."

"Well, if it decides to move this way," he said almost sarcastically, "I doubt you'll miss it."

She cocked her head and put her hands on her hips. "Were you born a boor?" Then with a toss of her long red hair, she strode away through the dimly lit hangar to her plane.

"Wait a minute," he called after her. "You have to lock the bar on the inside of this door after I leave."

Annoyed that her high-dudgeon exit had been interrupted, she stomped back to him. He went to the door and pointed to a lever. "Throw this to the right. The bar will lock in place. Even Buster won't be able to get in."

Then he was gone, leaving her to fume. She threw the lever, glad to lock him out, then started back to her plane.

Not even Buster would be able to get in? All of a sudden she felt creeped-out. Why would he even mention it? Did that alligator actually sometimes come into this hangar?

Nervously she looked around as she hurried

toward her plane. It was a relief to ascend the stairs, then pull them up behind her. Alone at last, she tumbled onto the bed in the tail without even pulling off her flight suit.

Enough was enough.

CHAPTER FOUR

HANNAH AWOKE in the morning to find herself eyeball-to-eyeball with a huge pair of reptilian eyes. For a few seconds, she was absolutely certain she was imagining them. Then the hair stood up on the back of her neck.

The alligator seemed to be grinning at her, his mouth hanging open. She froze as still as a statue, hoping he would think she was dead, not sure if that would work for an alligator, wondering how the heck he'd gotten on her plane, wondering how the heck she was going to get *off* her plane.

Then the alligator lifted his head and let out a deep, inhuman roar that seemed to bounce off the walls of the small cabin and shake her eardrums so hard it hurt.

Oh, Lord, was that a threat? Did alligators roar before they attacked? She felt the most childish urge to pull the covers over her head and convince herself she was hallucinating this.

Despite her best efforts not to move, a whimper

escaped her and she pulled back. But, to her amazement, the gator didn't leap at her in attack. No.

Buster looked wounded.

She shook her head, convinced her eyes were deceiving her, but nothing changed. The alligator looked hangdog. Hurt.

"Buster?" she said cautiously.

The gator's head came up, and he eyed her with something that seemed like hope.

Astounded, Hannah considered the possibility that this relic of the dinosaur era had learned something about human behavior. What other kind of behavior would he know, never having had another alligator to talk to?

Cripes, she *was* losing her mind. Reptilian brains didn't have emotions.

Did they?

Slowly, taking care not to startle the beast by moving too quickly, she pushed back the blanket she had pulled over herself sometime during the night. Buster watched, but made no move.

Slowly, she stood on the bed, which had replaced a row of seats against the rear bulkhead, wondering if she could leap across him to the aisle before he could turn in the confined space.

The option failed to excite her. She'd never been any good at the long jump, never mind jumping from a dead start.

Buster cocked his head, watching her from one eye, then let out another deafening roar. At once she rediscovered her ability to jump…backward. Pressed against the rear bulkhead, she studied her nemesis while wondering what it would feel like to be devoured alive. Not pleasant, certainly.

But once again Buster looked hurt, as if her moving away was not what he wanted. Well, of course he didn't want it. The farther away she was, the harder she would be to catch and eat.

Then he did something she would have thought impossible, something that nearly curdled the blood in her veins. He reared up and got his front legs on the bed.

"Oh, God!" The prayerful words escaped her lips, and all thought of not being able to jump disappeared in a wash of adrenaline. Before she had another coherent thought, she ran across the bed and leapt over the gator, reaching the floor—and his tail—in a flash. She kept running up the aisle toward the door, hoping the hydraulics would open the hatch before Buster caught up.

Another roar followed her, this one almost a groan. She could hear scraping as scaly skin began to slide around on the industrial carpeting.

She slammed her hand on the emergency button and watched the hatch begin to lower. *Hurry! Hurry!*

The sound of scraping alligator skin was growing closer. Afraid to wait any longer, the instant the stairs were halfway lowered, she climbed out onto them and then jumped.

Her ankles stung as her feet hit the concrete floor. She wanted to keep running, but now that she was no longer confined, she couldn't help but turn curiously to see what happened.

Moments later, Buster's head appeared in the hatch. If an alligator could have sad puppy-dog eyes, this one did. The sound that escaped him now was nothing like his earlier roar. It was, she thought wildly, the alligator equivalent of a whimper.

Hardly reassured, she backed up. Lumbering as if stairs were unfamiliar, Buster began to descend the now fully opened gangway.

Hannah backed up. Swiftly. If she had an ounce of common sense, she'd flee at once from this hangar and send that annoying Buck Shanahan in here to deal with Buster.

Which, she decided, much as it might wound her pride, she was going to do.

Then she remembered from countless TV shows that alligators could move very fast. Faster than one might think.

That did it. She turned and ran for the door, her feet barely touching the floor. Behind her, scaly scrapes followed quickly. Buster apparently had no intention of letting her out of his sight.

She reached the door, but of course it was barred.

She worked the lever as quickly as she could with sweaty palms, and at last managed to throw it back. She could hear Buster right behind her, but she refused to look back. That would only waste valuable escape time.

With a mighty shove, she pushed the door outward and darted through it.

The heat and humidity of the tropical morning felt like a punch in the face. She hardly noticed it as another growl propelled her away from the hangar, toward the office. As she ran, she vaguely noticed that the clouds had come no closer, but appeared darker than yesterday. Heat waves shimmered above the runway in the heavy air.

And scales still scraped behind her.

All of a sudden, Buck Shanahan appeared around the corner of the office. He was dressed in the same khaki as yesterday, though the clothing looked fresher.

"What the hell—?"

She ran right past him, saying, "Get rid of that prehistoric beast. *Now!*"

It didn't help to hear his laugh as she flew toward the office door. Once inside the air-conditioned building, she collapsed on a chair and put her head between her knees, feeling as if she were on the edge of fainting…or vomiting, either of which would embarrass her to death.

Closing her eyes, she clung to self-control.

A few moments later, Buck sauntered into the office and closed the door behind him.

"Did you kill him?" she demanded.

"Hell, no. He's an island icon. They'd lynch me."

She lifted her head and waited a moment for the world to stop swimming in the adrenaline sea. "He was *on my plane!* He tried to get *on my bed!* And he was roaring at me…."

"Roaring?"

"Roaring."

He started laughing.

She managed a glare and resisted the urge to throttle him. "What's so funny?"

"Well, Sticks, alligators roar for only one reason."

"What? They want to eat what they see?"

"Nope." He grinned around the ever-present cigar. "It's a mating call."

Hannah's jaw dropped. It was entirely possible that it dropped all the way to the floor, but she didn't bother checking. "What?" she asked finally, hoarsely.

"I guess he thinks you're the prettiest thing he's ever seen."

"Oh. My. God." Hannah put her head in her hands.

"Hey, it's a compliment."

"What? That he thinks I look like an alligator?"

Buck chuckled. "Relax. I'll get you some coffee and breakfast. He'll hang around for a while, then wander off to a cool pond before he overheats."

"He was on my plane!"

"So you said."

She really, *really* wanted to draw and quarter this guy. No sympathy. No human feeling. Laughing at her fright. Wasn't she entitled to be frightened when a huge alligator appeared beside her bed? Only a fool would be sanguine about that!

"You're crazy!" she declared finally, a wimp-out when compared to strangling him.

"Probably." He didn't appear at all disturbed. "Blame it on the tropical air."

"You must have blacked out one too many times."

That got his attention and he glared at her. "I was a Top Gun, Sticks. I *never* blacked out."

"Maybe you just didn't know it."

"Flying what I was flying, I'd have known it." He scowled at her. "What's with you, anyway? I told you Buster's a fixture around here."

"Not on my plane, he isn't."

All of a sudden, Buck's frown slipped into a cockeyed grin. "You must smell real good to him."

That was the point at which, if some weapon had been handy, she would have landed herself in prison for life. The only alternative was to storm out, but before she lifted her rump from her seat, Buster's roar sounded outside.

Buck shook his head. "He's really determined."

"Tell him I'm not interested in his species."

Buck, still grinning, asked, "What species *are* you interested in?"

"Nothing from Mars," she shot back.

"Ho! You read that stuff?"

"Shut your mouth, Shanahan, before I shut it for you."

"You know something, Sticks? My mouth is usually shut. It would help if you would stop provoking me."

"What? Now it's *my* fault you're an idiot?"

He put his hands on his hips, and now she could no longer read his face. The tip of his cigar bobbed up and down as if he were chomping rapidly on it.

"You," he said finally, "are walking proof of why *I* avoid Venusians."

"If I'm lucky, the mother ship will rescue me soon."

"It won't be soon enough for me." With that he walked out of the office, leaving her alone to stew in her own juices.

The last of the adrenaline washed out of her system, and she crumpled like a deflated balloon.

She didn't need this.

AS BUCK STRODE toward the hangar, hoping that the schematics would reveal some kind of quick fix for Hannah Lamont's plane so he could get her out of here as swiftly as possible, Buster was shambling away into the shade of the tropical foliage in the direction of the nearest pond. He'd spend the rest of the day there, keeping cool and dining on the occasional fish or too-slow bird.

Damn woman, he thought. She even had Buster confused. Whatever had made the gator board her plane? Or go into the hangar to begin with? Buster was far too canny a beast to box himself in like that.

Shaking his head, Buck entered the hangar and marched over to the computer. Sometime during the night, the download had finished, leaving him with a heap of schematics to run over.

He sighed as he looked at the printout. Personally, he preferred the older planes. Simpler. Easier to repair. He could even machine parts himself for his DC-3. That stack of printout was nothing but an indictment of modern complexity.

Then he felt like a hypocrite. After all, he'd flown some of the most complex machines in the world, and had loved it. He just didn't think he could repair one with the facilities at hand.

Bending, he lifted the stack from the basket on the floor and carried it over to the metal desk, where he dropped it. Switching on the desk lamp, he sat and began to pore over the schematics, checking for the likeliest point of failure before he started tracing the system.

Craig arrived on the dot of eight as he always did. He was probably the only person on this island, apart from Buck, who believed in being prompt. Everyone else seemed to suffer from a "whenever" mentality.

Which was fine for everyone else. It would have driven Buck up the wall in an employee, however. Sometimes he thought he just ought to give up and live on mañana time like the rest of the world. It would probably be better for his general health, not to mention his teeth.

"You're looking uptight, boss," Craig said, the first words out of his mouth.

"You'd be uptight if you had to deal with that vixen."

"Yeah?" Craig grinned. "Got you on your toes, huh?"

"She's got me p.o.'d is what she's got me. And while I'm on the subject, can you tell me what the hell Buster was doing in the hangar?"

"In here?"

"Yeah. What's more, he was on the Lear this morning. In fact, he was Hannah's alarm clock."

Craig's jaw dropped. "You're kidding."

"No, I'm not kidding. Big as life, there he was, and what's more, he was making his mating call."

Craig's eyes widened, then he started to laugh. Much as he wanted to stay annoyed, Buck started to laugh, too.

"The gator has the hots for her?" Craig choked out as he laughed. "Nobody's going to believe this!"

"Well, I saw it."

Craig chuckled. "Hey, did you hear on the radio? Tom Regan dropped thirteen hundred to Bill Anstin last night."

"You're kidding," Buck said. "Tom's not great, but he ought to be able to clean Anstin's clock. What happened?"

"Anstin was feeling cocky after playing here yesterday, so he and Tom Regan were playing five-ten-limit at the casino until the tourists left. Regan challenged Anstin to a heads-up match. Five-ten, no-limit. Thousand dollar buy-in. Regan was down three hundred and decided to rebuy, then two hands later he's holding King-Queen on a flop of King-King-Nine. He pushes it all in—"

"And the other guy had pocket Nines," Hannah said.

Buck hadn't heard her approach, and turned. "What're you doing here?"

"I heard him come in," she said, angling her head toward Craig, "and heard the two of you laughing. I thought I'd check and see if y'all have made any progress on my jet."

"Ah," Buck said, pointing to the stack of schematics. "Not yet."

"But I'm right, aren't I?" she said, turning to Craig.

He nodded. "Yeah, Anstin had nines full."

Buck couldn't resist a smile. As much as he hated to see Bill Anstin win, it was even better to hear that

Tom Regan's three kings had cost him a thousand dollars against Anstin's full house of three nines and two kings. Regan was the island's mayor, and Anstin owned the casino. The two of them were, in Buck's view, trying to ruin Treasure Island by turning it into a major tourist resort. And that was what yesterday's card game had been about.

Just as bad, Regan and Anstin kept hounding Buck to waive the landing fees for the tourist charter planes that Anstin booked. And Buck simply couldn't afford to do that. It was a long-running bone of contention, and anything that made either of them miserable was just fine with Buck.

"So this was on the radio?" Hannah asked.

"Yeah," Buck said. "Why wouldn't it be?"

"Wait," she said, holding up a hand. "Is that Bill Anstin? The World Series bracelet winner?"

Damn, Buck thought. Beautiful, a pilot, and she knew poker. A trifecta of danger. "Yeah, that's him. Took his winnings and built the casino here. Lords over it like he's God's gift to gambling."

Hannah laughed. "As if! He'd never have made the final table if he hadn't rivered that straight flush against Chris Ferguson. Ferguson flopped the nut flush, and Anstin hit runner-runner."

Buck couldn't resist a smile. Everyone on the island knew the story of the final table, where Anstin was dealt one monster hand after another, taking down two previous world series winners en route to the championship.

But few people remembered that hand against Ferguson, a hand that Anstin should never have played to begin with, and certainly not the way he had. Holding the Queen of Spades and the Four of Hearts, he pushed in all of his chips, trying to bluff on a flop of Jack-Six-Three, all Hearts. Former World Series winner Chris Ferguson called him holding the Ace and Queen of Hearts, an Ace-high flush. Anstin caught the Deuce of Hearts on the Turn, and the Five of Hearts on the river, giving him a straight flush, Deuce-Three-Four-Five-Six of Hearts.

Anstin's odds of hitting the cards he needed to win were one-in-five-hundred. It was one of the legendary bad beats in World Series history, but it had happened on an outer table, away from the television cameras, and it was largely forgotten outside of poker circles.

If Hannah Lamont remembered it, she must be a serious player. And since she was also a business owner, she might be good pickings.

"So you like poker?" he asked.

"I'm from Texas," she replied, as if that said all that needed to be said.

He nodded. "We have a game here, a couple of nights a week. If you're interested."

"Buck…." Craig said cautiously, as if sensing what Buck had in mind.

"Just a few friends," Buck added, ignoring him. "We play three-six, no-limit."

"Sure," she said with a casual shrug. "I'll give it a try. It's not like I have much else to do."

"Tomorrow night at seven," Buck said. "Back of the hangar."

"I'll be there."

As if she could be anywhere else.

CHAPTER FIVE

BUCK COULDN'T help it. As the vixen walked away toward the door, all he could see was the gentle sway of her hips. And of course she couldn't leave without another word.

All of a sudden, she stopped and turned. "Is there anywhere I can get a shower?"

The idea of her in a shower filled his mind with all sorts of images that belonged in a men's magazine. For a few seconds his tongue clove to the roof of his mouth.

"Sure," said Craig, drawling. He pointed to the emergency gravity shower over in the corner of the hangar, a defense against caustic spills and burns.

Hannah put her hands on those luscious hips. "Thanks, but no thanks."

"You can use mine," Buck heard himself say, another one of those Delilah-induced moments. It was like being under an evil spell.

"You don't mind?"

He shook his head. Mind? He'd have to be out of

his mind to mind. "Go through the back door of the office. The bathroom is off to the right."

"Thanks."

She shifted directions and headed back to her plane, prolonging his agony. When she re-emerged from the Lear, she was carrying a duffel.

"I thought," she said as she passed him, "that I'd be vacationing in Aruba. I guess it'll be here instead."

Vacationing here? Running up the side of the volcano and jumping into the crater was beginning to sound like a pleasant alternative. Certainly a safer one. But then he remembered Edna. Nope. No running up the side of a volcano for him.

Then, thanks to all powers that be, Hannah disappeared through the door. All of a sudden the air lost its thickness and he could breathe again. He ignored the strange look Craig was giving him.

"Let's take a look at these schematics."

"Wouldn't it just be easier to look for signs of the spilled fuel?"

Buck gave him a look. "Sure, go ahead. Be my guest. In the meantime, I'm going to find out exactly what we're getting into here so I don't mess it up."

Craig sighed and pulled over a stool, the metal legs scraping on concrete. "No seat of the pants, huh?"

"Not with this one. I want that woman off this island in one piece just as soon as I can manage."

"Yeah, right."

Buck glared at him, and Craig wisely shut his yap.

BUCK'S APARTMENT behind the office was pin-neat, although darkened by a shortage of windows…probably deliberate because of storms.

Hannah couldn't resist looking around a little out of curiosity. The man had apparently brought Navy habits with him into civilian life. Every bit of furnishing was utilitarian. Nothing appeared to be out of place. A check of the refrigerator showed it was spotless, and also offered the bounty of some fresh fruit. Grabbing a pear, mindful that it was probably terribly expensive given how far it must have come, she ate it, loving the way the juice trickled down her chin.

Having seen everything else, she was no longer afraid to look in his bathroom. It, too, was spotless, and the shower stall gleamed. The hot water felt like heaven and she took longer than she might have otherwise. When she at last emerged, she was pink from the heat and her fingers were beginning to prune.

When she had toweled off she decided that since she wasn't going to be spending the expected time in Aruba, she might as well wear some of the nicer clothing she had brought.

Like the sarong she'd bought years ago in Jamaica, a lovely combination of blues and greens. Sandals…and a barrette in her hair that was decorated with a small but colorful flower.

A glance in the mirror told her she looked okay,

so off she went to find a ride to town, because if she had to spend all day with Buck Shanahan, there was going to be blood on the floor.

Then she returned to the hangar and said, "Can someone give me a ride to town? I need some necessities."

Buck glared. Craig jumped to his feet. "Sure," he said.

AS THE JEEP bounced along, rounding one tight switchback after another on their way down the mountain, Craig glanced over at Hannah, obviously trying to decide whether to say something. Finally, he spoke.

"You really ought to find a way to bow out of Buck's poker game tomorrow night," he said.

"Why?" she asked. "I like poker. It's fun, and I'm going to be bored beyond belief if I don't find something to do."

"I understand that, Ma'am, but…."

"First, it's Hannah, not Ma'am. 'Ma'am' is my mother, or my grandmother. Second, I'm not going to be offended if you guys smoke cigars and tell bawdy jokes, if that's what you're worried about. I have three brothers. I think I've probably heard it all."

"It's not that," he said. "Look, if you're bored, I'll give you a ride to the casino tonight. They'll still have the poker tables open in the restaurant. Play there. Don't play in Buck's game. Buck's game is the toughest on the island, bar none. He says it's just a few friends, but they play hard and they're all damn good. I don't play in Buck's game. My wife would kill me if I did."

"I don't feel much like being stranded away from my plane if the hurricane should happen to pick up speed," she said. "And I never gamble with money that I can't afford to lose."

"Well, that's what you'll do if you sit at Buck's table," he said. "Take my word for it."

"You never know, maybe I'll get lucky," she said.

By this time they were riding along a dusty street framed on either side by small, colorful shops. Not many people seemed to be out and about, however. Maybe they were all working. Or maybe they were battening down for the storm.

"You'll need to, Ma'am…Hannah. Well, here's the island grocery. Do you need me to show you around?"

She smiled. "I woke up with an alligator staring at me. I think I can navigate the wilds of a grocery. But thanks anyway. Meet back here in an hour?"

"Sure thing," he said as she climbed out.

So this was going to be a major tourist resort? she wondered as she looked around. It looked more like a Caribbean version of Shantytown, U.S.A. Across the street from the grocery was the requisite tourist T-shirt shop, and a few other shops appeared to specialize in island-themed knickknacks, but by and large the town center looked tired and more than a bit run-down.

The grocery itself was a small shop, more the type she commonly saw in Europe than the big box supermarkets she was accustomed to in the U.S. The shelves were plywood on two-by-four frames, closely packed with what seemed to be a hodgepodge of items in no discernible organization. But she was able to find the few staples she needed—bread, some cold cuts, milk, juice, mustard, coffee, cream and sugar—and the prices were not much higher than she'd have paid in Houston. Considering that everything had to be flown or shipped in, that surprised her.

The grocer, an elderly man who introduced himself as Horace, the sole surviving descendant of Hank Hanratty, leaned over the counter to chat as she set her selections down. "So you're the fruitcake who ruined last night's game. I hear Buck had sevens full."

At first surprised, then a little irritated, Hannah answered, "I had to make an emergency landing, yes."

The old eyes, a faded blue, smiled at her. "Does him good to get shook up once in a while. You'll have a run for your money, though."

"A run for my money? Over what?"

"Buck. That volcanologist has her cap set for him."

Hannah bristled. "I can assure you, I don't have my cap set for anyone. I just want to be on my way to Aruba."

He nodded as if he didn't believe her. Now he was definitely smirking. "Maybe not," he said doubtfully. "Casino's damn near shut down now, you know. Are you sure that's all you want for getting through the hurricane?"

"It's a hurricane now?"

The old man nodded. "Just hit Cat One a couple of hours ago. I thought you pilots paid attention to the weather. You ought to buy some water. That's the first thing to muck up every time one of these things blows through."

"I have no place to put it."

"I'll stack it for you," he said agreeably enough. "Craig can load it in that Jeep of his for you when he gets back. You need three gallons per person per day. So that's you and Buck, figure four days… twelve gallons."

"Umm," Hannah said, but the old man was already stacking cases of bottled water by the door.

"Next is non-perishable food," he said. "Canned food is better, but we want to avoid the salty stuff. That would increase your water consumption. So let me see…two people for four days…."

A cardboard pallet of assorted canned meats and vegetables grew beside the cases of water.

"You keep saying 'two people,' Horace. Why do you assume I am buying for Buck, too?"

"Least you can do for costing him the game," he

said, without looking up, still stacking cans. "Plus, the way to a man's heart is through his stomach."

"But I don't want to get to his heart!" she objected.

"Yeah, whatever," he replied. "Now, what kind of flashlights do the two of you have?"

"I," Hannah said, emphasizing the word, "have an emergency flashlight in the aircraft, and my own in my travel kit. I've no idea what Buck has, though I'm sure he is more than adequately prepared."

"Need two good six-volt area lanterns, and two hand-helds," he said, fetching them. "And spare batteries for each. And candles, just in case."

"Mr. Hanratty...." she began.

"Horace," he said, still working feverishly. "You'll also want things to do, in case you get bored. A couple of decks of cards, some dice. I'm sure Buck has poker chips but just in case I'll toss in a set."

"I like to read," Hannah said, feeling as if she was being sold the entire store.

"I've got just the thing for you," he said. "I've got the complete series of David Sklansky books on poker, as well as Mason Malmuth's *Essays on Gambling*. And I guess I should throw in Doyle Brunson's *Super System 2* as well."

"I like to read *novels*," she said.

"I have *The Cincinnati Kid*," he said.

"Saw the movie," she said, wondering if Horace

had any leisure activities in his store that did *not* involve poker or gambling.

"And I have another one here, *Wildcard.*"

"Let me guess," she said. "Another poker novel?"

"Nope," he said, smiling proudly. "It's an international conspiracy thriller, but people see the title and I can't keep it in stock."

"I'll take it," Hannah said. "Anything's better than nothing."

"Hey," he said, looking wounded. "A lot of folks said this was a damn good book."

"I'm sure it will be," she replied.

"Okay, so that totals four hundred fifty three dollars," he said.

"*What?*" Hannah shouted, blanching.

"I'll round it down to four-fifty, since you're with Buck."

"I am *not* with Buck!"

"You will be when this hurricane hits," Horace said. "Cash or charge? I take all of the major cards."

"Mr. Hanratty—Horace—I don't want this stuff and I'm not going to pay for it!"

His watery blue eyes lit up. "Great. But it's already on the pallet. So you pay me or we play for it."

"What?" She was floored.

"Yeah. I'm always up for a good game. Best two hands out of three."

"You're joking."

He scowled at her. "I don't joke about poker. Nobody on this island jokes about it. If you're smart, you'll take a tip and remember that."

"But...I don't want this stuff!"

"It's a package. All or nothing. Stud. Best two out of three."

Hannah felt the competitive urge overtaking her. "Who will deal? I want an impartial dealer."

"Hah! I knew you were the right type of gal!" He cackled gleefully and pulled a brand new set of cards from behind the counter and began to peel the wrapper off. "Just step outside and grab the first person you see."

"While you're opening the deck? What kind of fool do you think I am? Dealer opens the deck."

He laughed again, apparently delighted. "Fair enough, Sticks."

"Sticks? Who told you that?"

"No secrets around here. Okay, fresh unopened deck. Now go get your dealer."

It didn't help her confidence any that he was rubbing his hands together.

It was easy to find a dealer. The first woman she ran into on the street was more than ready. She introduced herself as Gerda Miller, and confided she was a part-time dealer at Bill Anstin's casino. A woman of about forty with an impressive bust, she was already rolling up her sleeves as they walked into the grocery.

Horace Hanratty had set up a card table and two chairs near a front window where the light was best. An unopened pack of cards waited, as did some chips.

"Wait a minute," Hannah said. "I agreed to the best two out of three."

The old shopkeeper grinned at her. "What fun is it if you can't bet and bluff?"

Hannah hesitated, then decided he was right. "But only three hands. I don't have all day."

"Three hands. I hope you know how to bluff, Sticks."

"Oh!" said Gerda Miller, "this is the Sticks who caused Buck's full house to blow away last night?"

Hanratty looked at her. "Who did you think she was?"

"Just some tourist."

"Well, she's not. And after what she did to Buck last night, I think this game might help square things."

Hannah wanted to roll her eyes but refrained.

But Gerda took issue with that remark herself. "I'm glad Buck's cards got blown away. If we don't get that casino, I may be out of a job."

"Don't be foolish, woman. You already have a job at the casino."

"But how long do you think that tiki hut charm is going to keep drawing boats?"

"As long as there are cheap people who want to take the cheapest cruises in the world."

"I'd get paid more if we had a better casino."

Hanratty snorted. "You'd get paid more if someone besides Bill Anstin was running the operation. Now deal, dammit."

Gerda snorted but opened the pack, pulled out the jokers and instruction cards and began to shuffle with all the aplomb of a professional. "Ante up," she said.

Hannah looked at Horace. "We didn't agree how much the antes would be."

Horace picked up a red chip, casino quality clay. "Ten. We've each got fifty of these things. Short game."

"That's what I wanted." Somehow she suspected she'd just been told they weren't going to play only three hands. But she loved poker, any kind, and found it both relaxing and challenging. A slightly longer game would only keep her away from Buck Shanahan that much longer, and she couldn't find anything in that to be upset about.

She riffled her chips, waiting as Gerda dealt the first three cards, two face-down, one face-up.

She was looking at a seven of clubs face up. Somehow, since Buck had started everyone calling her Sticks because of his sevens, she thought that was a sign of good luck.

She wasn't superstitious. Of course not. No way.

When she peeked at her hole cards, the two that

were face down, her heart began to hammer. Two more sevens. She had trips. An excellent hand, and right off the top with four more cards to come.

Horace shoved in a stack of chips. "Two hundred."

Hannah, able to see only the four of diamonds he had face up tried to imagine what hand he could be betting so much on. A flush draw? A straight draw? She pursed her lips, then called him.

Another card, this time a Queen of Hearts, more betting, and again, until all the cards were on the table and the last two hole cards were dealt. Hannah looked at the two diamonds on the table, one of them part of Hanratty's hand, and one of them part of the board cards, then considered that in her hand she already held two diamonds. The likelihood that he had a flush was…small, she decided, and called his final bet. They were both all in.

She lost. Hanratty held a flush after all. He spread out his five winning cards and smiled beatifically. Then he looked at her trip sevens and said, "Oh, bad beat, Sticks."

"Yeah, right. Well, I guess I have to pay you, because I don't have any more chips."

"Oh, I can take care of that. I did say two best out of three."

"You did." She agreed reluctantly, sure this old schemer had something up his sleeve. He rose and went to the stack of bottled water. Putting his hand atop it, he said, "Each of these twelve packs buys you..." he paused, thinking about it.

She could almost see the wheels spinning, as if he were deciding how much he thought he could take her for. She was just about ready to get up from the table and pay the four hundred and fifty dollar bill, when he said, "Tell you what. Three of these buys you another five hundred."

Despite every instinct to the contrary, she settled back in her chair. "How much do they cost?"

"Six bucks apiece."

"You're on."

So he carried the three cases of water to the already overloaded cart, then returned to the table. Hannah reminded herself she really wasn't risking anything. After all, she'd either pay for the groceries or get them for free. And she could well afford the groceries, little though she wanted them.

Hanratty counted out another fifty red chips and shoved them her way. He smiled. "Ante up, Sticks."

Two hands later, having added twelve more cases of water to the pile by the door, Hannah decided enough was enough. "Okay, Horace," she said, walking to the door. "I'll get it back next time."

"Nah," Hanratty said. "Get it from Buck instead, when you sit in his game tomorrow night."

She turned. "How did you—"

He smiled. "No secrets, remember?"

She shook her head and walked out into the tropical heat. Then froze in her tracks as a woman planted herself directly in front of her. The woman scowled at her.

"Why are you trying to take my man?"

CHAPTER SIX

HANNAH STARED at the woman who confronted her, taking in details swiftly. She appeared to be about Hannah's age or slightly older, though it was hard to tell since the woman's skin showed signs of long-term sun exposure. She was athletically built, wearing a blue work shirt, khaki shorts and hiking boots with thick socks rolled over the top. In her hand was a tool that looked like the perfect murder weapon…a strange hammer-like thing with a huge, curved ice-pick in place of the claw.

Hannah instinctively stepped back. "Who are you?"

"Edna Harkin. Volcanologist. And where do you get off going after my man?"

"I'm not going after anyone."

"Yeah, right. I've been hearing stories."

"Stories?" All of a sudden, Hannah was fed up with this island. "If you've been hearing stories they must be coming from the voices in your head!"

Edna waved her hammer. "I've been hearing them from everyone in town!"

"Well everyone in town could hardly know what they're talking about since I only got here last night!"

"And stayed at Buck's place."

"And stayed in the hangar in my own plane, sleeping with a freaking alligator!"

Edna nodded. "Right, but Buster didn't hurt you."

"Does everyone know everything about everyone on this island?" Hannah asked in exasperation.

"Only about you," Edna said, matter-of-factly.

"So what are your plans for that hammer?" Hannah asked.

It was as if Edna Harkin suddenly realized the thing was in her hand. She gaped at it, then swiftly tucked it in a leather holster attached to her belt. "Sorry."

"You should be sorry! Where do you get off waving deadly weapons at total strangers?"

"I forgot I was holding it! And who the hell are you to tell me what I can do?"

"Just a passing stranger who feels as if she's fallen down Alice's rabbit hole. What is it with you people? Is there something in the water? In the air? Or were you all sent here by a mental hospital that had had enough?"

"Hey, you don't have to be insulting!"

"Why not? I've been accused of things by people I don't know, roped into buying supplies I don't need, and yelled at by a mad woman waving a hammer."

"I'm not mad!"

"No, but you *are* furious," drawled a deep voice.

Hannah spun about and found herself looking into the exceedingly handsome face of Bill Anstin. In that instant, she totally forgot Edna. "Bill Anstin!" she said, feeling a little amazed. "I was at the rail when you won the World Series of Poker."

He smiled, a wide, winning smile. No wonder his nickname in the poker world was *Handsome Anstin.* His looks were too good to be true. Unfortunately, he seemed to know it.

"Nice to meet you," he said, giving her the kind of once-over that always made her skin crawl. "You must be that pilot who blew away our game last night. Sticks, isn't it?"

"Umm, no. Hannah Lamont." She shook his hand, wishing she didn't feel impressed in spite of herself. Luck might have won him the World Series, but he was still a winner. He still owned the coveted bracelet—which, she noticed, he was wearing.

"Hi, Edna," Anstin said to the volcanologist. "Come down from the mountain for the storm?"

Edna gave a short nod. "Time to hole up. I also need to get some more people out here. I think the mountain is starting to get active again."

"Well, nobody's going to get in here till after the storm."

"I know that. But I still need to make some calls." Edna looked at Anstin as if she wished he'd drop from the face of the earth.

Anstin gave Hannah another once-over. "Buy you a drink, Sticks?"

"No, thanks. I've got to get back to my plane."

"Maybe you'll come play at the casino when the storm has passed. I can give you some tips on your game."

"Thanks. Nice meeting you."

Anstin strolled away looking as if he owned the place. Edna sidled up beside Hannah. "Look out for that guy. He never tells the truth when a lie will do. I swear, he lives life on a bluff."

Hannah nodded. "He seems…oily."

"Greasy. Globs and globs of emotional grease."

Hannah looked at her. "Are you really worried about the volcano?"

Edna shrugged. "Prediction is pretty much a guessing game. I need a team out here."

Hannah hesitated. "This is not making me happy."

Edna shrugged. "It's thrilling the heck out of me. But I'm a volcanologist. We're not wimps."

Hannah chose to ignore the insult. "What if it erupts during the storm?"

"Then…." Edna shrugged again. "How much trouble we'll be in depends on the kind of eruption. I mean, this mountain is sometimes explosive, like Mount St. Helens, and sometimes more like the volcanoes in Hawaii…just slow lava flows. You can outwalk those if you need to. But honestly?"

"Yes?"

"I don't think anything's going to happen immediately."

"Thank God. I like excitement, but not that kind."

"You better not like the Buck kind of excitement either," Edna said, frowning at her in a way that suggested to Hannah the hammer had *not* been in Edna's hands by accident. She took a step back.

Edna left, tossing one more warning glare over her shoulder.

Craig looked at the pallet of supplies when he pulled up in his Jeep a few seconds later. "Are you planning on moving in?"

"It's hurricane stuff." Hannah felt embarrassed. "Horace said we'd need it."

"Oh." Craig looked dubiously at it. "Buck already has supplies. And he has a couple of cisterns to catch rain water. The town never ran water up to the airport. It was too far."

Hannah now felt supremely annoyed. "I'm going to go back in and strangle Horace. Wait for me, will you?"

Craig reached out and touched Hannah's arm. "Don't do that. We'll take the stuff up with us. Whatever we don't use, we can get Horace to take back for credit. Other folks will probably need it after the storm."

And that's how Hannah came to be loading a bunch of food, water and paper products onto Craig's

Jeep, muttering under her breath at the lunatics on this island.

"What did you think of Edna?" Craig asked as they drove back up the winding mountain road.

"After she got past wanting to kill me, she merely made me nervous."

"She's a weird one, all right. She's a fruitcake who's been trying to say for the last five years that the mountain shows signs of erupting. So far the thing hasn't even vented steam. And Buck hates her."

"Buck hates everyone."

"No, he doesn't. But Edna keeps coming on to him and he's tired of it."

Hannah cocked her eye his way. "Doesn't he like women?"

"Not since his divorce."

"That explains a lot. What happened?"

"I'm sworn to silence," Craig said, drawing his thumb and forefinger across his lips as if zipping them. "But get a couple of extra beers in him sometime and he'll probably tell you."

Hannah didn't like the sound of that. "Does he drink a lot?"

"Actually, no. But once in a while...well, sometimes a guy has to howl at the moon."

BACK AT THE HANGAR, relieved—or so he told himself—to have everyone out of his hair, Buck waded through the schematics of the fuel system for Hannah's jet and soon had some ideas of what might have gone wrong. There were things even the best mechanic might not spot before they happened, especially if he was working on a plane for the first time, and if maintenance logs had been, well, doctored.

He suspected Hannah had been taken for a ride on this particular plane, insofar as whether routine maintenance had been properly and completely performed all along. It wouldn't be the first time someone had cut a corner. She was damn lucky not to have ditched.

Of course, he wasn't going to tell her that. Give Delilah an inch, and she'd take a mile.

But now that he had some ideas, he was itching to get at it. Where the hell was Craig? Was he planning to take Hannah on a complete sightseeing tour of this ugly piece of rock or what?

Rising from the desk, he stretched and headed outside to take a look at the sky. Over in the east it wasn't pretty at all. Frowning, he went to the office to get a weather update. On his way, even from this altitude, he could see that the Caribbean was probably pushing twenty-foot waves or higher, with heavy chop. Today would not be a good day to be at sea.

Soon enough he was looking at isobars again, noting how they had tightened up. Noting that Tropical Storm Hannah had finally pushed up to hurricane status. Hurricane hunters were posting winds near the center at over eighty miles an hour. Glancing at the clock, he saw he'd have to wait another two hours for the latest update.

Not pretty. Not terribly ugly yet, but not pretty. He sat back in his chair and plucked a fresh cigar from the humidor, tucking it between his teeth. He loved a good hurricane. He just didn't love a bad hurricane. At this point Hannah was a minor threat in terms of the island. Folks here had been battening the hatches for this kind of stuff for a long time.

And sitting on a volcanic cone like this limited the problems of flooding. The rivers would get high, the pools and ponds would overflow, but there'd be no serious mudslides, and the water wouldn't stay on the island long enough to cause real damage. Well, except for storm surge. That would depend on how Hannah hit and where her cyclone was strongest when she hit.

Storm surge might wipe out the casino. That almost made him grin, the vision of all those tiki huts washing away.

You're evil, Buck, he told himself. Shouldn't wish ill on anyone. But Bill Anstin drove him nuts, as did the mayor, especially since they were determined to turn this island into another carbon-copy Caribbean casino resort. A Vegas-type operation. Complete with has-been headliners.

Hence the poker game he had been playing last

evening against Anstin. Everything of import on this island was decided by poker. So the city council (all of whom held their positions by virtue of their final positions in the last island-wide tournament) had dictated that the decision about a new casino would be decided by a tournament. Finally, after several weeks of play, it had gotten down to Anstin and Buck, heads-up. The rules at that point said the winner would be decided by best out of three heads-up matches. The idea was to reward skill over luck.

Luck. Yeah. He'd had some and then that damn woman had come roaring in over his head on a wing and barely enough gas fumes to cause a person to cough.

But if that new casino ever came to pass, Buck was determined to find a different volcano to park himself and his airport on. Too much civilization would run him off faster than an eruption.

Not that they were going to have one. Edna had been trying to conjure an eruption for five years now. The mountain failed to cooperate. Her constant alarms had not only resulted in folks on the island utterly ignoring her for crying wolf, but the entire volcanology community apparently had written her off.

At last he heard Craig's Jeep roar up and pull to a stop beside the building. Rolling his cigar around in his mouth, Buck moseyed outside, looking for all the world as if he hadn't felt a wisp of impatience.

One look at the contents of Craig's Jeep transformed him.

"What the *hell* is all of that?"

Craig, who was just climbing out answered laconically, "Hurricane supplies."

"Hurricane supplies? We don't need any hurricane supplies."

"Horace took Hannah for a ride."

Hannah, her head suddenly popping up as she climbed out, said, "Actually, I didn't want to be a burden."

Buck saw Craig roll his eyes in a *yeah, right* sort of way. He debated whether to push the issue or let it go. He knew Horace Hanratty; the man could sell snow to Eskimos. If he smelled a valid credit card, there was no stopping him. Hannah had to be excused from the label of idiot simply because she didn't know Horace.

Or so he tried to tell himself. He snorted and rolled his cigar over to the other side of his mouth. Finally he said, "I've got so much water in my cisterns that if the storm knocks out the water system in town, folks are going to be coming to *me* for the stuff."

"That's what I said," Craig offered, stepping into what he apparently viewed as a brewing storm. "But Hannah didn't know that. And I told her whatever we didn't need, *someone* would need after the storm, if it hits."

Buck squashed the cigar between his teeth, reminding himself that a little civility was a good thing. Sometimes. "Okay, let's get it into the hangar. Hannah is getting wound up tight out there. We'll be lucky if she doesn't blow up to a Cat 4."

"Really?" The other Hannah's eyes widened. Caribbean green. Gawd.

"Really. Isobar lines near the eye are showing a rapid drop in pressure. This is going to be a wicked one."

Craig spoke. "I guess this will put paid to the poker game, huh?"

"Not on your life."

Craig gave Hannah a pitying look, but didn't say any more.

Buck went to get the big flat-bed hand truck he sometimes used to cart engines around, and together he and Craig loaded the supplies onto it. Hannah stood to one side, her hands in her pockets. Staying out of the way. Good. The last thing he needed was her getting any part of herself in his way. Especially those hips. Or those breasts he was just now noticing.

He didn't think he'd ever seen a better package climb out of a flight suit.

Things were stirring in him, things he preferred to be in control of, not controlled by. Feelings. Needs. Wants. Sheee-it!

Tugging the heavy cart into the hangar and tucking

it out of the way proved a welcome bit of exercise for him, taming the beast within. At least he thought of it as a beast; it was the kind of thing that got him into trouble, and seemed to have a mind of its own.

Once the supplies were out of the way, Hannah-the-pilot was right there asking about her plane.

"I got some ideas," Buck said. He took the cigar from his mouth and tossed it in a trash can. "Things that could've happened that your mechanic wouldn't have known could happen…especially if the maintenance logs were doctored."

Hannah's face darkened. "I had a feeling."

"Before you bought that thing?"

"After," she said sharply, taking his question as a criticism. Which he supposed it was, however oblique. "Afterward. Do you know how few people *really* do all the maintenance? I would have expected to find some oversights. Just a few. But there weren't any."

"Well, *some* of us do it all, but I agree, a lot of private planes don't get all the attention they should. Either because the owner is a cheapskate or the mechanics cut corners."

She nodded, for once agreeing with him. "Look at the major airlines."

"Exactly. There's a lot of reasons people run close to the edge. Anyway, I went through the schematics while you were out wasting your money, and found a few things to check out."

"Are you going to check it out?"

"Now?" He arched a brow. "Not likely, Sticks. Craig needs to get home to look after his family before Hannah hits, and I need to go down the mountain to help out. My neighbors are more important than your fuel line."

"Did I say they weren't?" Fire sparked in her eyes. A hot-tempered redhead. So what else was new?

"No. But I'm giving the reason before you ask. Some of the older folks are going to need help boarding up. So if you'll excuse me…."

"I'm going with you."

His jaw dropped. He didn't need this. "Now look…."

"I know how to use a hammer," she argued stubbornly. "And I'm in decent shape. If people need help, I'm going to help."

Buck looked at Craig, as if he might find help there, but the coward just shrugged.

Which was how Buck came to be driving down the mountain behind Craig, with Hannah Lamont perched firmly in the passenger seat of his pickup truck…resisting every urge to acknowledge her generosity.

CHAPTER SEVEN

HANNAH CHANGED back into her flight suit, it being the most rugged piece of clothing she'd brought with her, and endured the lumpy, bumpy ride back into town.

"Doesn't anyone work on the roads around here?" she finally asked.

He gave her a look that said she was being a pain. "You try living on an island where storms keep washing them away. Fixing roads takes time and money."

"With a casino…."

He glared at her and rotated his unlit cigar to half-mast. "The only person making money off that casino is Anstin. He doesn't care about anything that doesn't help the casino."

She blinked. "What about taxes?"

"Who pays taxes?"

Truly she had fallen through the rabbit hole. "But how does anything get done?"

"We get together and decide we need to do it. That's how we built the school that doubles as a storm shelter. By our own sweat and people supplying the materials they could afford to buy."

Hannah thought about that. "Rock soup."

"Basically. It works. But these aren't the kind of people who want a government or taxes. Except Anstin, anyway. He seems all kind of interested in having a government. Mainly because he doesn't want anyone gambling outside his casino. So we've got a mayor now. What a joke."

"Why is it a joke?"

"Because the guy couldn't organize falling out of a tree, let alone run a government. He doesn't have any power because nobody's stupid enough to listen to him."

"Oh." She peered at him curiously. "You don't think a little bit of government could help?"

"Why? Most of us here came to get away from all that crap."

"But...but what about police? Fire department?"

"We have a volunteer fire brigade, and who needs police?"

Most everyone, she thought, wondering if she had flown into total anarchy. But before she could pursue the subject, they were in town, driving down a residential lane, swerving to avoid potholes.

"Look," he said, "when something needs doing, we have a referendum."

"Oh, so you vote?"

"Hell, no. We play poker. That's what I was doing last night. The island is pretty much split on whether Anstin should be able to build his fancy high-rise casino. So the council said it should be decided by a poker tournament."

Hannah blinked. "Okay. But you vote for a city council, right?"

"No. We have a tournament for that, too. Top six finishers get the job."

"That hardly sounds like winning." She turned in her seat to look at him. "I hear you're a pretty good player. So why aren't you on the council?"

"Because that's one tournament I'm not stupid enough to play in."

Hannah faced forward again. An island where everything was decided by poker. Now she was certain she'd landed in an asylum. On the other hand.... She smiled to herself. It would be kind of fun.

Buck changed the subject. Pointedly, she thought.

"These older homes," he said, waving out the window at white-painted clapboard-sided houses with green shutters already closed against the coming storm, "were built shortly after Hanratty came here. Men who knew a lot about ship-building put them up, and they've withstood everything nature has thrown at this island. The strongest winds just make them bend and creak. It's the newer homes we have to worry about."

She could see why. Even low cinder-block structures, of which there were few enough, didn't look especially strong. Other homes appeared to have been built on the cheap, and it was into that neighborhood that Buck steered the truck. People were out, trying to board their windows with plywood that had obviously been used before. Some appeared to be getting on in years, and it was these people Buck stopped to help.

They greeted him warmly. It was obvious everyone knew him and liked him. Hannah wondered just what it was about him that they liked. She certainly hadn't seen much to recommend him, other than rugged good looks and a set of narrow hips that awoke something primal in her.

Funny, she thought, that she had never before noticed how sexy a man's hips could be.

Buck introduced her as a pilot who was laying over for the duration, and called her Sticks. Not that it mattered. Everyone on the island seemed to already know that she was "with Buck," that she'd awakened with Buster, and that she'd fallen for Horace's slick patter at the grocery. It was as if she were living in a fish bowl.

The third elderly couple they helped were Joyce and Dil Fenster. Hannah judged them to be in their eighties, and only too glad to allow Buck and Hannah to lug plywood and screw it over windows.

"Been here forty years," Dil said as he "supervised." He apparently wanted Hannah to know all about him and Joyce. "I worked as a shrimper out of Destin, Florida, but me and Joyce got tired of me being away for six weeks at a time. So we saved up to buy our own boat we could live on and fish from at the same time."

"Yeah," said Joyce, who still looked as if she could haul in a net. "Then we found this place. Been stuck here ever since." She laughed, as if it were an old joke. "Now our son runs the boat and our grandkids turned coat and went to work at the casino. What kind of job is that, I ask you? Taking hard-earned money away from other people."

"Now, now," Dil said to her as if he'd said it a thousand times, "those people come to the casino knowing what the odds are."

"Still don't think it's right," Joyce said. "It's not fair like our poker games. I just can't imagine them taking a rake out of every hand. It's pure thievery if you ask me."

Hannah, already perspiring in the humidity and heat, drove screws with a drill while Buck balanced the plywood.

"It'd be better," Dil said, "if Anstin were on the up and up, though. Now if he transported private jets for people like you do…that would be an honorable calling."

Hannah almost dropped the drill. Cussing under her breath, she reseated the screw and started again.

"Hurry up," Buck said. "I'm not Superman. This thing is heavy."

"Quit your complaining." She turned to Dil, knowing better than to ask how he knew her business. Instead, she asked, "What do you mean Anstin isn't on the up and up?"

"No regulations," Dil said as if it were self-evident. "If he gets his way and builds that big hotel and casino, we're going to *have* to get a gubmint. Now won't that be a hairy shame."

"Yeah," Joyce agreed. "All this time we ain't needed anybody sticking a nose into our business. This Anstin is going to change all that."

Buck spoke. "We ought to tar and feather him and ride him off the island."

Dil laughed wheezily and Joyce emitted a belly laugh. "You put tar on him," Joyce said, "and he won't sink!"

"You got a point there," Buck agreed.

"Done," said Hannah, climbing down the ladder.

"Thank God." Buck let go of the plywood and shook his arms. "You ever hear of lactic acid build-up?"

She smiled sweetly. "Maybe you should do heavy work more often."

He glared at her. For once there was no cigar. He must have lost it somewhere.

While they stood in this eyeball-to-eyeball contest, neither of them willing to blink first, Joyce let out a little shriek.

"Oh, my word, Buster, what are you doing here?"

Hannah blinked first. The hairs on the back of her neck stood up and she whirled, looking for the alligator. Yup, there he was, crawling his scaly way across the thin grass toward her.

She was never quite sure how she got there, but in an instant she was on top of the ladder, saying, "Get that thing away from me!"

Buck laughed. "He wouldn't hurt a fly."

"No? Then what does he eat?"

"Mostly people food," Joyce confided. "Everyone feeds Buster."

Hannah glared at the three people and then the alligator. "That's a mistake. Some day when you don't give him food, he'll bite off your hand the way he did Hanratty's."

Joyce looked at Dil. "You don't think he'd really do that, do you?"

"Nah. We been here forty years, girl. Don't you go taking strange notions just 'cuz Sticks here is frightened of poor old Buster."

Hannah blinked. "Poor old Buster?"

"Yeah," Dil said. "He's Robinson Crusoe. Castaway on an island with none of his kind."

"Crusoe had Friday."

Dil laughed again, sounding like a poorly pumped accordion. None of this, of course, was helping Hannah who watched warily as the gator kept coming straight for her. She had no doubt that he could knock the ladder over and put her on his menu in an instant. "Buck, *do* something!"

"Every time a woman wants me to *do* something, I get into trouble up to my neck. Just what am I supposed to *do?* Whack him on the snout?"

That didn't sound very wise to Hannah, even in her current predicament. "Why won't he leave me alone?"

"Maybe he likes your perfume."

"I'm not wearing any!" And the gator crawled closer.

Buck was silent for a couple of heartbeats. "That's your *natural* smell? Jeez. I thought it cost a hundred dollars a bottle."

Dil and Joyce cackled. Buster opened his huge jaws and roared.

"Oh, my," said Joyce. "Sticks, honey, he's got the hots for you. I knew it when I heard he wanted to sleep with you last night. You are definitely his type."

At that instant, mortified beyond belief, Hannah could have cheerfully sunk through the ground never to be seen again. "I smell good to an *alligator?*"

Dil spoke. "You smell pretty good to me, too." Joyce elbowed him.

"Obviously," Buck said, "we need a way to distract him."

Hannah agreed wholeheartedly. The gator took another couple of steps in her direction. "*Do* something," she begged. The ladder was beginning to feel weak, then she realized she was shaking. That embarrassed her even more.

It was then that Buck moved. Quicker than a flash, he darted past the gator, wrapped a strong arm around Hannah's waist and tucked her against him like a football. Seconds later she was in the pickup truck with the door closed.

"Stay here," he said as if he were giving an order to a subordinate. In the midst of her fright and astonishment at the way he had seized her and carried her as if she weighed nothing at all, she felt a spark of anger. He didn't have to treat her like that!

She leaned out the window, shouting after him, "You could at least be polite!"

"I *was* polite. I saved you."

Simmering, angry both with herself and him, she settled back against the seat and folded her arms. It did nothing to improve her mood that Buck and Dil finished the plywood while she had to watch.

Or that Buster made his lizardly way toward the truck and then stopped, just looking up at her with those intense saurian eyes.

Why me? she wondered miserably. *Why couldn't*

I have landed on any other island in the Caribbean? What did I do to deserve a crazed alligator and an even crazier man?

Or maybe she had that backwards. At this point she didn't care. All she wanted was for her plane to get fixed so she could escape this insane asylum.

What really clinched it for her, though, was when Joyce got a bucket full of water and dumped it on Buster. "We don't want him to get too hot," she explained cheerfully.

"Yes we do," Hannah said out the truck window. "Then maybe he'll go find a pond."

"I don't know," Joyce said, "but it's like he doesn't want to take his eyes off of you."

"Yeah, he's probably measuring me for his dinner plate."

Joyce laughed uproariously, but Hannah didn't see the humor in it. Being stalked by an alligator was not at the top of her list of desirable experiences. In fact, it was somewhere near the bottom, now filed next to "meet a serial killer."

As soon as Buck finished helping Dil and Joyce with their house, he climbed into the truck and announced, "I'm taking you back to the airport."

"I don't want to go."

"You aren't any help to me with Buster following you around. You'll be safe up there."

"Really?" The word dripped sarcasm. "Like I was safe on my plane this morning?"

"You can lock yourself in before he can get back up there. You'll be fine."

"Your concern touches me."

He turned. "Look, Sticks, I didn't ask you to land on my island, but you did. Now you're just going to have to deal with things the way they are. Shutting up would be a good start."

Ooooh, she wanted to throttle him. Slap duct tape across those lips. Lips, that while they were thin and masculine, seemed to be offering a constant invitation to exploration. Yeah, she'd slap duct tape across them. Then he wouldn't be able to talk and she wouldn't have to keep seeing that mouth. As a bonus, he wouldn't be able to stick another cigar in there and chew on it. Lord, what a nasty habit!

In fact, she decided as they bumped up the mountain road again, in danger of getting a concussion, he was just plain nasty. Sexy, but nasty.

And why was she feeling this godawful, unwanted, horrible attraction to him? She preferred men who treated her well, not sarcastic, nasty, cigar-chewing ape-men. She was interested in men who gave her roses and….

Who was she kidding? Few men were interested in her. They took a look, liked what they saw, but after one date they backed away. She intimidated them. Well, except for pilots. And the last one of those she'd made the mistake of dating had proved to have a "special girl" in nearly every city on his route, in addition to being married.

After him, she'd pretty much given up on testosterone-based life forms. But now here she was, feeling an irresistible tug toward a man who had more warts than a frog.

Stupid.

Another jolt nearly banged her head on the roof of the truck. Maybe a concussion would do her some good.

One thing was certain, she didn't like being taken back to the airport as if she were a misbehaving child.

CHAPTER EIGHT

THE AIRPORT enjoyed beautiful views from every direction. Upward was the craggy mountain, below, spread on three sides, the green-blue of the Caribbean shallows. On the northwest shoreline, the town looked almost like a toy village, and the casino, on the opposite side of the tongue of the narrow island, blended its brown tiki roofs with lush green tropical foliage. At times she even thought she caught a glimpse of a sparkling waterfall down there between the town and casino.

She pulled a couple of the plastic chairs out of the office, sat on one and put her feet up on the other, and soaked up the sun and the balmy day. For once she didn't even bother with sunscreen to protect her fair skin. Annoyed, she was also feeling strangely reckless, and the recklessness seemed to grow as she watched the storm still so far out at sea, still just a blip on the horizon, but growing steadily closer.

She'd been through hurricanes before, in Houston, but she discovered that the approach of one felt entirely different when she had nowhere to run. It wasn't as if she could drive a few hundred miles inland and miss the worst of it. If it came this way, there was nowhere to go.

Effectively, she was trapped. And trapped with a man who awoke crazy feelings in her. At one instant she was furious with him, and the next she was noticing him in ways that made her want to blush.

Even the thought of him put a scowl on her face. She closed her eyes and folded her arms tightly across her breast, listening to the breeze in her ears.

Up here it blew constantly, but it seemed to have grown a bit stronger. She wondered if she was imagining it.

Finally she opened her eyes and saw a squall line approaching. One of the storm's feeder bands? She wasn't sure. Then, a moment later, she heard the roar of an engine and the sound of squeaking springs as a vehicle approached.

Buck? She wanted to pretend disinterest, but she couldn't keep herself from watching the road. Moments later there appeared the most amazing sight: a black BMW, the last thing she had expected to see on this island. Anstin, she thought uneasily. Somehow she didn't want to be anywhere alone with that man.

Then she noticed that the BMW looked as if it had been batted around a few times by a vengeful giant cat. Surely Handsome Anstin wouldn't drive anything like that?

She was soon proved right, for as the car pulled up and parked near her, she saw a small, thin, older man at the wheel. He climbed out wearing, of all things, a suit. That garb didn't fit this island at all, she thought. But maybe he was hoping Buck could fly him someplace where he had important business.

That guess soon proved to be wrong.

"Oh, hello," he said, walking toward her. "You must be Buck's new girlfriend. The pilot."

"Pilot, yes. Buck's new girlfriend, no, not even when hell freezes over." Some long-buried superstitious part of her brain suddenly shrieked a warning that making statements like that tempted fate. She ignored it. She'd be out of here in a couple of days, free of this un-gilded cage of an island. Free of Buck Shanahan.

"Edna will be glad to hear that," he said.

"She already has."

"I doubt she believed it. Why should she believe you?" He looked at her from dubious eyes. "Then what are you doing here?"

"I'm not sure that's any of your business."

All of a sudden the little old man puffed up. "*Everything* is my business. I'm the mayor."

So this was the guy who must have taken first place in the tournament for political office. Hannah felt torn between tweaking him and ignoring him. "Where I come from," she drawled finally, using her best east Texas accent, "nothing is a mayor's business unless the city council brings it to his attention."

He scowled. "It's different here."

"I've noticed. The lunatics are running the asylum."

Now he was definitely irate. He even stomped his foot. "Now you listen to me, young lady...."

Hannah slowly put her booted feet on the ground, then unfolded to her full height. She was no Brunhilde, but she still towered over the little man. "Why don't you watch how you talk to me? In fact, why don't we start this entire conversation over from the beginning, you officious little loser."

He blinked rapidly. "Loser? How dare you! I'll have you know I won this office."

She shrugged. "Yeah, and you lost thirteen hundred dollars to Bill Anstin last night. That makes you a loser in my book."

She wouldn't have thought a human being could turn so red without a third-degree sunburn. "That has nothing to do with you!"

"You made it a matter for me when you said that everything was your business because you were the mayor, Mr. Mayor. Now, do we start this conversation over, or do I simply walk inside and lock the door?"

He made a whole bunch of frustrated sounds, some of them quite entertaining. She especially liked the one that sounded like a whistling teakettle. His fists were clenched tight as if he wanted to hit her. Hannah half-wished he'd try. She'd deck him before his fist came anywhere near her. Besides, she told herself as she forced her own fists to relax, it was more fun sending the guy on tilt. He was still smarting over his loss, and right now she could practically see the steam coming out of his ears.

But finally he said through his teeth, "I want to talk to Buck."

"You're still out of luck. He's in town."

"Well, dammit."

Hannah shrugged. "Not my fault you're still on a losing streak."

She could have laughed then, she really could have. Poker players, *real* players, were usually better at rolling with their losses. This guy couldn't handle it. She was willing to bet she could roll him up in just a few hands. That's when she realized she was thinking liking an islander. God help her!

The mayor continued to make his impossible series of noises, his face going from red to purple and eventually to white. Finally he choked out, "You better watch it, Sticks, or I'll clean out your bankroll."

"I've heard that before. It never happens. Besides, what makes you think I'd want to play with a loser like you? You're a fish. Dead money. I like a bigger challenge."

If glares could have killed, she'd have been dead, buried and returned to dust in that single instant.

"Give Buck a message for me."

She shrugged again. She really did *not* like this little man.

"Tell him he's damn lucky your plane blew away his cards."

That piqued Hannah's interest. "What do you mean?"

"That's none of your business!"

He was puffing again. She wondered if he'd learned that from watching a blowfish.

"*If* you were a *real* card player, I wouldn't have to explain." Turning sharply, he started back to his car.

Then he paused and shouted back, "And tell that damn Buck Shanahan that it's on his head if we lose this island!"

"You're just angry because Anstin cleaned you out."

"He did *not* clean me out. I never gamble what I can't afford to lose."

"Why do I have trouble believing that?"

The little man didn't bother to answer. He stormed toward his car.

"And if that's the case," Hannah couldn't resist calling after him, "why are you gambling with your island at stake?"

He didn't answer.

"By the way," she called after him, "I didn't get your name."

He faced her. "Regan. Mayor Tom Regan."

"Good to know whom to avoid until I can get off this island. Have a good day, Tom."

Again that confused blinking, but this time he almost ran to his car. Apparently dealing with the lunatic locals hadn't prepared him for dealing with Hannah.

But, Hannah thought as she resumed her comfortable position on the plastic chairs and closed her eyes once again, very few people seemed to be able to deal with her.

Just as she was getting really comfortable, a squall line hit. Sighing, she grabbed the chairs and carried them into the office. Some days you just couldn't win.

BUCK WAS SCREWING the last sheet of plywood onto a window for another one of the elderly residents, a woman named Mariki who looked as if she were as old as the volcano. Her origins remained a mystery, but even in frail old-age she displayed the distinctive beauty of a multiracial heritage.

"Are you sure you don't want to come up to the airport with me?" he asked for the third time. He really didn't like the idea of Mariki trying to ride out the storm alone. "We'll probably play poker all the way through the hurricane."

Mariki laughed, a dry, brittle, but charming sound.

"I been riding these storms before you were born, boy. Comes the one that takes me, I be ready."

He wasn't ready, Buck thought, descending the ladder and folding it so he could put it back in his truck. He treasured this woman's friendship. "How about coming because I don't want to be alone?"

She laughed again. "Now I know you be telling me tales. You be alone the way the fish in the sea be alone. Pah. You get back up there. I be fine here."

There was no budging her. Buck considered staying down here to keep an eye on her, but knew he couldn't. Someone had to keep an eye on the airport; in days to come it would be their only link with the outside world. Yes, the satellite phones might work once the storm had passed, but the only way to get medical and other help swiftly would be if relief planes could land here. Waiting on boats might take too long.

So he had to content himself with asking the neighbors to keep an eye on Mariki, as if they weren't already, then he climbed into his truck and headed back up the mountainside.

The first squall moved through swiftly, bloated with rain that was soon running heavily down the gullies to either side of the road. The potholes were already getting worse, and he stuck a cigar between his teeth to protect them from the jolting. The sky cleared again just before he reached the airport, but he didn't think it would be for long.

Hurricanes had long arms extending hundreds of miles from their centers, pulling in water to feed the hungry eye. Each one of those sodden bands brought rain nearly anywhere they passed, and sometimes high winds and tornadoes. Hannah—the hurricane Hannah—was just beginning to vent her spleen.

The other Hannah, the one who awaited him in his office, would probably begin venting *hers* the instant he set foot within. Damn women. They might look like roses but they were all thorns.

He considered just going straightaway to the hangar, but told himself not to be a coward. So she yelled at him. He guess he kind of deserved it for the way he'd summarily brought her back up here as if she were the problem and not the alligator.

What was it with that gator anyway? He'd never heard of one behaving like this. Although all bets were off with Buster. Buster never had another gator to teach him gator ways. Instead he'd had an island full of people who thought of him as a pet, some of whom even professed to feel sorry for him.

Buck, too, might have felt sorry for him, except Buck had been married. Buster didn't know how lucky he was not to be sharing his pond with a female.

Buck braced himself and stepped into the air-conditioned office. To his amazement, he didn't get yelled at. Instead, Hannah was leaning over the counter, studying the latest weather updates.

He cleared his throat. "Anything interesting?"

She looked over her shoulder, those amazing green eyes instantly captivating him. "Yeah. I'm glad I'm not on a boat out there." She straightened and motioned him to take a look.

He whistled, unhappy with what he saw on the weather fax. Hurricane Hannah was wound up tighter than a top, and all that energy was going to have to expend itself somehow, somewhere.

"Eyes this tight," Hannah said, "are rare."

"I know."

"The advisory says she's a Cat One now, and they think she'll develop into a Cat Four. But, if I'm reading this right, she might not be that well-developed when she hits us."

"She's coming straight on?" He took the bulletin and began to scan it. "Twenty-four hours. That's a lot of time to grow."

She nodded, looking truly concerned. "What should we do?"

"I don't know what we *can* do. I built this airport on the leeward side of the volcano for a reason, and the hangar and office are tied down with three-quarter-inch steel cable. It's not going anywhere. So maybe it's time to get people up here. We're above the storm surge. We're shielded from the worst of the wind. And thanks to Horace, we have supplies aplenty."

"You're going to open a storm shelter?"

"Right," he said. "Somebody has to take care of these people, and it's for damn sure that Anstin won't be bothered. We have to get busy, Sticks. And fast."

"We?"

He looked at her. "You're going to help me."

CHAPTER NINE

HANNAH STOOD with her back to the large hangar door, arms spread, facing Buck with her plane looming behind him.

"I treasure life as much as the next person," she said, "but you're not taking my plane out of this hangar."

"Hannah…."

"It doesn't belong to me anymore. I've got a contract that says it belongs to some French playboy. I've already accepted half the payment. You can't put it out in the storm!"

He paused. Then, "Don't you have insurance?"

"Not if I knowingly expose it to danger."

"Oh, well, that's okay then, because you couldn't help it that a freak fuel leak put you right in the path of a storm."

She gaped. "Are you serious? Are *you* going to explain to the adjuster why my plane wasn't in the hangar?"

"I would if I needed to."

"I'm not taking that risk. You'll have to tug it right over my body."

The corners of his mouth had been doing strange things since she'd flown to the door and pressed herself against it to protect the plane. Finally those strange twitches gave way to a laugh.

"What's so funny?" she demanded. "I don't think this is funny at all!"

"I gathered that." He chuckled again and wiped the corner of one eye. "But…"

"But what?" she interrupted. "You're not taking that plane out of here!"

"Hannah. Think back. Did I say I was going to?"

A bit of her anger seeped away, and she ran the conversation back in her head, as best she could remember it. "You said you were going to move it."

"Yes, *move* it. To one side. To make more room. If you hadn't flown instantly off the handle I would have explained."

"Oh." Now she felt like a complete idiot, standing there with her arms spread out as if willing to be nailed to the door.

"Yeah, oh." He shook his head and sighed. "You listen so well, I wonder how you get through business negotiations."

Embarrassment vanished as anger surged. "Now look, buster…."

"Buster is the alligator. I'm Buck, remember?"

Shaking his head, he walked away into the dim hangar toward the bank of light switches. One by one he flipped the switches, until the level of illumination in the hangar approached full daylight.

Gradually she relaxed her death grip on one of the door reinforcing bars.

"I just want to move it closer to my DC-3," he said. "The wings can overlap. It'll make more open space for kids if they want to toss a ball or something."

She shuddered. Tossing a ball. Dents. More repairs. Her profit margin was beginning to shrink before her very eyes.

"Come on, Hannah," he said. His voice was almost gentle.

She sighed and gave up. People mattered more than property, and despite her recent behavior, she had never forgotten that.

"Sorry," she said. "You're right. If it comes down to saving a life or saving the plane, the plane loses."

He wrapped an arm around her shoulders and gave her a quick squeeze. "I knew you had a heart."

"If that's what you want to call it."

He shook his head, smiling, as if he knew better.

But once she stopped being an idiot about that plane, she flung herself wholeheartedly into his plan. If the storm really was going to be as bad as it was beginning to look, the people near the waterfront had to be moved.

"How many people is that?" she asked.

"I'm not sure. Most folks haven't built right on the water, but I think we need to start evacuating the nearest first."

She nodded. "Do you have an extra vehicle?"

"No, why?"

"Because I thought I could go down and get some folks."

"First let me call a few friends of mine to get the ball rolling. Then we'll go into town and help where we can."

"Sounds good to me."

It struck her as the height of absurdity that he had to use a satellite phone to call into town. Why hadn't someone put up a repeater so they could use wireless?

Then realization struck her. They'd have to play a poker game for it. Maybe they already had. Maybe they'd decided that their original phone system was just fine and they didn't need the expense of running a line up to the airport. Especially since Buck had a satellite feed for weather anyway, and his phone probably piggy-backed on it without any trouble.

Besides, a wireless repeater would probably turn into a heap of scrap metal in a truly strong storm. And it wouldn't be cheap, either.

She scratched her head, watching him call a couple of friends and describe the situation. Listening to him, she suddenly realized this town had a pyramid system.

When he hung up, she said, "Who thought up the pyramid calling idea?"

"Horace did." He shrugged. "It's the same way we handled it at military bases. Each person on the pyramid calls two others. You'd be amazed how fast word gets around."

"You should have just put it on the grapevine. I swear everyone on the island would know already."

He grinned. "Sometimes it seems that way."

"*Seems?* Let me tell you, Buck, word spreads faster around here than a hurricane wind."

"When there's something interesting going on, yes."

"I'm not interesting."

He looked surprised. "Not interesting? You flew in right over my head, ruined my card game, made it necessary for me to meet Anstin in another match while the entire island is waiting on the outcome. That's not interesting?"

But his words had jogged her memory, causing her to mentally leapfrog to the mayor's earlier visit. "By the way, Tom Regan stopped by today."

"What did that idiot want?"

"To tell you that you were lucky your hand blew away."

"Lucky? I had a full house."

"He implied Anstin had something better. And he asked me to remind you that the whole island is riding on you."

"Hell. He's bluffing. Anstin could say he had any hand he wanted to at this point."

"So could *you,*" she pointed out, smiling brilliantly.

He glared at her. "What's with you? Are you accusing me of lying?"

"Maybe bluffing."

He blew air between his lips in disgust. "As I know you know, there's very little that can beat a full house."

"If he had the Eight and Nine of Diamonds, he had the straight flush," Hannah said.

"And what are the odds of that?"

"One in one-thousand-three-hundred-twenty-six. But he's known for his lucky suck-outs. Maybe he did have you beat, in which case I saved your island."

He paused for a moment, as if impressed that she could accurately cite the probability of Anstin's straight flush, off the top of her head. She found that moment delicious, having finally set him back on his heels.

He let out a sigh. "And Anstin's the biggest liar to set foot on this island since Hank Hanratty himself."

Hannah winced. "If Horace is anything like his ancestor…"

"Rumor has it he is. On the other hand, all those supplies you bought will probably be really useful. Folks will bring what they have, but it's usually never enough."

"No. It costs a lot to buy hurricane supplies." As

she had learned, and she'd only bought for two. Horace's version of two, anyway.

Buck flashed a grin. "I heard about that. A word of advice. *Never* play cards with Horace. The guy has the devil's own luck."

"So it seems. So why isn't he the one playing in the game for the island's future?"

"Because he only plays Stud. The island tournaments are all Texas Hold 'Em."

She nodded. It made sense. No-Limit Hold 'Em was the most popular form of poker, especially since several TV networks had begun to broadcast tournaments. It was also deceptively complex. A child could learn the rules in two minutes, yet the game was so subtle that it was the format for nearly every major championship tournament. It was no accident that a relative handful of top professionals made repeated appearances at the final tables.

"I guess I should grab a broom and get started," she said. "Not that your hangar is dirty, but if people will be sleeping on the floor…."

"No offense taken," he said, walking to the supply closet. He took out two push brooms. "Which end do you want to start at?"

BUCK WAS NOT surprised when Horace Hanratty was the first to arrive, his truck growling and clattering up the narrow road, fully laden with supplies. He was, however, surprised to see that Horace had brought a cash box along.

"Hey," Horace said, smiling amiably, "I'm sure people will need more food and water than Sticks bought for you. Some will bring their own, but you know some won't. So I thought I'd be prepared, you know...."

"Prepared to charge hurricane shelter prices, I'm sure," Buck said.

"Now when have you ever known me to take advantage of someone in distress?" Horace said, looking wounded.

"This morning," Hannah called from across the hangar where she was setting out stacks of plastic cups on a long table that Buck had provided. "I witnessed it first-hand."

"Oh, Sticks," Horace said, putting a hand over his chest. "I had no idea you were in distress. Honestly."

"It's been my experience that whenever a man ends a statement with the word 'honestly,' he's lying," she said.

"We don't call it lying here," Horace said. "We call it bluffing."

"Uh-huh," she said with a determinedly non-committal smile, returning to her work.

"Look," Buck said quietly, as he helped Horace unpack. "You know as well as I do that a lot of the people who'll be here can't afford supplies of their own. Not even at your regular prices. I'm opening this shelter to take care of the people who can't take care of themselves. Don't put me in a bad spot, buddy."

Horace chuckled. "I was just saying that to rile Sticks. You're donating your hangar. I'm donating the supplies. But let's not let Sticks in on that. She's too cute when she's morally indignant."

Buck nodded. "Yeah, she does have that down to an art form, doesn't she?"

"A man could do a lot worse," Horace said, grunting as they lowered a six-burner propane grill from the truck onto a dolly. "A whole lot worse."

"And your point is?" Buck asked as they balanced the grill and began to maneuver it into the hangar.

"My point is, don't be a blind fool," Horace said. Then, dropping the subject, he added, "We'll put this just inside the hangar door. I brought extra propane tanks, and a hose and coupler setup. The tanks stay outside."

"I'll find some tie-downs," Buck said, nodding.

"You won't have to," Horace replied. "I brought my own. Half-inch steel chain. I will have to mount hooks on the hangar wall, though."

"Help yourself," Buck said.

Buck returned to lugging the supplies into the hangar as Horace set himself to the task of securing the propane tanks. For his part, Buck thought Horace was a damned fool about Hannah. Yes, she was nice to look at. Very nice, in fact, and even that was an understatement. But she was also very much accustomed to living her own life, and he had seen way, way too much of that with his ex-wife. *She* had been busy living her own life while he was at sea. He wasn't going to buy that pack of trouble again.

On the other hand, Hannah didn't seem to have the cruel streak that his ex had had. Even when they were dating, he'd sometimes stared, jaw agape, at the things she would say about his squadron mates and their wives.

On their first date, she'd described one of the wives as "a bubble-headed cockpit sucker," a remark which, had he not doubled over in laughter, would have registered as not the kind of comment that a would-be wife should make. But no. Buck had been entranced by her beauty, by her "sense of humor," and blind to the downright meanness that lay just beneath the surface.

So just how was he ever supposed to trust his own judgment again? He had almost *knowingly* walked into a marriage with an abusive, lying, cheating witch, and all of that handwriting had been on the wall, if he'd only poked his head from beneath the sheets long enough to see it.

He looked over at Hannah, trim and firm, with just the right curves, a graceful tilt to her head as she assembled the plastic shelving that Horace had brought. She moved with a grace, an economy of motion, that could take a man's breath away. A dancer, he thought. She moved like a dancer, as if every step, every sway, every gesture had been choreographed by a gracious Muse for the benefit of any admiring eye.

And yet, unlike his ex, she seemed utterly unaware of her beauty. There was no temptress in her. Far from it. She had been a near virago from the moment they'd met. She didn't try to ply feminine wiles, with coquettish bats of her eyelashes. She spoke her mind and stood her ground, and the consequences to her femininity be damned. And that only served to make her all the more attractive.

Damn it.

There was work to do, a lot of work to do, and here he was daydreaming about a woman who had literally blown into his life without so much as a by your leave. And she had no ties to this island, save for a disabled aircraft. The moment Buck had the engines on the Lear up and humming, she would be gone, Treasure Island put firmly in her past with no regrets or reminiscences.

And wouldn't that be the ultimate, cruel twist of a God whose sense of irony was beyond debate? That Hannah Lamont, aviation virago, would indeed be the woman matched to Buck's heart, only to watch her fly away into the azure Caribbean sky, never to return?

Yes, he thought, that would be just about the most perfect crowning touch to his checkered history with women. An omniscient God, possessed of a sense of humor, doubtless knew this as well, and had set out this practical joke, a cosmic laugh at Buck's expense.

And he was not going to fall for it. No way. He would fix her jet and get her gone as fast as he could possibly manage it. And then he would beat Bill Anstin, and things would settle back to normal, or what passed for normal on this island.

That was how it would be.

Buck had made up his mind.

But she was *so* damn cute.

CHAPTER TEN

AS ANOTHER FEEDER band swept through, the refugees began to arrive. Not everyone owned a vehicle. In fact, Hannah gathered that relatively few did. Battered cars and trucks, full of people and supplies, turned around as soon as they dumped their loads, and headed back for more.

Buck directed traffic, sending all the provisions over to the shelves Hannah and Horace had set up. At the other end of the hangar, Hannah helped people make up bed rolls, set up lawn chairs, and otherwise stash their most prized personal possessions.

Periodically, rain drummed so hard on the roof that it was hard to be heard even when shouting. At other times the wind moaned around the corners, and the hangar creaked like old bones.

Hannah noted with surprise that there really weren't all that many children. The island's population seemed to consist mainly of older people, or at least those dwelling closest to the water were older. That made sense, actually. The first houses would have been closest to the beach, closest to the boats. And Buck *had* mentioned a school that also served as a shelter, so the island boasted at least enough children to fill a school. Perhaps those families had chosen to stay at the school.

The children who had come to the hangar, however, soon proved they were less interested in tossing a ball than pursuing the island's favorite pastime. Each time Hannah passed a group of them huddled together, they were playing cards. The stakes were comic books, baseball cards, sticks of gum, sometimes matchsticks, and even, on occasion, cheap plastic chips.

Hannah didn't know whether to be appalled or to laugh. The idea of kids gambling shocked her. At the same time, given the way things were run on this island, these kids were merely practicing for careers in governance.

Then she *did* laugh.

At least these children in the hangar exhibited good manners and good sportsmanship. In its own way, this was no different from playing a game of Monopoly or War to decide who did the dishes. She remembered plenty of kids who had done so during her childhood. All under the benign eye of parents who would have blanched had anyone suggested it was gambling.

So she shrugged and let it go.

"I need a weather report," she announced when she ran into Buck again.

"Need your fix, huh?"

She just rolled her eyes.

"Me, too." The rain had let up for the moment, so the two of them escaped the cacophony that filled the hangar and went back to the office, this time through the rear door in the hangar that led directly into Buck's snug little home. Hannah noted that he'd studiously avoided using that entrance when she was around, until now. She'd never guessed he had a direct way from the hangar to his house. She supposed she should be honored, she thought as she trotted after him into the office.

Buck rounded the counter and pressed the button on the weather fax. It immediately started spitting out paper.

All of a sudden, the smile froze on Buck's face. He looked past her toward the front door of the office, and his jaw dropped.

Hannah immediately spun around. Several seconds passed before her brain registered what her eyes were seeing. The front door had apparently not been locked, and now, pushing his way through it across the threshold, was Buster the alligator, his mouth full of wildflowers.

Like a bouquet, Hannah thought wildly. Buster took a step toward her.

That was it. Hannah leapt onto the counter and scrambled over it, landing in a surprised Buck Shanahan's arms.

"Oh, my God," Hannah whispered.

"Shh," he said. He didn't put her down.

Moving slowly, Buster edged his huge body into the office. His gaze never left Hannah.

Hannah murmured, "Why do I feel like prime rib on the hoof?"

"I think you're more the blushing bride. To Buster, anyway."

She didn't know if that was a compliment or an insult, nor did it matter. Right now she couldn't take her eyes off the approaching dinosaur. Her heart was hammering so hard she thought it would break free.

Until today, she would never have said that reptilian eyes could look soulful. These did. Buster made a relatively quiet groan, which nevertheless rattled the windows, then dropped the flowers on the floor.

"I don't believe this," Buck whispered.

Then, slowly, with great reluctance, Buster backed his huge length out of the office.

Once outside the door he opened his mouth, revealing gleaming teeth, and offered another of his mating roars. Having made his point, he then turned and went looking for a friendlier venue.

"Wow!" Buck said. "If half the island hadn't seen

this, no one would believe it. Buster just brought you a bouquet."

The equally strange part was that there was no doubt it *was* a bouquet. The flower roots were still attached, making the whole thing look exceedingly forlorn, but for all the power of his jaws, Buster had managed to handle the blooms without crushing them.

Hannah stared, seeking balance.

"I'm underwhelmed." She tried to sound amusing but failed miserably. Slowly her heart started to return to normal. Then she realized she was still being held by Buck, with his arms beneath her shoulders and legs, and her arms tight around his neck. Almost tight enough to strangle him.

Apparently Buck became aware of the same thing at the same instant, for he stopped breathing. Half terrified and half hopeful, Hannah turned to look at him. His gaze was fixed on her, the alligator forgotten. His hold tightened, just a little bit, and she began to have fantasies of being dragged off to his bedroom, tossed on the bed and taken in animal passion.

A shiver of delight passed through her, and heat pooled at her core. It was the first time in her life she'd ever thought she might like to be mauled by a caveman.

Slowly Buck's face came closer. A kiss. He was going to kiss her. Roman candles started to go off in her head at the mere thought. Yes!

He astonished her. His mouth didn't slam down on

hers, nor did it grind against her. There was none of the stuff you saw in the movies. Instead his lips touched hers lightly, a touch more seductive than demanding.

And seductive it was. Her entire body seemed to melt as the tentative kiss continued, a brush, a flutter, and who would ever have thought a man's lips could feel so soft?

Her brain had definitely left the building. Shivers of longing began to race through her, unlike anything she had ever known. At that moment she would gladly have laid herself on the altar of this man's desires.

Slowly, the kiss deepened. She let her head fall back willingly, accepting all that he might give her. Fire suddenly streaked through her as his fingers brushed the side of her breast. He was no longer so much holding her as cradling her. All he had to do was turn and carry her into his home behind the office…

Then reality raised its ugly, disgusting, unwanted head. He jerked his head back as if stung, and looked at her with something so much like horror she wondered if she'd grown snakes in place of her hair. Then, so quickly that she gasped, he set her unceremoniously on her feet.

Before she could embarrass herself further by asking what was wrong, he disappeared through the door behind them, closing it with a definitive slam.

Hannah stood there shaking, shocked by the swift change in mood, wondering if there was something terribly wrong with her. Why had he rejected her that way?

Humiliation filled her and she wanted to find a hole to hide in where she could lick her wounds unseen. That feeling lasted for a full minute, maybe a little longer, as she stood looking from the firmly closed door to the pathetic little bouquet Buster had left.

She was losing her mind! That was it. She was dealing with two reptiles, not just Buster. And the one on two legs had no excuse at all. Why was she putting up with this?

Suddenly furious, she marched toward Buck's door and banged on it. When he didn't answer, she threw it open and marched inside. He was standing at the bar in his kitchen and swung around when she stormed in.

"I don't remember inviting you in," he said sarcastically.

"After what just happened I don't need an invitation. I need an explanation."

"Explanation for what? I kissed you. Big deal."

"You stupid man! You can't just kiss a woman like that then drop her as if she's only a bag of potatoes!"

"Why not?" He shrugged. "It shouldn't have happened to begin with."

"Maybe not, but it *did* happen, and I want an explanation of why you hightailed it the way you did. Do I stink? Is my breath bad? What the hell, Shanahan, I'm not a toy to be tossed in a corner at will."

"Toy?" He shook his head. "If I thought you were a toy I wouldn't have stopped."

Somehow that didn't ease her anger any. Instead it enhanced her frustration. "You know what? You are an uncouth, arrogant, cigar-chewing waste of human flesh."

He started to laugh. That didn't help either. "And you," he said between laughs, "are a virago. So where does that get us? If it wasn't for the storm, I'd suggest that we move to opposite ends of the island."

"Ooooooooooh!" The groan of frustration escaped her as her hands knotted into fists. "You're impossible!"

She turned to march out, unwilling to be within sight or sound of him any longer, but his next words stopped her dead in her tracks.

"Watch out for Buster," he said casually. "With this cloudy weather he gets around more."

She froze. Her feet stuck to the floor as if glued. "Buster," she said. She remembered the bouquet then, but worse, remembered that the office door was still open to the outside world. Even now that beast could be waiting for her. A shudder ran through her.

"Is there something wrong with the air on this island?" she demanded, facing him again. "I haven't met one normal person since I got here, and that includes Buster."

"I dunno. You don't exactly seem normal yourself."

At that instant she wished she were a ninja and could throw herself over the kitchen counter and teach him a lesson.

"I'm perfectly normal."

"Really? Who told you that?"

He was laughing again. The devil of it was, when he laughed he was even more attractive than his usual grumpy self.

And speaking of grumpy…there *was* something in the water or air. "I don't usually act like this," she snapped.

"No? Is that the effect I have on you? Maybe for my own safety I should cast you adrift in a rubber dinghy."

He was impossible. Absolutely impossible. What did Edna see in him? But she knew *exactly* what Edna saw in him, because she was seeing it, too. If anything on this island was making her crazy, it was Buck Shanahan.

"Look, Sticks," he said, "why don't we declare an armistice? Just until this storm is over. Otherwise all we're going to do is play the insult game. 'I'll see your insult and raise you one.' Do we really need that?"

She deflated then. She *had* been acting like an idiot, and there was no excuse for it. All she had done was humiliate herself further. She might as well be wearing a big sign around her neck that said I want to sleep with Buck.

Gawd! She wanted to sink. What was it about this guy? He could light her fuse faster than a match.

And of course, it was right then that there was a sharp rap on the door and Edna Harkin walked in.

CHAPTER ELEVEN

"WHAT IS GOING ON here?" The words blurted from Edna's mouth as her eyes narrowed to something feral. Hannah felt as if she were facing a lioness on the hunt.

Worse, Hannah couldn't even protest, not given what *had* happened. For an instant, she froze, feeling like a schoolgirl who'd been caught by her mother doing something racy with her boyfriend. But only for an instant.

Then she remembered the kiss.

"We're having some private time," Hannah heard herself saying, groaning inwardly as she said it.

"Well isn't that just cozy?" Edna replied.

"Yes, quite," Hannah replied.

She glanced over at Buck, who seemed as if he were watching a tennis match being played with a live hand grenade. *Good,* she thought. *Let him simmer.*

Then she turned her attention back to Edna. "If you really *must* know, Buster brought me a bouquet. For some reason, two of the reptilian species on this island seem to find me attractive. Apparently Buck was so thunderstruck by the romantic notion that he kissed me. And…my God in Heaven!…what a kiss it was!"

Edna looked more ready to erupt than any volcano Hannah had ever seen. "You have *no* right to kiss my man!" she announced with a voice that echoed off the walls and drew a crowd of teens to the back doorway. They clustered in the little laundry room off the kitchen, watching eagerly.

"*Your* man?" Hannah asked. "First, *your* man kissed me, so you'd need to take that up with him. Second, if that kiss was any indication at all, he's less *yours* than you'd like to think!"

Teens who had been exchanging matchsticks and gum over hands of poker were now passing them back and forth in excited whispers.

"Umm," Buck began, "may I…."

"*No!*" Hannah and Edna answered in unison.

"You stay out of this!" Edna added for good measure.

"But this is my…."

"Shut up, Buck!" Hannah added. "Now, Edna, I think you should apologize for barging in here like this and interrupting us."

"*Apologize?* Are you out of your mind? I have every right to barge in when some floozy tourist is making time with my man!"

"I'm not a floozy tourist," Hannah said, crossing her arms defiantly.

"And I'm not...." Buck began.

"Shut! Up!" Hannah and Edna said in unison.

More sticks of gum passed between the teens. The youngest of them, a boy with Jamaican mocha features who might have been fifteen, seemed to be getting the best of whatever wagers were passing in their tense, whispered exchanges. That kid would have gum to last a lifetime, at this rate. Hannah winked at him and continued her assault.

"I'll have you know that I am a businesswoman," Hannah said. "I run a multi-million-dollar corporation, largely on my own hard work. And I'm *stranded* on this damn island because of a mechanical failure and this storm. So, in the manner of most CEOs who find themselves stranded on tropical islands during storms, I'm taking advantage of the local scenery!"

"Now wait a...." Buck began.

"Don't!" Hannah said, turning to face him. "Don't say another word. Think of yourself as the sexy gardener being fought over by the wives of the landed gentry. Mouth shut. Penis at the ready when called for."

At that, the teens let out a howl, and the mocha-skinned boy collected two more packs of gum. Hannah considered shooing them, but couldn't bring herself to do it. This was the most fun she'd had since she'd landed on this benighted rock.

"Such filth!" Edna said. "You think my man is a

mere sex toy to be played with while you're here? I'll have you know he's a…he's a…he's a…."

"If he's such a gem," Hannah said, "why are you at a loss for words? What, exactly, do *you* like about him?"

"Well, he's…."

"A single white male on this rock you've found yourself trapped on," Hannah said.

"But…."

"Oh please," Hannah stormed on, "don't tell me you really *love* him! He's a troglodyte. A sexy troglodyte, to be sure, and he damn sure kisses like a teenage wet dream. But he's still a cigar-chewing, grease-covered, broken-down ex-fly-boy troglodyte. He won't even give you the time of day, for crying out loud!"

"Eleven nineteen," Buck said, glancing at his watch.

"*Please!*" Hannah said, whirling to face him again. And then, just for an instant, she caught the glint in his eyes. *He was enjoying this, too!* "Can you keep that cigar-laden, melt-my-loins-kissable mouth shut for two minutes?"

"Aye-aye," he said.

"Well, I *never!*" Edna said, stomping a foot.

"What a shame," Hannah replied. "You'd have probably had more dates in high school."

At that, Edna's howl of rage was matched only by the cackle in the doorway. The boy probably now owned everything in the hangar, including her Lear.

"That's *enough,*" Edna said to them. Then, turning to Hannah, fire in her eyes, she added, "You have insulted my honor, and my man. I challenge you to a duel."

"Geologists' picks at twenty paces?" Hannah said, placing a hand on her hip. "Somehow I doubt that will accomplish much."

"No! Heads-up poker, no-limit Hold 'em, best three of five matches." Edna paused, then added, "And the winner gets Buck!"

"You're on," Hannah said.

"Fine," Edna said, turning on her heel and storming out through the crowd of boys.

The mocha-skinned boy gave Hannah a thumbs up. She smiled to him before he turned and led the other boys out into the hangar. When she looked back, Buck was lounging in his chair, legs crossed, a cigar stuck between grinning teeth.

"So what was that all about, Sticks?"

She laughed. "Damned if I know. But do keep your...equipment...at the ready, gardener boy."

"You know," he said, "you never paused to ask if I minded being the stakes in your little game with Edna."

"You're right," she said. "I didn't."

THEN, BEFORE SHE COULD think about what that meant, she strolled out the door, pausing in the kitchen to pick up Buster's bouquet, before walking out into the hangar and climbing into her jet. Only then, when she was alone, did she let herself think about the last half-hour.

Now what the hell have I done?

The only logical answer lay in the pair of saurian eyes reflected from behind her.

"Buster," she said, looking at him in the mirror, "you are making me crazy."

If an alligator's groan could have said "I'm sorry," that one did.

She turned to face him. "Look, I've pretty much figured out by now that you're not going to eat me, right?"

Buster seemed to nod.

"But here's the thing. I know you like me. But I'm really not your type. At all. I'm a mammal. You know, warm-blooded, hair instead of scales, the class that your kind normally thinks of as food?"

Buster nodded again, and Hannah found herself feeling as if she were trying to explain why she could not marry someone of another religion, while at the same time knowing this situation was entirely different. In fact, the entire idea of conversing with an alligator felt totally absurd to her. But what the hell? She'd just agreed to a poker duel for the rights to Buck Shanahan. Could talking with an alligator be any crazier than that?

"What I'm saying, Buster, is that I'm going nuts

on this island. I just agreed to a poker game with Edna, and the winner gets Buck."

Huh? Buster seemed to moan.

"Yeah, I know, it's crazy."

Buster nodded.

"I don't even know Buck, let alone whether I'd really like him. He thinks I'm a virago, and he's right, and I'm sure he wouldn't like me that way."

Maybe, Buster's eyes seemed to say.

"But God is he sexy. And that kiss! Wow!"

Please, Buster moaned.

"Oh, I'm sorry," Hannah said, reaching out to stroke his leathery head. "How thoughtless of me."

Mmhhmmm, Buster moaned, and at the same instant Hannah realized what she was doing. She almost jerked her hand away, then thought that would only hurt his feelings more. And she definitely did not need a resentful alligator in her midst.

Unbelievably, Buster's tail began to twitch. Not quite wagging, thank God, because a wagging alligator tail would have made a hash of the jet's cabin. Just a twitch.

"You like this, don't you?"

Mmhmm, he moaned.

"So what am I going to do?" she asked. "Buck's made me nuts more than Edna has, for crying out loud. Even if I win, have I really won anything?"

Hard to say, Buster's eyes whispered.

"I guess I could lose on purpose."

Grrrr.

"Right," she said, running her nails back and forth over the softer hide at the side of his neck. "Bad idea. Forget I mentioned it."

Mmhmm.

"I wonder how good she is. Edna, I mean. Is she a good poker player? What are her tendencies? What hands does she like to play? What are her tells?"

Can't help you there, his eyes said.

"Yeah, I know," she said. "But I need to find out. That's something my father told me. Never sit down at a table full of strangers for money that matters."

Mmhmm.

"So who knows her, Buster? You seem to be the all-seeing, all-knowing eyes around here. Who does she play poker with?"

No answer.

"C'mon, Buster. A girl needs some help here!"

If a low, rumbling, hissing growl could have formed words, they would probably have been: *Right, now you expect me to give you names, in a language you would understand?*

"You're right," she said. "But you could point them out to me, right?"

Mmhmm.

"You're with me in this, right, Buster?"

Ohhh yesss.

"Even if it means I end up winning Buck?"

Sigh. Yes.

"Partners, then?"

Mmhmm.

She held out a hand, and, impossibly, he placed a front foot into it. Partners.

"You're not so bad," she said, returning to scratching his neck.

Mmhmm.

"We'll get Edna, together."

Mmhmm.

"You'd agree to anything I said, so long as I keep scratching, right?"

Mmhmm.

CHAPTER TWELVE

CUTE AND SPUNKY, Buck thought, still chuckling in his room. *What a devastating combination.*

Fact was, he'd just witnessed one of the sexiest displays he'd ever seen, better even than that two-girls-and-handcuffs scene he'd watched at a bar in Manila. And this time he hadn't been twenty-three, drunk, and half a world from home.

So she'd accepted Edna's duel. Wow. That offered all kinds of possibilities. So far, the fly-girl virago had been a distraction, an annoyance, and a very uncomfortable temptation. Now, however, he began to consider that she might be something else: a playmate.

Not in the sexual sense, perhaps, although his groin had stirred when she'd said he was the sexy gardener, mouth shut, penis at the ready. It'd been all he could do not to burst out laughing at that moment, but he'd known that would ruin her performance. No, she could be a playmate in the better sense...a way to retain his sanity while his hangar was overrun with islanders hiding from the storm.

Yes, this could get very, very interesting indeed.

First, however, there was the scene in the hangar to be dealt with. He walked out to find that more people were arriving, many on foot or piled in the backs of pickup trucks, bearing what few possessions they could not leave behind. One family had brought a small coop with a half-dozen chickens. Another had brought a freshly slaughtered pig. That, he thought, was a good place to start.

"Horace," he said, pulling the grocer aside. "We need to get food started for these people. Any chance we can get a barbeque pit going for that pig?"

"It's not statistically impossible," Horace said. "But if we're going to roast a pig, we need to get some barbeque sauce going. And Ms. Ginny over there makes the best barbeque sauce on the island. Someone should ask her if she brought the fixins for it."

"You're right," Buck said. "Someone should. Why don't you take care of it? I'll round up some extra cement blocks for the barbeque pit, and get some people together to gather up wood."

"You got it, Buck."

Two hours later, the barbeque pit was built on the cement apron outside the hangar door, and the huge fire had been laid. Buck had even managed to make a temporary tent over the pit with remains of an old shed he'd been demolishing. The hope was that they could keep the fire from drowning in the veils of rain that were sweeping through, and keep the "tent" together long enough to finish the cooking. He and several other men worked at bracing the heavy wood-and-shingle roof sections from the old shack.

The pig had been dressed and soon was buried in the coals. Ginny Devaneau had indeed brought most of the ingredients for her renowned sauce. What she didn't have with her, Horace made good from his provisions. The sauce would be added to individual portions after the cooking. Ginny worked with two huge pots, taken from the school's kitchen.

As Ginny stood at the grill heating and stirring her sauce, and the cooking scents began to waft around the hangar, other women watched surreptitiously, hoping to finally get Ginny's secret. She simply chuckled and kept several bottles of spices safely out of sight in her apron pockets.

Buck was watching this silent contest with glee when Hannah emerged from the Learjet with Buster following her. She ignored his surprised look and angled her head toward the women around the grill. "What's going on there?"

"Ginny Devaneau's making barbeque sauce for a pig we're going to roast in a bit. The other women are trying to sneak peeks at her recipe. There aren't but a handful of secrets on this entire island. The recipe for Ginny's barbeque sauce is one of them, and by far the most tightly guarded."

"Tighter even than the combination to Anstin's casino vault?" she asked.

"Forty-two, thirty-eight, sixteen, thirteen, nine," Buck said. When she looked at him questioningly, he had to smile. It was so nice to shock her. "Yeah, that's it. His age, his ex-wife's age, and his kids' ages. In order."

"How did you…."

"Most of the island knows," Buck said, shrugging. "Like I said, there aren't many secrets here."

"This is one very strange place," Hannah said, stooping down to scratch Buster's back.

"Says the woman who accepted a duel for the rights to a man she can't stand, and has a love-struck alligator for a pet," he replied.

"Yeah, about that duel," she said.

Buck put up a hand and grinned. "Hey, I'm flattered. And with this storm about to sock us in for a few days, I can think of worse things to make book on."

"Make book?"

"I put a C-note on you at three-to-two," he said. "Horace set the line."

"I'm a three-to-two *underdog?*" Hannah asked. "To that psycho lava lover?"

"That's just the initial line," Buck said, laughing. "I'm sure the odds will shorten."

"I'm going to go talk to Horace," she said, rising. Even Buster looked offended.

He put a hand on her forearm. "Relax, Sticks. Look, it's better to be the underdog. In fact, it's better to be a huge underdog. We both know you're going to clean Edna's clock, unless the deck slaps her silly. If we play this right, you could end up owning Anstin's casino before all's said and done."

"I don't *want* to own Anstin's casino!" she said. "I'm not even sure why I took the challenge at all, except that I'm feeling stranded and feisty."

"Sure there's not more to it than that?" he asked with a grin.

Buster nudged her leg and looked up at her, as if telling her something. Buck couldn't figure out what, though, and understood her reply even less.

"I don't gamble what I can't afford to lose, Buck. But I damn sure do play to win."

I'M AN UNDERDOG, Hannah thought, storming across the hangar. That annoyed her beyond all reason. She had felt dismissed, disrespected, and generally like a curiosity ever since she'd landed on this island. If there was going to be a betting line on her poker ability, then they could at least get the line right.

Although the hangar was growing more crowded, she realized that people were opening a path for her. In fact, they were parting like the Red Sea, with widened eyes and momentary gasps. She wondered if perhaps she'd grown a third eye, but then she knew what it had to be. A quick glance over her shoulder confirmed her thought. Buster was following her like a love-struck puppy.

"Buster, heel," she said.

Huhhh?

She stopped and looked back. "Don't act like you don't understand me, Buster. If you're going to follow me everywhere, at least walk beside me where I can see you."

Ohhhh.

He shuffled up beside her, and she continued on her way across the hangar. Now, rather than wide-eyed stares, people were giggling and a few even applauded. That alone soothed her wounded pride some. That, in turn, cleared her anger and allowed her to think more clearly. Now she strode up to Horace with a purpose.

"Hey, Sticks," he said. "I see you've tamed Buster?"

"Tamed? No, I doubt that. He's still as dangerous as he ever was, right, Buster?"

The alligator seemed unsure of how to respond, until she gave him a look that said *just play along, kiddo.* Then he let out a wall-rattling roar. If she hadn't known better, she'd have thought he winked!

"Okay, Sticks," Horace said. "I get your point. So let me guess. You're upset about the betting line."

"You're damn right I am," she said. "I should be a much bigger underdog."

If she had told him that he had just grown a horn on his forehead, he would not have looked more surprised.

"That's right, Horace. I should be at least a three-to-one underdog."

"But...." he began.

Buster cut him off with another growl, and again looked up at Hannah, with eyes that said *this is what you want, right?* She flashed Buster a nod.

"Three-to-one, Horace." She leaned in and lowered her voice. "Bet the difference on me."

"You have something working here, don't you, Sticks?" he asked in a low whisper.

"Yup. But that's just between us, okay?"

He smiled. "My lips are sealed. Whatever plan you're working, it should be entertaining to watch."

"Let's hope so," she said.

In truth, the plan was only half-formed. Something Buck said had given her the germ of an idea...an idea that might just put Bill Anstin in his proper place for a long time to come. Images of the Newman-Redford classic, *The Sting,* floated through her mind as she walked over to the coffee machine and poured herself a cup.

Ooooh.

She looked down and saw that Buster was eyeing her coffee cup. "Don't tell me...you like coffee."

Mmhmm.

How on earth could an alligator have come to like

coffee? Of course. Duh. The islanders here put out food for Buster on a regular basis. Someone put out coffee, too.

"Let me guess. You want a donut with your coffee?"

Mmhmm.

Well, in for a penny, in for a pound. She selected a plain donut, thinking that the combination of sugar and caffeine would probably not be good for Buster's temper or metabolism, then found a bowl and poured come coffee into it. She crumbled the donut into the coffee and set both on the floor of the hangar for him.

"How's that, big guy?"

Mmmmmmmhmmmmmmmm.

She sipped her coffee as she watched Buster devour the coffee and donut, bowl and all, his jaws snapping the clay bowl as if it were candy. After a few moments, the bits of clay came shooting out with a contented half-burp, half-roar that left her speechless.

"Well," Buck said, appearing beside her. "I guess we know who should be the island's police."

She scowled at him, then looked down at Buster. One clear thought floated across her mind: *I have utterly lost my marbles.*

The worst of it, though, was that she couldn't seem to care. Talking to an alligator? Feeding him coffee and donuts? What the hey. This was Treasure Island, after all.

BURIED IN HOT COALS, 800 pounds of pig cooked reasonably fast and thoroughly. Not too long after dark, as the rain bands grew more threatening, Horace and the mayor stood at a groaning table, slicing off hunks of roast pig, while Ginny served large dollops of her famed sauce to all comers.

Although Horace looked as if he were running a mental cash register over the paper plates, napkins, plastic cups, utensils and the bushels of apples he parted with for dessert, the hangar had taken on a festive air. Even Buster was granted a pig hock to ecstatically gnaw on.

Sounds of laughter and playing children, along with the occasional snatch of song waged battle against the rain that hammered on the roof of the hangar. Hannah, sitting on the top step of her plane, watched it all as she ate, and thought that it was almost as if the people had created a cocoon of well-being around themselves that not even the storm could pierce.

She was sitting there, feeling a genuine spirit of bonhomie with the citizens of Treasure Island, many of whom she had met during the course of this fractured day, when her mood turned sour, thanks to the arrival of Bill Anstin.

He climbed up a couple of steps until he sat directly below her with his serving of roast pig and barbeque sauce.

"You need something?" she asked him in a less-than-friendly tone.

He looked up at her, offering a thousand-watt smile. "Not at the moment. I just wanted to share the view."

And it was a rattlesnake's nature to bite. She waited for the bite.

But for awhile he said nothing more, merely tucking into his meal and carefully wiping his hands on a paper towel as if he couldn't bear to have sticky fingers even between bites. She also noted that he had received one of the best slabs of meat, the succulent, sweet ribs. She wondered which old lady he'd stolen it from.

Then she wondered at her own reaction. Other than a few leers, she had nothing against Anstin. Well, except possibly for his ego. And possibly because he wanted to ruin Treasure Island with a huge casino and hotel.

Although why the latter should matter to her at all, she couldn't conceive. This island would soon be a fading spot in the rear window of her plane as she flew on to Aruba.

Anstin meticulously finished his rack of ribs, gnawing the last shreds from the bone. Then, as he wiped his hands on yet another paper towel, he smiled up at her, unaware that he had a piece of meat, reddened with sauce, stuck between his front teeth. "I've got to hand it to Buck," he said. "That was a great idea."

"And to the person who brought the pig, and to Ginny for her sauce, and to all the people who helped."

"That goes without saying. But it was his idea."

She eyed him suspiciously. "Why are you suddenly being so nice about Buck?"

"I have never been *not* nice about Buck. He's been a thorn in my side for several years now, but I have never been rude to him."

"Amazing." And he could lie like a rug. Well, of course. He was a poker player.

"Thing about poker players," she said sweetly, "is that you never know when they're bluffing."

He laughed, as if she had just made the funniest joke of the century. It was that laughter that convinced her this man was after something. The question was what.

"I hear you're playing Edna for Buck," he said when he stopped laughing.

Hannah shrugged. "So it seems."

"What will you do if you lose?"

"Get on with my life."

"Oh, come on. You must want Buck or you wouldn't be playing."

Hannah shook her head, wondering why something inside her was trying to squirm. "I never play for stakes I'm not willing to lose."

He raised an eyebrow. "Then you're not really a gambler, are you?"

She wanted to bean him then. She gambled every day of her life in the real world. She gambled on the planes she bought, she gambled on the price she charged for them, she gambled on whether she could keep her business going through thin times. She gambled daily on stakes that really mattered. What was a card game but a mere amusement?

"Maybe," she said, "you don't really understand what gambling is."

Anstin looked offended. "Believe me, I know. I won the Main Event at the World Series, didn't I?"

"Big deal. That's not gambling."

"What?"

"Heck no. You pay your fee of ten thousand dollars so you can play poker for a week. That's not gambling. That's paying to play."

He squawked, sounding almost like a dying crow. "I was gambling for the winner's pot and the bracelet. I gambled on every turn of a card."

She shrugged. "You paid to play. You didn't put up anything you weren't willing to lose."

His face turned a bright red and he was no longer giving her anything resembling a lascivious look. "You're wrong," he said. "I'm gambling against Buck for this island."

"You're gambling for the right to build a huge casino here. And if you lose, you'll just find another island to build on. In short, you won't lose anything,

Anstin. But the people on this island could lose an awful lot."

He glared at her. "What have they got to lose? Poverty?"

"Peace," she said. "And a tightly knit community. You want to take that all away from them. But *you* have nothing to lose."

That did it. He rose, turning his back on her and storming toward the trash bins with his paper plate and napkins.

A moment later, Buck appeared at the foot of the stairs. "What did you say to Anstin? He's muttering under his breath and stomping his feet."

Hannah shrugged. "I just told him he wasn't a real gambler."

Buck gaped at her. Then an uproarious laugh escaped him. "You go, Sticks," he said between laughs. "You rock!"

Then the lights went out.

CHAPTER THIRTEEN

BUCK HAD BEEN happier in his life. He'd been more miserable, too, but that wasn't foremost on his mind at the moment. Right now he was angry at the island's humidity which had somehow managed to rust part of the generator despite all his careful care and oiling.

Wiping sweat from his brow, he banged again on the side of the cam trying to loosen it enough to turn. Everything in this climate deteriorated rapidly unless you were on top of it every minute. The dampness and the salt air made corrosion control a full-time job all by itself.

He was angry at himself for not catching this problem sooner, and angry that he must have slipped up on his routine maintenance. Angry because all those people were sitting in *his* hangar using flash-lights that might be more important later. They were *depending* on him.

He squirted some more lubricant around the cam and banged again. This time he thought he saw some-thing shift.

A damn good thing, too, he thought as he wiped more sweat from his eyes. Another squall line was approaching and the wind had stiffened enough to make it hard for him to keep his balance.

Reaching out, he was about to turn the cam to see if it would work now, when he heard Hannah's voice.

"Buck?"

Looking up, he saw her stumble around the corner of the building, bent against the wind. Cripes, he thought irrationally, this was all *her* fault. In his mind, Delilah here was becoming insanely but inextricably linked to Hurricane Hannah and all the attendant problems.

In fact, the more he thought about it, the more convinced he became that his life had gone to hell the instant Hannah Lamont had flown in over his head. Before that, life had been relatively peaceful. Even Bill Anstin had been as easy to ignore as a cloud of gnats. He just kept batting him away.

But this.... He clenched his teeth and realized he didn't have a cigar to act as a cushion. See? That woman had turned his entire life upside down and inside out in twenty-four hours.

He decided then and there that if he could get this generator running, he was going to utterly ignore Hannah Lamont and get to work on her plane. Then as soon as the weather cleared he could go get parts. Or, if he was really lucky, he could fix the problem with what he had on hand and see *her* fly out tomorrow.

He decided he liked the second option best.

That woman was really getting under his skin, and he hated it. Visions of her curves kept haunting him in unguarded moments, and he knew he was angrier with her than he should have been. He was usually an even-tempered guy. But all that had blown out the window the instant that vixen set foot on his island.

"Buck?" she called again over the wind.

"What?" He sounded as grumpy as he felt.

"Are you having any luck?"

"What does it look like?" He was sure he was a sight: wet, bedraggled, grease-covered. Holding a sixteen-pound hammer.

"Not good."

"Then go back inside and wait."

"I can't exactly do that."

"Why not?"

"Because folks inside are a little uneasy about having Buster in there when the lights are out."

"So take him for a walk."

She threw up her hands and almost lost her balance. "I tried. He wouldn't follow me outside. Do you think he's stupid?"

"Well, then, people are just going to have to trust that he'll chew on leftover pig if he gets hungry.

Come to think of it, he seems to have quite a taste for Ginny's barbeque sauce."

"I don't believe you!"

He patted his pockets again, hoping against hope for a cigar to chew on. No luck. His luck seemed to have run out the instant Hannah landed on his island. "Look, Sticks, I gotta get this generator running. Ask some of the other macho meatheads in there to remove Buster. In fact, tell Anstin to organize a crew. That ought to suit his ego."

She didn't answer immediately, which was just as well because he took another swipe at the cam with the hammer. "Yessss!" he said as the cam moved another inch.

Hannah watched him, an odd expression on her face...or at least there seemed to be, except her cloud of red hair kept getting blown across it. He found himself wondering if that hair was as soft and silky as it looked...a big mistake, because he hit his thumb with the hammer.

A yelp escaped him. Hannah immediately struggled toward him. He viewed this as an onslaught: the enemy was about to overwhelm him.

"Stay back," he snapped. "You're a jinx."

"I'm a *what?*" She gaped, then glared.

"A jinx! Everything's gone wrong since you flew into this place."

"I could say the same!"

"So *you're* jinxed, too. I'm supposed to feel sorry for you?" He sucked his throbbing thumb. "Damn, damn, damn!"

"I didn't make this hurricane."

"Hah! I suppose you think it's coincidence that it has your name?"

"Sure, I asked the guys at the Hurricane Center to use my name, and make sure it was pinned to a storm that was going to hit the same island I didn't know I was going to be on."

This ridiculous argument—and he knew it was ridiculous even though his thumb was throbbing as if it wanted to explode and he was growing as mad as a hatter—might have gone on forever if the capricious wind hadn't chosen that moment to hurl Hannah into his arms.

She literally came flying toward him, a look of astonishment on her face. He reached out to catch her, dropping the hammer on his foot. A yelp escaped him.

"Damn it!" But before he could accuse her of jinxing him yet again, she was pressed hard into his arms. He had the brief mental image of one of those Garfield stuffed animals that people liked to stick on the back windows of their cars…an image of Hannah, arms widespread as she tried to steady herself…and then she was glued to him by the wind, just like Garfield on the rear window.

Foot forgotten instantly, he wrapped his arms

around her, trying to steady them both against the savage assault of Mother Nature.

Then, in an instant, everything except Hannah vanished. The wind could have ripped the building apart, the rain could have come down like Noah's flood, the volcano could have erupted…but he wouldn't have noticed.

Hannah was in his arms. His awareness narrowed to her curves, lusher than he would have expected since she was so lean, almost coltish, in her build. But there was no mistaking at this moment the press of full breasts, the roundness of a woman's hips….

One last warning shrieked in his head like the Klaxon on a submarine in an old movie, or like the warning tone that preceded the call to general quarters on an aircraft carrier. Then it, too, was gone and he was lost. Samson was no longer a jerk, and Delilah was winning the day.

Because it was as if everything inside him went into total meltdown…except his manhood which began to throb with a hunger he'd almost forgotten and decided to nestle itself right against the softness of Hannah's belly.

Her head tipped back, eyes wide with astonishment. Her hands clutched his shoulders. Then, with all the aplomb of a former Top Gun, Buck braced himself and took the death-defying dive toward the enemy.

He kissed her. Oh, did he kiss her. It was a kiss

that involved every cell in his body, every muscle he had. It took the breath from him and seemed to toss him straight to the moon at superluminal speed.

The warm cavern of her mouth welcomed his tongue to a duel that merely fueled his aching need. When she squirmed against him it was a semaphore from her body begging for more. Lost, lost, in an airless bit of heaven, his mind filled with stars and swirling galaxies, his body aching…aching…aching….

Then Mother Nature intervened rudely, slapping him on the back hard, causing him to stagger forward.

Hannah tore her mouth from his and cried out as she was thrust against the generator.

Reality returned hard and fast, and an instant later they were both leaning against the wind, staring at one another as if…as if they were stunned.

Her green eyes were huge, astonished. Her mouth looked a little puffy, which only made him want to seize it again. Then a tremor passed through her and she turned swiftly, breaking the spell. He could see that she was as frightened as he suddenly was.

"Hannah…" Something stopped him. Now was not the time to beg for more, and some last ounce of sense warned him that an apology would be exactly the worst thing he could offer right now.

She drew a deep breath, as if gathering herself. She turned her head in his direction, sliding a hand up through her hair to pull it from her face and giving him a coquettish look. "God, Buck. Kiss that generator, please! Or else hook *me* up to those power lines!"

No one, *no one,* had ever responded to his kiss like that. In fact, by the time his marriage lay in ruins, he'd convinced himself that he was an utter failure as a man. But something in her windswept face gave him a shiver to his very core.

"Yeah. It's almost there." Slowly the throbbing of his thumb and toe grew more insistent.

She looked away, then faced him again. "Are you okay? The hammer...."

"I'm fine." He was doing well. He could breathe again. The ache was still there, but it was easing. A little anyway.

"Can I help?"

The worst offer she could have made. He knew he was *that* close to turning into a caveman and taking her bent over the generator.

The storm took a hand, slapping him in the face with a big raindrop.

"I'm almost done," he said. "Go back inside and keep your gator out of everyone's hair."

A spark flared in her eyes. "He's not *my* gator."

Good, she was getting annoyed again. It was what he wanted, needed, for his own safety. "Whatever. I'll have the lights on in a few minutes."

"Everyone else's lights, you mean."

She didn't say another word, but simply flashed

him a smile that itself should have started the damn generator, and struggled away into the wind.

He watched her round the corner of the building. Then he was alone again with the forces of nature.

And not all those forces were on the outside.

BACK INSIDE the hangar, Hannah paused just inside the door, pretending to survey the groups gathered around various kinds of lanterns, some gas, some electric. She couldn't see Buster anywhere.

But inside she was shaking. Like a leaf. Her encounter with Buck had exceeded any such encounter in her life. She wondered how to handle it, because she could already feel the urge to return to him, to try another one of those kisses to see if it had been real.

To return and find out if she could become that swamped in desire once again. Between her legs she still felt soft, ready to yield. The press of her bra on her breasts had become oddly sensual, and each brush of fabric on her skin heightened her awareness of the need he had awakened in her.

She wanted him. Oh, how she wanted him.

But want was not enough, she told herself. It had to be more than that. And with Buck that was all she had. A need like a spark in dry tinder, and if she gave into it, she would be the one burned. Of that she was sure.

Straightening, she looked around again, and spied

Horace. He was camping out with his store of goods next to the pallet of things he had sold her earlier.

"The generator will be back online soon," she said.

A number of nearby people took up the word and passed it through the hangar which, lit only by the lanterns, seemed like a cavernous maw.

"You might," Horace said, "get your alligator out from behind this pallet before he eats the food."

"What's he doing back there?"

"Apparently he didn't feel safe without you."

"Yeah, right."

Horace shrugged. "He hid as soon as you went outside. It's the only reason we're not having a riot in here."

"I thought you folks thought of Buster as a pet."

Horace snorted. "Outside is one thing. Locked up inside is another."

She couldn't really argue with that, she supposed. "He ought to be full of pork."

"You'd think." Horace jerked his head. "Take a look."

So she went around the pallet and found Buster, almost invisible in the little bit of light from Horace's lantern that reached back there. He opened one sleepy eye, let out a contented groan, then went back to sleep.

"He's not going to bother anyone or anything right now," Hannah said as she came back around the supplies to Horace. "He's so full of roast pig all he wants to do is sleep."

"You're sure of that?"

"He said so."

Horace cackled. "I gotta tell you, Sticks, I ain't never seen that animal take a shine to anyone like he took to you. He'd probably let you lead him around on a leash."

"That would be cruel."

"What's going to be really cruel is when you fly off into the sunset and leave that poor animal heartbroken."

Hannah had the strangest feeling that Horace wasn't talking about the gator just then. She peered at him, trying to read his face, but he looked as innocent as the day was long.

Which meant, she thought as she considered her earlier encounters with this man, that he wasn't talking about the gator at all.

He was talking about something else. And she wasn't sure she wanted to hear the message.

CHAPTER FOURTEEN

A HALF-HOUR LATER, the lights flickered, then came on. A cheer spread through the hangar, enough even to make Buster open one eyelid for a moment. Seeing that Hannah was still there, he let out a happy moan and closed his eyes.

They thought he was sleeping, which was fine. It gave him time to think. That was the one thing that bothered him about the two-legged kind. They did everything so *fast.* They lived fast. They died fast. And worst of all, they thought fast.

That made him feel stupid.

Well, that and not having a mate. Everyone had a mate. That was normal. But not Buster. He had an existence, but not a life.

And then *she* came. She recognized intelligence, at least, even if it had taken her forever to comprehend the simple truth that he did not think of her as a food source. There was plenty of food available here, and most of it involved no risk whatever. He hadn't survived all of these years by fighting needlessly, and she would have fought.

No, there was something about her. Something unlike any other being he had ever known. And he wanted to be with her. With her, he mattered.

The question, then, was how to keep her. She had come in on the silver thing, and most people who did that also left quickly. She didn't seem to be setting up house, so she probably wanted to leave quickly, too. And he wasn't foolish enough to think that she would stay for him. No. They'd made peace, so far, but that was all.

But the other one…the man…now there was a possibility. She might stay for the man. If he could get them together. And keep them together. There had to be a way. And given time, he would think of it. He just hoped he had time.

BUCK RETURNED to the house, dripping wet and covered with grease, and made a beeline for the shower. At least the pump was working now. Ten minutes later, he walked out and found Edna sitting in his living room.

"You know I'm the favorite to win that match?" she said, without so much as a greeting.

He shrugged. "Yes. I bet on Hannah."

"You want her to win, don't you? I can't imagine why. She's just going to fly away and break your heart. And I'll still be here."

"Edna…." he began.

"Is it because of my work?" she asked. "What was it she called me, 'a loony lava lover'?'"

"I think she said 'psycho lava lover,' but whatever."

She rose and approached him. "Buck, you know I want you. You're the smartest man on this island, which may not be saying much, but at least we can have a conversation."

"So I'm the best of the sorry lot?" he asked. "Gee, thanks, Edna."

"No!" she replied, dropping back into the chair. "I didn't mean it that way."

She looked as if she was about to cry. Worse, he felt as if he ought to comfort her. He couldn't do that, of course. It would only encourage her delusion that he found her attractive. Still, he found it all but impossible to stand there, impassively, as her lip began to quiver.

Fortunately, he was rescued by a shriek from the hangar. He took off at a brisk jog, still barefoot, Edna hard on his heels. He didn't have to ask where the shriek had come from; the knot of people around the nose of the Lear announced the location of the crisis as clearly as any public address system.

Buck shouldered his way through the crowd and found a young boy, no more than six years old, lying on the floor of the hangar, clutching his shoulder. To Buck's horror, Buster had the boy's hand in his mouth, and seemed to be pulling, despite the desperate cries of the boy's mother. Hannah was kneeling beside the boy's head, looking into his eyes.

"He climbed up on my jet and fell off," she announced when she glanced up and saw Buck.

"Quit it, Buster!" he said, moving toward the gator.

"No!" Hannah yelled. "Look. He's not breaking the skin. He's helping get the shoulder back into joint."

"He'll take that boy's hand off," Edna said.

"If he wanted to do that," Hannah replied tartly, "he'd have done it already. If you want to help, get some ice. Otherwise, stay out of the way."

Hannah manipulated the boy's shoulder and nodded to Buster. "Once more, big guy."

The boy screamed as Hannah turned the arm a fraction while Buster pulled, then suddenly went quiet. "It's...fixed," he said between gasps.

"It's still going to swell," Hannah said to his mother. "You need to keep it iced tonight. But he'll be okay." Then, looking over, she added, "Buster, you can let go now."

But the alligator already had, and now the boy was wiggling his fingers on Buster's tongue, as if petting him. If Buster didn't exactly like it, Buck thought, at least he was tolerating it, patiently holding his mouth open until the boy slowly, slowly withdrew his hand, wincing as the shoulder joint moved.

The boy's mother gathered him into her arms,

tearful words of love mingled with frightened scolds for his having climbed on the jet. But Buck saw only Hannah, still kneeling on the hangar floor, looking at the boy and his mother, her eyes softer than he had ever imagined.

"Need to keep those kids off the planes," Horace said, stepping forward.

"Thank you, Captain Obvious," Hannah replied.

Buck couldn't resist chuckling. "You're both right. We'll have to keep a closer watch on them. Meanwhile, Sticks, want to explain to me why you had that boy's hand in Buster's mouth?"

"I had to," she said, defiance settling on her face. "I needed him to pull while I manipulated the joint back into place."

"I could have pulled," he said.

"You weren't here. Two other people tried, but they let go as soon as the boy started to grimace. Buster was the only one willing to do what needed doing."

"Not the only one," Buck said. "You did, too. Where'd you get your first aid training, anyway?"

"At the International Academy of Oh, God That Hurts," she said with a shrug. "Or, by its more common name, the School of Hard Knocks."

"Got dinged up some, did you?"

She nodded. "Eight years of volleyball, high school and college. I separated my shoulder twice, diving to dig would-be kills."

"I guess we should give you a medal," he said, then bit his tongue. "Damn, Hannah, that didn't come out right at all."

"No medals needed," she said, rising. "We all do what we can, right? Isn't that how this island works?"

"When it works," he said with a laugh. "Seriously, Sticks, you did good work. Buster, too."

At that, Buster rested his chin on Buck's foot, looking up at him. Almost in spite of himself, Buck grinned then looked at Hannah. "Welcome to Treasure Island, Dr. Dolittle."

Edna looked at the two of them, an unhappy expression on her face, then turned sharply and walked away into the crowd of people. Neither of them noticed.

LATER, AS THE WIND picked up power and hard gusts turned to a steady blow, Hannah and Buck retreated to the small office at one corner of the hangar. This office, unlike the one from which Buck operated his business, was purely a repair room. Files bulging with records of past repairs, spare parts and lubricants filled shelves. It was a tight space, not exactly cozy, but with a couple of cups of coffee, they could sit here on battered chairs and keep an eye on things.

"I wish Craig hadn't decided to stay in town with his family," Buck remarked. "I don't like the sound of this storm." He gestured with his head toward the hangar, which was beginning to groan like an arthritic old man.

"Is his house safe?"

"It should be. He built a brick sh-" He caught himself. "Like a you-know-what."

"I've been hanging around aviators my entire life. You think I haven't heard that word before?"

He grinned over his mug. "Sometimes old training takes over. Anyway, his house is sturdy, and he's well above the line of the storm surge. He planned it that way."

"Then he'll be fine. Or maybe he went to the shelter with the rest of the people." The hundreds who couldn't possibly have fit in this hangar.

Within the howling wind came a sharp gust and the hangar let out a loud groan. Hannah looked up. "Are you sure about *this* building?"

"Trust me, I wouldn't have asked all these people to come up here if I weren't. I'm averse to having to rebuild things every time a hurricane comes through." He shrugged. "Waste of time and money. Besides, I don't want to lose my planes. So yeah, we can handle a Cat 4."

"I hope this doesn't get any stronger."

"It may, but only after it passes the island. You saw the weather printouts."

"I'd like to see another one now."

"I'm not sure the plywood will hold on the office

windows. I don't think either of us could avoid turning into Dorothy out in that wind, and I'm in no hurry to get to Oz."

"You don't seem afraid." She was beginning to feel uncomfortable herself from time to time, little butterflies of anxiety in her stomach when the wind slammed the building especially hard.

"Well, you know, there's really no way to be perfectly safe, Sticks. My feeling is, when your number's up, it's up."

"Did you learn that philosophy when you were flying for the navy?"

"I don't know that I'd call it a philosophy. And if I had to guess when I started thinking about it that way...well, it could have been when I lost a couple of close friends in high school. Kayaking accident. They'd kayaked in rapids hundreds of times. No reason that day should have been any different...except the rapids were more dangerous than they looked, and the current a lot faster."

"I'm sorry, Buck."

"It happened a long time ago. The point is, they weren't being reckless. Or at least had no idea they were. And bam. It happens all the time. So why worry about it?"

Hannah sipped her coffee, thinking about it. "I guess I see your point. I do things that other people would consider risky. But I don't think they're risky because I know what I'm doing. Yet look what might have happened yesterday."

"It could just as easily have happened to you trying to cross a street in Houston. Or slipping in your bathtub. I think the trouble with too many people is that they want life to be completely safe and risk-free. Well, you can lock yourself up in a bullet-proof cave and never come out, but you're going to die eventually anyway."

Hannah couldn't prevent a giggle. "Probably sooner than later if you never come out for fresh air and exercise."

He laughed. "There you go!"

For the first time, a look of true understanding passed between them, and Hannah felt a pleasant warmth settle into her center. If anyone had asked her earlier if she and Buck Shanahan would ever find mutually agreeable ground, she'd have told them they were nuts to even wonder.

Which was truly strange when she considered that they were both apparently addicted to planes and flying.

Maybe the truth of it was they didn't *want* to like each other. Ships passing in the night and all that.

"I always wished," she said, feeling a little shy to be admitting so much, "that I could have flown one of those fighter jets you flew."

He smiled then. A warm, untroubled expression. "I'll tell you, Sticks, there's nothing like it. Sometimes in my dreams I'm still looking down the runway on the carrier deck, feeling the engines strain and pull as I throttle up, waiting for the catapult to throw me into the air. Sometimes I still dream of making a night landing in rough seas, watching the landing lights bob in front of me, sometimes disappearing as a huge wave crashes over the bow. And I've got to watch the ball. Always watch the ball, and somehow time myself to that pitch and roll...." He trailed off, his eyes bright and shining as if he were envisioning it all over again.

"You miss it, don't you?" she asked quietly.

Slowly his gaze refocused in the present. "Sometimes," he admitted. "Sometimes. If you wanted to fly fighters, why didn't you join the navy or air force?"

"Because my dad needed me to step in on the business. He was ill and getting worse. Besides, not everybody is lucky enough to be handed a good business. He hung on long enough that his customers learned to trust me, so...." She half-smiled. "I'm one very lucky lady, in that regard."

"Maybe so. Or maybe you earned your luck."

Surprise took her aback. She'd never expected to hear a compliment from him, but that one was as clear as if it had been engraved in gold. She could feel color rush into her cheeks, and for an instant she was oddly tongue-tied.

"Thanks," she managed finally.

"Just stating the obvious."

She needed to lighten the moment. "So you're not still angry with me for nearly taking off your head?"

One corner of his mouth twitched. "Last time I looked, my head was still attached."

The lights flickered then, and the whistling of the wind grew to a loud moan. Rain clattered against the steel walls sounding as loud as hail.

Buck looked up as if he thought he might be able to see the storm through the ceiling. "And it's going to get worse," he said, as if to himself.

CHAPTER FIFTEEN

HANNAH SPOKE. "Are you getting uneasy?"

She looked at him, as if hoping to find confidence in his response. He realized his worry must have been showing more than he knew. Time to ruck up.

"Nah," he said. "It's just that...well, to be honest, I'm already sick of this storm. Sometimes they move through fast, but this one's been dragging her heels since she first wound up."

"And that makes it worse."

"Far worse. And worse than that, it makes them endless. I'm going to check the weather again."

She followed after him, as if she were as impatient as he to know what was going on. His house was dark, but he didn't turn on the lights, instead using the flashlight he carried. To the relief of both of them, the plywood still protected the large panes of glass in the front office.

"Why didn't you put storm shutters on those windows?" she asked him.

"I ran out of money. Besides, I don't especially care

if this office blows away. It's easy enough to rebuild. And it's barely attached to the house behind it."

Thankfully, she didn't ask him to explain why he'd built his home like a blockhouse but not his office. The house might have been a bunker, except for the few shuttered windows. He didn't want to have to explain why he lived in what was essentially a cave, that the thick walls of his home mirrored those of his heart.

To his relief, they found that the weather fax had automatically spit out a few pages during the evening. The pressure gradient lines were frighteningly close together near the eye, which was now about 160 miles southeast of Treasure Island.

"She did it," Buck said grimly. "Look at these wind speeds. A strong Category Three."

"And strengthening," Hannah added, reading the text from the weather service Buck subscribed to. "The eye is moving at about seventeen miles per hour. We're going to get flooded." She lifted her gaze, concern written on her features. "What about mud slides?"

"There's not enough mud on this island to slide, thanks to Big Mouth. That's the least of our worries."

"And the storm surge?"

He looked down at the papers, gauging the data against his mental map. "Not too bad on the inhabited side. The wind should mostly blow the water down the coast. And from the way the projected path is arcing...." He closed his eyes a moment. "The town should be safe from the surge unless something changes drastically. But we're going to get the very devil from the wind and rain."

"So we all just ride it out."

He pursed his lips. "It's not like we can fly out now for a long weekend at the Hyatt in London."

She seemed put off by his attempt at levity. Well, that was how he dealt with stress, and he wasn't going to apologize for it. He'd spent enough time apologizing to a woman for every breath he took. Never again.

She seemed to be biting back something she wanted to say, and though he wasn't sure he wanted to hear it, he had to ask anyway.

"Cat got your tongue, Sticks?"

Her teeth clenched and she paused for a moment before answering. "No. There just doesn't seem to be anything useful to say, does there? Storm, us, survive. That's about it."

"You could say that." He shrugged.

HANNAH SAW SOMETHING in that shrug. In a moment of blinding insight, one which had been delayed only, she was sure, by the incredible humidity of the air, the fury of a hurricane, and being stalked by a love-sick alligator, she realized something about Buck Shanahan: he was using his biting sarcasm to keep her at a distance.

Well, duh, she thought as she tagged behind him

back into the hangar while the outer bands of Hurricane Hannah shrieked their rage around the corners of the building. Brilliant insight. She ought to get a Nobel Prize for that one.

And she ought to be glad that was his attitude. At least she'd be safe from him for the next twenty-four hours.

Ridiculously, she felt a twinge of sadness about that, and told herself it was just all the stress. She had no room in her life for a man right now, and certainly not one who had a chip bigger than a two-by-four riding his shoulder.

Buck brought them more coffee from the urn outside which was being husbanded by Horace, and they settled once again into the repair office. Not quite looking at her, Buck spread the weather printouts on the small, oil- and grease-stained desk. While she tried to peer over his shoulder, he pored over them, as if trying to read the entrails of a chicken. Finally, from his hip pocket, he pulled out some of the earlier weather faxes, sadly crumpled.

"What are you doing?" she asked.

"Making my own weather guesstimate."

"You're a meteorologist?"

He shook his head, still not looking at her. "No, but I've read a lot of weather maps in my day. I just want to calculate the surge. None of the big forecasters really worries about a tiny underpopulated island like this one. I'm always having to make mental adjustments for our local conditions."

She sat on one of the creaky old chairs and watched. "I can give you local conditions," she said lightly as the building groaned angrily in a renewed blast, rain pelting the walls and ceiling like stones. "Rainy, windy, dark and plenty of cold shoulder."

At that he looked up, and for an instant something flickered in his blue eyes. Fear? Anger? She wasn't sure. All she knew was that it was intense, and she felt strongly that she shouldn't have awakened whatever it was.

A delightful shiver ran through her.

"Look, Sticks, we've got to rub shoulders as best we can for the next day or so. Riding out one of these storms isn't easy even with your best buddy. For a couple of strangers it could get really difficult."

What was he trying to say? She wasn't sure she knew, so she shrugged. "Just trying to lighten the atmosphere. It's rather soggy."

He rolled his eyes and bent back to the map. With a clatter, she put her mug down on the desk. Then feeling stupid for her behavior, she picked it up again and was about to sip when she abruptly realized that the world outside had grown dead silent.

"Do you hear that?" she asked.

"What?"

"Nothing."

"Nothing?"

"Nothing. That's my point."

He cocked his head. "Rain band must have finished passing through."

"Right. Or a tornado is coming."

"On this hunk of rock? There's no place for one to build up steam."

"Waterspout then."

"Oh, cripes. Is there no end to your imagination?"

"If you lived where I do, you wouldn't like it when a storm gets completely silent and still."

He tossed down the pen he'd been writing with on the edge of one of the printouts. "Just what the hell can we do about it, Hannah?" Frustration seemed to be coming out his every pore. "Tell everyone to run? Where to? Frankly, whether you like the idea or not, we're all in God's hands now."

She bit her lip. "I was just pointing out…." Her voice trailed away. She was being difficult and she knew it. And why was she being difficult? She also knew that. She had to force the admission out through a throat that wanted to clamp down on each self-revealing word. "I'm…afraid."

His face softened right then, and for an instant she had the wild hope he would come and hug her. Somehow being sucked up into a tornado or blown away in a hurricane didn't seem so bad if she could just hold on to him. Or have him hold on to her.

But he caught himself, and she tasted bitter disappointment. "I know, Sticks," he said. "I know."

At least he hadn't laughed at her. Or told her she was being silly.

Another gust of wind caused the wall beside them to ripple. At that instant it was all she could do not to throw herself into Buck's arms.

"Not much longer," he said, trying to sound bracing.

"Not much longer before what?"

"Before the eye hits us."

She closed her eyes then, looking inward, wondering if she was ready to meet her Maker.

"WHAT'S GOING ON in that head of yours?" Buck asked a few minutes later. If it were possible, the air seemed to be growing even heavier.

"What makes you think anything is going on?"

"Well, you're intelligent, so it's highly unlikely your brain is just a blank."

"Actually, I was just thinking about old movies. *Singing in the Rain,* actually." She didn't want to continue the train of thought with him. Especially since it was silly anyway.

"What brought that on?"

"Can you explain the way your brain synapses work all the time?"

He grinned crookedly. "Point taken."

"This has been a long day," she remarked.

"I'll second that."

"Don't you get it, Shanahan? The weather in these storms is unpredictable. The overall picture may be clear, but there's no predicting what might happen at any given location, like the few square feet we're standing on. The winds do crazy things, especially as the eye gets closer, and it doesn't have to be a tornado or a waterspout to be dangerous."

He just nodded, as if he already knew that. She would have liked him to say something just so she could jump on him. She needed to let her anxiety out somehow, and a good verbal fight might be just the ticket.

It would also be stupid and childish, and she knew it. Unfortunately, being stupid and childish mattered less and less the more the building groaned.

"You're easy to rile, Sticks."

"Just don't tell me I'm cute when I'm mad."

"I wouldn't dream of it."

"Good."

He turned his attention back to the weather maps. Or so he pretended. "You're far too beautiful to be called cute."

She froze. She forgot the hurricane, forgot the heavy air and suffocating humidity, forgot water-spouts, tornadoes, winds, floods, and even her busted airplane. *Beautiful.*

As many times as she had looked in a mirror in

the course of her life, she had never seen beautiful. She had seen a wild mane of red hair that could only be tamed by a ponytail holder and four barrettes. At some point, she'd given up and let it be.

Her face, she'd always believed, was ordinary. Not the stuff of Hollywood, certainly. Just ordinary. As for her figure…she had labeled that average.

So what was Buck talking about?

Just then the wind strengthened, buffeting the building hard. The slab under her feet rumbled deeply, as if moved by the strain on the building.

"Oh, God," she said.

"It's just the wind."

Just the wind. *Just* the wind? That was the whole problem, wasn't it?

His gaze settled on her, and something in his face gentling. "You'll be safe in here. I promise."

She wanted to laugh the whole thing off, to tell him he was mistaken about her state of mind, but that would have been a lie. Instead the truth tumbled from her lips. "For a few seconds there, I honestly thought this building was coming down."

He nodded. "It was wicked."

She liked him then, for justifying her fright rather than dismissing it. "Sometimes you're almost human, Buck."

"Yeah, well, don't tell anyone, okay?"

CHAPTER SIXTEEN

SETTING HIS MUG aside, Buck rose. "Let's get the hell out of this room before we get cabin fever."

"Sure." She stood, realizing that every muscle in her body was screaming with tension. Moving around would do her some good. It might also distract her.

"Are you two in?" Horace asked when they emerged from the office.

"In what?" Hannah replied.

"The tournament," Horace said, showing her the list of names he'd penned on Buck's white board. "It's a freeroll, and the winner gets Ginny's barbeque sauce recipe."

"She's going to give that away?" Buck asked, incredulous.

Horace smiled and shrugged. "Okay, I worked on her a bit. It's not as if I haven't known it for years. I sell her the fixins, after all. Only condition she set was that everyone who enters has to swear they'll never tell another soul."

"You old fox," Buck said. "Sure, we're all going to get bored soon anyway. I'm in."

"And you, Sticks?" Horace asked.

"Sure. It's a freeroll. I can't pass that up."

And she couldn't. Freeroll tournaments—where there was no entry fee—were rare in live poker. Poker players wanted something to play for, and the prize pool for the winners was the sum of the entry fees, minus the cut taken by the casino to cover the costs of hosting the tournament.

Soon she found herself seated at a makeshift table—the folding tables from the coffee bar had been cleared, and the island's residents had scrounged up plywood and laid it over stacks of boxes for the rest—listening to a sound like a thousand crickets.

It was the sound of dozens of players shuffling their chips as they waited for the action to start, and she had long found it one of the most soothing sounds in the world. It carried her back to her college days, where she'd hustled food and laundry money—and a few hundred a month—playing in dorm rooms and pool halls. Her father had taught her the game when she was six, and she'd been an able and eager student.

The game fascinated her. As the legendary Doyle Brunson had said, poker was not a card game played by people; it was a people game played with cards. It called on both sides of the brain: the intuitive processes of reading opponents and estimating what cards they held, and the mathematical processes of computing the odds based on those reads. The best players, the ones who consistently made the final tables in major tournaments and won millions in high-stakes side games, were brilliant at both.

Hannah did not consider herself in their league, but she could hold her own against average players. And while the players at her table were a bit better than that, she found herself steadily accumulating chips when opportunity knocked, and folding her cards quickly when it didn't. Although she hadn't played with any of them before, she quickly learned their styles, tendencies and mannerisms, which combined to give her a pretty good idea of what cards they were playing in a given situation.

Nearing the end of the first hour, she had tripled her stack and was the chip leader at her table. She felt confident, in control of herself and the game.

And then Horace tapped her shoulder. "Gotta move you, Sticks. Rack your chips and come with me."

She couldn't object, as it was a standard practice in poker tournaments. As players were eliminated, the tournament director—Horace, in this case—shifted players to other tables. This process went on until all but a single table of players remained, the final table.

Still, she felt a lurch in her stomach as she found herself seated next to Buck, and directly across the table from Edna, both of whom had large stacks of chips in front of them.

"Hey, Sticks," Buck said as she sat. "Join the club."

"Yeah, gee thanks, Horace," she said, tipping her chips out of the plastic racks and handing the racks back to Horace.

"I see you've been getting good cards," Edna said, looking at Hannah's stack.

"Yeah, the dealer liked me," Hannah replied. "He seems to have liked you, too."

"We'll see," she said.

And with that, the challenge was laid on the table for all to see. Hannah took a breath, then simply nodded. In a full table game like this, she couldn't afford to get drawn into a one-on-one battle with Edna Harkin. That was a recipe for disaster if someone else picked up a powerful hand. If Edna wanted to head hunt, that was her decision. But Hannah wasn't going to join in.

Buck was dealing this hand, and Hannah watched as the other players peeked at their cards and decided whether to play the pot. The first three players folded, and Edna quickly put in a raise.

Too quickly, Hannah thought.

Edna then stared directly at Hannah, as if daring her to call the raise. Every instinct told her that this was a classic case of "strong means weak," that Edna had a weaker hand than she was representing.

After the next three players folded, Hannah quickly glanced over at Buck. If he'd looked at his cards yet, she couldn't tell. He was probably smart enough not to look at his cards until the action came to him, so that he couldn't give away any information, just as she had done thus far.

Hannah lifted up the corner of her cards and saw the Jack and Ten of Diamonds. Not a bad starting hand, she thought, especially since she held position on Edna. Edna would have to act first on every betting round, which gave Hannah more information before she had to make a decision. Edna's raise hadn't been excessive—less than a twentieth of Hannah's chip total—so Hannah made the call.

"Oh, boy," Buck said, now looking at his cards. "Looks like the fireworks have begun. I think I'll pass on this one, ladies."

He pushed his cards into the pile he had collected from the other players who had folded their hands and, after the two players to his left folded, piled the chips that Hannah and Edna had bet along with the blind bets.

"I guess you two want to see the flop," he said, discarding the top card, then peeling off the next three cards and spreading them on the table.

Hannah didn't look at the cards right away.

Instead, she watched Edna look at them. The fleeting twitch of Edna's eyebrows, coupled with a momentary glance down at her chips, told Hannah that Edna had hit the flop…that the three cards Buck had laid out had strengthened Edna's hand considerably. Edna feigned a quick frown, then tapped the table with her fingertips.

"I'll check," she said, as if disinterested.

The corollary to "strong means weak" is "weak means strong." Edna had acted strong before the flop, meaning she'd probably been betting a mediocre hand. Now she was acting weak, which meant she'd probably flopped a monster.

Only then did Hannah look down at the three cards on the table. The Eight, Nine, and Queen of Diamonds. Hannah held a straight flush, Eight-to-Queen in Diamonds, the best hand possible. The stone cold nuts.

"I guess diamonds are cheap," she said. She looked at the chips already in the pot in front of Buck, as if counting them, although she already knew exactly how much was there. "Okay, what's in the pot already? Three hundred? I'll make it one-fifty."

She counted out six black chips, worth twenty-five dollars each, and pushed them toward the center of the table, watching Edna the entire time. She was playing the reverse of "strong means weak," acting strong so that Edna would read her for having a weak hand, when in fact there was no card in the deck that would cost Hannah the pot.

Edna shrugged and pushed out six black chips, calling Hannah's bet, adding a casual, "Whatever. It's a freeroll anyway."

Hannah was now certain that Edna had flopped a set—three of a kind—either Eights or Nines. She was equally certain that Edna did not know that Hannah already had her hand beaten, and that Edna was drawing dead, with no hope of winning the pot.

"Let's see the turn, Buck," Hannah said.

"Your wish is my command," Buck said.

Once again, he discarded the top card, this time turning a single card and putting it on the table. Once again, Hannah didn't look at the card, but instead watched as Edna looked at it. A quick intake of breath, and at the same time, a glance at Hannah's remaining chips. Hannah didn't have to look at the cards on the table to know what had fallen: another Eight, Nine, or Queen, giving Edna a full house or even four of a kind.

"Four-fifty," Edna said, pushing out nine black chips.

Hannah glanced down at the turn card. The Eight of Hearts, just as she'd expected from Edna's reaction. She looked at Edna. "How much do you have left?"

Edna counted her chips, her hand quivering a bit, and now Hannah knew exactly what she held:

pocket Eights, with the two Eights on board giving her four of a kind.

"Eleven-fifty," Edna said.

"Let's play for all of it," Hannah replied, pushing three stacks of twenty black chips into the table, for a bet of fifteen hundred.

"Sure, why not?" Edna said, pushing in the rest of her chips. She turned up her cards. "Four of a kind beats a flush…Sticks."

"Yes, it does," Hannah said, turning over her own cards. "Unless it's a straight flush."

The other players at the table gasped as they saw Hannah's cards. Edna seemed to study them, her face frozen in disbelief.

"You b…."

"C'mon, Edna," Buck said quietly. "It's just a game, remember?"

"Yeah, fine," Edna said, finally getting out of her seat. "Whatever. This one doesn't matter."

"Nice hand," Hannah said, glancing up as she stacked the pile of chips Buck had pushed to her. "Just not quite nice enough."

After Edna stormed away, Buck turned to Hannah. "That was a bit of insult to injury, don't you think?"

"You're right," Hannah said. "I'm sorry."

"Don't apologize, Sticks," Horace said, standing

beside the table. "That's the most fun I've had all week."

It *had* been fun, Hannah had to agree. But she'd been wrong to rub it in. Her father had taught her better poker etiquette than that. She'd make a point to apologize to Edna later. Once she felt like she could do it sincerely.

"Okay, folks," Horace called out. "Ten minute break."

THE BREAK, however, was going to be a lot longer than ten minutes. The line at the bathroom beside the repair office stretched halfway across the hangar. Worse, with their minds no longer distracted by the game, folks were noticing the storm's fury again. Uneasy glances around each time the building creaked or the wind whistled especially loud made heads turn. The younger children had mostly fallen asleep on mats, bedrolls or any blank space of floor near where they had been playing Monopoly. The teens, many of whom were playing in the freeroll, seemed to have lost interest. They were beginning to cluster in the far corner of the hangar around someone's boom box, which was issuing sounds that reminded Hannah more of a collapsing bridge than music. A sign of her age, Hannah thought wearily. She was willing to bet her favorite music had hardly sounded any better to her dad.

She sighed, stretching, and joined Buck beside the coffee urn, reaching for a reusable plastic cup. Her conscience, she realized, was really beginning to twinge over her behavior a few minutes ago.

"Sorry," she said to Buck. "I'll apologize to Edna before we start up again. I guess I'm overtired."

He shrugged. "I shouldn't have said anything to you. I'm not sure what's going on between you and Edna, but I've never understood women anyway. Don't worry about it."

That sparked her irritation. Buck irked her all too easily, but that was a conundrum she really *was* too tired to ponder right now. "What's to understand? Despite books to the contrary, we're not a different species, okay? You don't have eyes on stalks and I don't have green skin, and we speak the same language."

"Theoretically."

"Oooh, you can be maddening."

"So can you. Where does that get us?"

"It gets me off this island as soon as I can go."

"Good. I came here for peace and quiet."

"Sure you did. I've got my own theory about that."

He glared. "Oh, yeah?"

"Yeah. You're hiding from something, Shanahan. You came here to hide."

"You don't know what you're talking about."

"You think not? Adrenaline junkies don't just disappear to underpopulated Caribbean islands to make grocery runs on an antique plane."

"You don't know the first thing about me!"

"Well, you don't know the first thing about me, either, but you're quick enough to offer opinions."

He shook his head sharply. "As I recall, this entire argument started because I was *apologizing* for doing that very thing."

She froze, her mouth open, words evaporating before they could emerge.

"You'll catch flies," he said, touching her chin with his fingertip and pushing her mouth closed.

She still wanted to lash out with her tongue, but the words wouldn't come. Worse, the sinking realization that he was right was filling her. Her mouth opened again, then snapped closed.

"I've got an idea," he said. "Why don't we both just agree that we're doing our best not to like each other. Then we don't have to fight to make the point. And frankly, I'm getting tired of these spats."

She had to try twice before she was finally able to croak, "Agreed."

"Good." He seemed satisfied. She wasn't at all sure she was. The argument felt unfinished, as if something very important had been hanging in the air, just out of reach, and now it had vanished in a pop.

Inexplicably saddened, she followed him back to the poker table.

As if he were speaking to a stranger, Buck remarked as they sat, "I think it's going to be a long night."

Listening to the moan of the wind and the protests of the building, she agreed. "A very long night."

HANNAH KNEW she should have been a shoo-in to make it to the final table. She had a mountain of chips, courtesy of Edna, and yet it was evaporating before her very eyes. Ill-timed raises, missed draws and a flush that had lost to a full house at the river had combined to carry her from chip leader to short stack within a half-hour.

She realized her heart just wasn't in the game anymore. Not after the pointless spat with Buck. She'd thought they were past the arguing-for-the-sake-of-arguing stage, but apparently that wasn't going to happen. Well, screw it, she thought.

She looked down at her next hand and saw a pair of Jacks. The most difficult hand in No-Limit Hold 'em, it was a hand that looked much stronger than it was. Most top pros agreed that it was a hand you didn't want to have to play after the flop, because it was not likely to improve, while the hands that might play against it often would. Worse, it was difficult to know whether you were ahead or behind in the hand after the flop.

Hannah measured her stack mentally, realizing that a standard opening raise would commit almost half of her stack. If she were called, she would not have enough chips left to chase someone off of a strong drawing hand, even if she were still ahead in the hand. And if she folded at the flop, she would have so few chips left that she would be forced all-in on the next playable hand, regardless. Better to do it now.

"I'm all-in," she announced, pushing her chips into the table.

"Gotta call you, Sticks," Buck said immediately.

When the rest of the table had folded, they turned up their hands. Not that Hannah had any doubt what she would see. He had a pair of Kings.

She didn't even wait for the community cards to be dealt. Instead, she rose from the table and walked away to the repair office, closing the door behind her.

"WHAT THE HELL got into her?" Horace asked. "I'd have put money on her to make the final table."

Buck shook his head. "Damned if I know. But I'll tell you one thing I *do* know about women."

Horace grinned. "Other than the good stuff?"

Buck snorted. "Get your mind out of your pants."

"Why? It's happy there. What were you gonna say about women?"

"Their skin may not be green, but their brains must be."

Ignoring Horace's befuddled expression, Buck went back to riffling his chips, waiting for the game to restart.

Damn women anyway, he thought. No matter how you tried to deal with them, they were ticking time bombs, just waiting to blow up in a guy's face for no apparent reason.

CHAPTER SEVENTEEN

WHATEVER FUN the hurricane might have been passed abruptly when a bone-jarring *crash* reverberated through the hangar. Buck's head snapped around and he saw a ten-foot-long dent in the far wall, probably the result of an uprooted and windblown tree. Buck glanced at his watch and saw it was 2:00 a.m. The worst was hitting right now, and people were looking as if they wished they were anywhere else on the planet. Buck couldn't blame them. As well as he'd built this hangar, one crazy wind gust exceeding Category 4 force, and they might all be tumbling down the side of the mountain.

Buck considered going outside to verify the source of the dent, but the shrieking wind and deafening drumroll of rain convinced him otherwise. They were feeling the inner eyewall now, and he had no desire to tempt fate. Slowly, as if crawling up out of their holes after an artillery barrage, the people in the hangar gathered their breath and tried to quiet terrified children.

The tournament was down to the final table of ten. Buck had deliberately lost all his chips a short while ago because his competitive spirit had given way to fatigue and the realization that he didn't want Ginny's recipe. But Esther Dubois had been hankering after that recipe for years, so Buck had decided to lose to her. He went all-in on a bluff when he was as certain as he could be that Esther had a hand. And did she ever: pocket Aces.

She'd cleaned him out. He'd pretended to be disappointed, but the fact was, he just needed a place to stretch out and rest.

Unfortunately, with the storm raging outside, he doubted he could do more than catnap. Few in the hangar had been sleeping, and the crash against the hangar wall had awakened those few. Long since out of the poker game, they were sitting near family and friends, waiting as if they were on death row.

And maybe they all were. He deserved to burn in hell if he'd brought these people up here only to get them killed. If he'd overestimated the strength of this building. Merely having designed it to withstand this kind of assault didn't mean it would.

He headed toward the small repair office, then drew up short when he saw Buster stretched across the doorway as if on guard. Hannah was still in there, he reminded himself as if he'd forgotten it for even a minute. Surprisingly, she hadn't gone to sleep on her plane, but had instead encouraged a family with four small children to camp out there. Very generous of her, considering she'd been trying to protect that plane like a baby, and considering what four small children could do to a space, given the opportunity.

Overhead the lights flickered, and for a heart-stopping moment everyone looked up, wondering if they were about to be cast into the dark again. It shouldn't happen, but it might.

This storm would be hell to take in the dark. It was bad enough as is. He could almost swear that sometimes he saw the entire building sway as it shrieked in protest.

He looked down at Buster, who lay between him and the recliner beyond the door.

"Can I get by?" he asked. Stepping over the gator would require exposing a very sensitive part of his anatomy to a reptile that could move faster than an eyeblink. He might not have any use for that part of himself anymore, but he was still rather emotionally attached to it.

Buster looked up, as if measuring him. For long moments, that gator didn't move. Buck felt as if he was being put on some kind of prehistoric scale and weighed.

"Hmmmmm," Buster thrummed deep in his throat. Then, slowly, more slowly than was necessary, the gator moved backward, clearing the path to the door.

Strange, Buck thought. But then, this damn gator had been acting entirely too human during the hours since Hannah had arrived.

"Thanks," Buck said, deciding that talking to Buster was a safer alternative than ignoring him.

"Hmmmmmm."

As soon as Buck slipped into the office, he could hear Buster slither back to his guard post.

Hannah, he saw by the light of the desk lamp, was sound asleep in one of the two battered recliners. Not even the tree slamming against the hangar wall had awakened her. That surprised him; she'd seemed as edgy as any of them about this storm.

Unable to help himself, he stood over her for a few minutes, noting the delicate lines of her cheek and throat, noting the surprisingly thick red lashes that rested on her flawless skin. A raving beauty, he thought. And raving in more ways than one. But that was one of the things he liked about her. She had plenty of spirit, annoying as it could be.

But at the same time, he realized that spirit in her allowed the tender side of him to emerge. It was as if her determined self-sufficiency and independence made it possible for him to be gentle.

He'd never felt that way with his ex. She'd played up to his "manly" side, his machismo. And he'd been stupid enough and young enough to feel like a banty rooster ruling the henhouse. There'd never been time for this side of him. He'd been too busy trying to make his ex feel like a princess while beating his chest with pride.

Hannah had an entirely different effect on him. They might squabble and fight, but he could also look down on her sleeping form and feel tenderness tighten his throat.

He wasn't sure he liked that. Being vulnerable wasn't something he wanted to be ever again. Certainly not with a woman. Certainly not with a woman who'd be leaving in a day or two.

So he resisted the urge to touch her cheek to reassure her in her sleep. Resisted the urge to gently touch her flaming mane, or find a blanket to tuck around her so that in the wee hours, when her body was in its deepest sleep, she wouldn't feel chilled.

Sighing, he edged around the desk, trying to avoid looking at the weather printouts because they'd only get him thinking once again about just how bad this storm could get.

Settling into the other recliner, he closed his eyes and listened to his world groan around him.

Tomorrow, he promised himself, the instant the worst of this storm passed, he was going to get to work on that woman's airplane, if for no other reason than that he needed to send temptation away.

He couldn't leave, so she had to go. Was that so hard to understand?

Somehow it seemed like the knottiest problem in the universe.

And on that thought, he at last began to drift into sleep, still wary, still alert, but blessed sleep nonetheless.

THE MORNING brought calm, and Hannah awoke to the sound of snoring and birds. The snoring, she quickly discovered, was Buck, passed out beside her on the other recliner. The birds, however, were outside. And if there were birds, then the hurricane had passed.

She considered waking Buck, but decided against it. Although he hadn't said a word, having his hangar overrun with evacuees had to have been stressful. He was used to a kind of independence that being responsible for dozens of stranded people didn't permit. If the time of danger had passed, let him rest.

Quietly, she made her way out into the hangar. She was surprised to discover that the islanders had already opened the hangar door, not because she didn't think them capable of doing it, but simply because she thought the sound of those doors opening would have awakened her, or at least Buck. Apparently, somehow, they'd found a way to do it quietly. Or she'd just been so exhausted that nothing short of the roof tearing off would have broken the bonds of Morpheus.

"Hey, Sticks," Horace said as she wandered

through the hangar. "You missed a heck of a final table last night."

"I was too tired," she said. Looking around the hangar, she added, "We don't look too much the worse for wear."

"It was pretty bad around three," he said. "Edna wanted to come in and get Buck, but I told her to leave the two of you alone. I figured you needed some quiet time."

"It wasn't like that," she said.

He shrugged. "It was. It wasn't. It doesn't matter to me, Sticks. I said it before and I'll say it again—a woman could do a damn sight worse than Buck Shanahan. Way I figure it, he could do a damn sight worse, too."

"Speak of the devil," Hannah said, watching Edna approach like the storm clouds that had just passed by.

"Did you have fun with my man last night?" she demanded.

Hannah was in no mood for verbal jousting this morning. She shook her head. "Honestly, Edna, I didn't even know he was there until this morning. I was sound asleep by the time he got in there, and he's still asleep now. So give it a rest, okay? I think the island has more important things to worry about than who slept near whom last night."

She turned to Horace. "Has anyone gone into town to survey the damage yet?"

"Not yet," he said. "I got through to Craig on the radio, and he said it wasn't too bad right where he was. But he hadn't gone down to the waterfront yet."

"Are you in the mood for a ride?" she asked.

Horace looked over at his shelves. "Who's going to watch my stuff?"

"You were donating it anyway, weren't you?"

"Well, yeah, but there's donating in time of need, and then there's people stuffing anything they can grab into bags and cars before they high-tail it out of here. I've still got to make a living when this is over, Sticks."

He had a point. Somehow, though, she didn't think the islanders were likely to take advantage that way. Treasure Island was too communal a society to foster that kind of behavior. It might be a community of gamblers who resolved civic issues with poker games, but it was hardly the gun-toting, Aces-up-the-sleeve kind of gambling town typically portrayed in Hollywood movies. In fact, in spite of or because of its many quirks and foibles, it was the type of place that would be easy to call home.

"Tell you what," Hannah said. "How about we leave Edna in charge of your stuff. I'm sure she'll wake Buck if there's a problem."

"Damn right I will," Edna said. "Though how I wake him…well, I'm not the type to kiss and tell."

"I'm not worried," Hannah said breezily. "Buster's

still guarding the office door. He won't let you in unless he thinks there's a good reason to."

Then, before Edna had a chance to reply, Hannah turned to Horace. "Let's go. We need to find out how much work we'll need to do before these people can go back home."

THE FIRST SIGHT that greeted Hannah was an uprooted palm tree lying at the base of the hangar wall, beneath the huge dent it had caused. "I can't believe I slept through that," she said.

Horace shrugged. "You were tired. C'mon. Let's get into town and survey the damage."

If the road had been rough before the storm, it had become a bone-jarring, teeth-rattling mess to the extent that Horace began to drive with only two wheels on the pavement and the other two on the shoulder, which looked badly washed out. It had drained, however, given the slope, so there was no mire to bog them down.

Everywhere Hannah looked, damage was visible: uprooted trees, palms stripped nearly bare of fronds. A few trees had lost their tops, twisted loose at the trunk.

Amazingly, nothing blocked the road, so they made it to town in reasonable time.

But there...there the hurricane had left its mark. The storm surge may have missed this side of the island, but the wind had whipped hard on Big

Mouth's face, and gravity had taken the wind-blown debris down the side of the mountain into the town. Here and there roofs were missing. The oldest houses, as Buck had said, had withstood the storm best, but the smaller, newer ones were a mess. Even cinder-block houses had been damaged. Plywood had been ripped from windows in places and the storm had blown right in.

People had already begun to emerge from the school's shelter and were picking their way through streets, or looking through the wreckage of their homes.

"Ain't never seen one this bad," Horace muttered.

"It's awful." Hannah pressed her hand to her mouth, trying to take it all in. She'd seen hurricane damage before in her life. It wasn't as if none ever hit the coast of Texas. And who could forget the devastation of New Orleans by Katrina? Or the delayed rescue response?

These people were on their own. There was no cavalry to ride to the rescue here, unless the Red Cross flew in. There were no supplies just over the horizon, no hospitals. This was it.

And it was horrible.

"I don't think we lost anybody," Horace remarked.

"How can you know that?"

"Because anyone who wasn't with us last night was in the shelter down here. Nobody on this island is stupid enough to simply ride out a storm that strong in their homes."

"Some said they wanted to."

"Sure, until their neighbors pulled them out and dragged them away. Happens every time."

"The rebuilding is going to be hard."

Horace shrugged. "We built it in the first place, we can build it again. Lots of strong, willing bodies around here."

They negotiated the wreckage-strewn streets, making their way through the town.

"Where are we going?" Hannah asked.

"To see what's happened to the casino. Betcha it's gone."

He sounded as if he took delight in that possibility, but there was no wondering about his reaction when they reached the former location of the casino. His face fell.

"Hell," he said, "kicking Anstin's butt is one thing. This is worse than I expected."

Hannah stared at what had been Bill Anstin's little empire. The small hotel still stood, though a second-floor room looked as if it had been impaled by a palm tree, its roots protruding from the wall. The former gaming area was a debris-strewn mess. Nothing remained of the tiki huts, save for a few supporting posts that hadn't been broken off near ground level.

Horace tried to laugh, but it came out as a sigh.

"I don't especially like Anstin myself," Hannah said, agreeing, "but I couldn't wish anyone this."

Horace nodded. "I'm not wishing him anything. But more than a few of us will point out that, while his casino blew away, it can be replaced in a matter of weeks. Folks on this island can build him tiki huts like that." He snapped his fingers. "Maybe he'll reconsider his grand hotel designs. How long would it take to replace a hotel? And how much would it cost?"

Hannah nodded, understanding now. "You've got a point, Horace."

"I've always got a point. Doesn't mean most idiots will listen, though. And Bill Anstin's the biggest idiot of them all."

Hannah couldn't help a chuckle. "I can't disagree."

"'Course you can't. Nobody in their right mind does. But he's made some jobs for the younger folk, and it's nice they're not all packing up to leave for the bigger islands. So we'll build him his damn tiki huts again."

"All the equipment is safe?"

"Most of it, I'm sure. He moved that into the hotel conference rooms. It ought to be safe."

"Good for him," Hannah said. "But the town. We have to help in town."

"Yeah." Horace put the truck in gear. "That's the

first thing. Shelter and food. Buck'll be a big help with that."

"What about your groceries?"

Horace scowled. "Do I look like the Red Cross?"

"Horace Hanratty, I'm ashamed of you!"

"Like I care. You want a white knight, go talk to Buck. Damn fool's always trying to save someone."

Hannah frowned most of the way back to the airport. As she climbed out of Horace's truck, she looked back just long enough to say, "You'll pay for that attitude, Horace."

"Yeah, right."

He jammed down on the accelerator and headed back to town. His store hadn't taken much damage, and apparently he felt whatever was left in there needed protecting.

THE REST OF THE DAY passed in a whirl of activity. Families whose homes were still livable moved back in. Those whose homes had been damaged spent the day trying to make repairs, then traipsed back to the hangar at nightfall.

Hannah spent the day helping wherever she could, as did Buck. Each piece of rubble was checked for possible usefulness before being added to a growing pile on the beach just above the waterline where it eventually would be burned.

Hannah glimpsed Buck making notes on a pad

several times, and finally, as she took a break from moving debris she wiped her brow with her forearm and asked what he was writing.

"A list of what we'll need for rebuilding." He looked at her. "Tomorrow we're flying over to Aruba for supplies. Wanna ride along?"

A grin split Hannah's weary face. "I thought you'd never ask. Will you let me take the controls?"

An answering grin creased his face. "A woman after my own heart. You betcha."

That evening, her heart feeling inexplicably lighter, Hannah sat around an outdoor campfire and sang songs with the other people still camping at the airport. They started with the bawdy, but as the stars rose higher and brighter in the sky, a kind of solemnity fell over the people.

When a lone tenor began singing "Amazing Grace," Hannah felt a tear roll down her cheek.

They had all been lucky. Very lucky.

The woman next to her clasped her hand, and soon hands were joined all round as voices raised in hymn.

The community had survived, even if the houses had not.

And in those moments, that was all that mattered.

CHAPTER EIGHTEEN

THE MOOD EVAPORATED as Bill Anstin's Jeep pulled up on the apron not too far from the bonfire. Much as people disliked him, no one could deny that his casino had borne the brunt of the damage. While the hotel had seemed intact from the outside, but for the tree protruding from the second floor, it was a different story inside.

Broken windows had provided an opening for wind-swept rain which had drenched the landward rooms and leaked into the ground floor rooms, including the conference rooms where the gaming equipment had been stored. It would be days before they knew how many tables would need new felt covers, and how many slot machines had been ruined by water damage. Worst of all, the kitchen was right beneath the room where the tree had crashed in. The ceiling had given way, and between the water damage and the ceiling collapse, the hotel kitchen would be out of service for weeks.

Everyone knew what kind of mood Bill Anstin

would be in when he got to the hangar. Buck stiffened as he saw Bill approach, steeling himself, because he knew what Bill would ask for. Worse, he knew he couldn't decline.

"I need to ask a favor, Buck," Anstin said by way of greeting. "I need to ask you to lend me your hangar, to house the casino while I'm rebuilding."

"I'd like to say 'No,'" Buck began, but Anstin interrupted.

"Look, Buck, I sank all of my World Series winnings into the casino as it stood. The hotel's still standing, but I can't feed anyone and half of the rooms will need to be totally refurbished, right down to the drywall. I can't afford to do that unless I have the tables running. I'm insured, but you know how that works. It'll be months before I see a dime there."

Buck held up a hand. "I know, Bill. I know. I don't want your big high-rise and all that goes with it, but a lot of these people depend on that casino for their income. I'd be hurting all of them if I said no. But I'm going to need some concessions from you, too."

"What do you need?" Anstin asked.

"We can fly people in for gambling junkets," Buck said, "but they're going to need somewhere to stay while they're here. So we have to get some bungalows built, and quickly. The airport offers a great view of the Caribbean so that's a selling point at least. And we'll have to move your kitchen equipment, what's left of it, up here. We'll need it to serve the guests, but more than that, we have a lot of islanders who'll still need shelter and food while we're rebuilding."

"Makes sense," Anstin said, nodding. "What else?"

"I get ten percent of the tourist proceeds," Buck said. "That should cover the lease of the hangar space."

"Sure," Anstin said. "If we get any tourist proceeds, which we may not."

"I'll take that risk," Buck said. "And one more thing. You hire islanders to do your repairs, unless there's no one here on the island who can do the work. I don't want the reconstruction money going to some offshore contractor. There's a reason the old buildings stood while your hotel got trashed."

"Buck…."

"That's the deal," Buck said. "I want the money going to local people, people who'll do the job right. We've got good folks here, Bill. Let's take care of them first."

"I have a standing contract," Anstin said. "My investors insisted."

Buck felt anger rising in his belly. "Tell your investors to fly down here and look what their people did, and how it held up. We built that school ourselves, and between that and my hangar, we got through this with no one dead. What would've happened if some of your guests had decided to stick it out in the hotel? Ask your investors that question. We do this with local people, or your damn investors can keep you afloat while they rebuild it their way. And you wouldn't be here if you didn't already have an answer to that question. Right?"

After a long moment, Anstin nodded. "They want evidence of a viable continuing income stream."

"Then there you go," Buck said. "If you want to be a big shot on this island, Anstin, then you're going to have to give something back. If you want a casino you can be proud of, then let these people build it. They'll be the ones running it for you, after all. Let it be their pride, too, and not just yours."

"I'll call them back and see what I can do."

"You do that, Anstin. And be convincing. Or you'll never see another dime from this island."

AS ANSTIN STRODE away to his car, a smattering of applause began among the group gathered around the fire. The sound rose as more hands joined in, until everyone was applauding Buck Shanahan.

He had an "aw, shucks" look to him by that point, and Hannah was pretty certain he would have been glad to run and hide. Finally he gave an embarrassed smile and bowed.

More applause, then, much to Buck's apparent gratification, attention returned to conversation about the rebuilding efforts. They agreed to an island town meeting the next evening at the airport, before Anstin was allowed to move his casino up here.

Buck looked satisfied with that. "Gonna have to put off our supply junket for a day, Sticks. We'll get a much fuller shopping list after the meeting tomorrow night."

She nodded, looking up at the sky. "Makes sense. Flying weather isn't so great anyway. It's clear blue sky here, but we'd be flying into the back edge of the storm."

"Yup," he agreed. "Aruba, Jamaica, or Cozumel, or maybe St. Maarten's, depending on the supplies we need and where Hannah has hit. No sense flying into someplace that's just been battered silly. They won't have anything either."

"Kinda makes you feel all alone out here," she said.

"We're on a small rock in a big ocean," Buck said. "Beyond that, we're on a small rock in a big, mostly empty universe. We *are* all alone out here."

"I try not to think of it that way," Hannah said. "What's that old joke—it may be just a hill of beans, but it's our hill and our beans? It's like a poker tournament. You can't do anything about what's happening on the other tables. All you can do is play the cards you're dealt."

He chuckled. "You're starting to sound like an islander, Sticks."

"Heaven forbid!"

"Speaking of, that was a hell of a beat you put on Edna last night."

She waved a hand. "The cards played themselves. I flopped a straight flush, and Edna turned quads. A blind monkey could've played that hand."

"Maybe so," he said. "But you knew she'd turned quads, didn't you?"

"Yes. Or a full house."

He shook his head. "No, you knew she'd turned quads, didn't you?"

Hannah found herself wondering why he was being so insistent. Was he sizing her up as an opponent? Or was it just idle curiosity? She decided on the latter.

"Yeah, I did. She was trying to keep calm on the outside, but I could almost hear the marching band and the fireworks going off inside her head."

"Nice when you have that good of a read on someone, isn't it?" he asked.

She nodded, realizing she had no such read on him. She hadn't at the table, and she didn't now. "Yes, it is. And it's scary when you don't."

He studied her for a long moment. Every poker player had heard about the great players who seemed to be looking right into your soul. That's how she felt. As if he was seeing every thought, almost before it formed.

Simultaneously she felt a shiver of delight somewhere deep inside her, and along with it a shiver of fear. She had always preferred to play life close to the vest. The idea that she might be an open book to someone, even only one someone, both enticed and frightened her.

She broke eye contact and looked around the hangar. "I guess we should organize people to start straightening out the hangar in the morning, for tomorrow's meeting."

"Not a bad idea. It sure as hell beats standing here trying to read each other's cards."

Well, she'd been right about that part, she thought, as they began to organize people into crews for tomorrow's tasks. Horace for once didn't butt in, but seemed content to sit back and watch, while sucking on a corncob pipe.

IN THE MORNING, bright and early, folks pitched in to stack bedrolls and other personal items against one wall to make room for the meeting. Buck towed his DC-3, the two small planes and Hannah's jet out onto the tarmac, clearing even more space. Children went around gathering discarded food wrappers and water bottles, and teenagers took turns on push brooms. In two hours, the hangar almost shone.

"The people here really do work together," she said, as she helped Ginny straighten the shelves of food that remained and restock the drink table.

"Of course," Ginny said, as if Hannah had asked if the sun rose in the east on Treasure Island. "We're a family. We have our spats, sure, but we're still family."

"Even Bill Anstin?" Hannah asked with a wry smile.

"You have any brothers or sisters?" Ginny asked.

Hannah shook her head. "Nope. I'm an only child."

"Aunts? Uncles? Cousins?"

"A whole slew of those," Hannah said. "Dad had two sisters, and Mom had three brothers. Why?"

"I bet there's at least one of those relatives that the rest of the family talks about in whispers, and only when he's not around. Am I right?"

After a long moment, Hannah chuckled and nodded. "Yeah. My uncle Mike. Mom's older brother. He went to Canada during Vietnam, when everyone else was gung-ho, my-country-right-or-wrong. Came back when the war was over and headed out to Hollywood, where he wrote television scripts. Now he's a big movie producer, but what does everyone in the family remember?"

"That he dodged the draft," Ginny said.

"Exactly."

"But I'll bet you all go to see his movies when they come out, right?"

Hannah smiled. "Yes. Mom had all of them on video. One of them even won an Oscar, way back when. We'd watch it at every family reunion, but only after Uncle Mike had gone home."

"That's how we feel about Bill Anstin," Ginny said, patting Hannah's hand. "He's a slimy toad, but he gave a lot of people jobs when he came here. So we sneer about him, and we all applaud when someone gets the best of him like Buck did. But he's still family."

Hannah found herself remembering Ginny's words as the meeting got underway. Once it finally did. It was like watching someone try to herd cats into a barn. Three times, Tom Regan walked to the makeshift podium they'd fashioned, and tried to get the people's attention. Three times, the people ignored him and went on talking among themselves.

Finally Tom whispered to Buck, and Buck put two fingers in his mouth and let out an ear-piercing whistle that seemed to climb right up Hannah's spinal cord, along with everyone else's in the hangar. The chatter quieted, and Tom walked to the podium again.

"I guess since I'm the mayor," he said, "I have to run this thing."

"Let Buck do it!" someone shouted.

Soon a chorus of voices joined in that opinion, but Buck shook his head. "He's the mayor. It's his job."

"Right," Regan said. "So let's get started. We're going to need to know who lost what, and who needs what to get back into their homes. We also need to know who still has a home, and how many extra people you could take in. We need to get the kids back into school, and Bill's going to set up the casino here, so we can't keep people in the hangar. So the first priority is getting people into homes."

At this point, Regan held up what appeared to be hieroglyphics written on a stained sheet of poster board. "I've prepared a housing plan. I need everyone who still has a home to move to the left side of the hangar, and the rest to move to the right side. Then we'll take a census of each side, and use these formulae...."

And that was the last thing anyone heard him say. A man standing in front of Hannah started to move toward the left, but his wife caught his arm and hissed "Stay right where you are."

Similar encounters were repeated all over the hangar, yielding a sound like of a room full of leaking tires. The sound grew to a murmur and then to a dull roar as women began to gravitate into clumps of twos and threes, then fives and sixes, then tens and twenties. Hannah was pulled along as if by magnetic force, listening.

"Damn fool will have people tearing each other's hair out in a week!" one woman said.

"Formulae!" another chimed in. "I don't even know how to pronounce it, but I sure as hell don't trust any formula or 'ay' or 'ee' or 'eye' that Tom Regan came up with."

"Calm down, girls," Ginny said. "Let Tom Regan

run his formul-ay-ee-eye till his eyes cross, and meanwhile we'll solve this problem among ourselves."

"As usual," one of the women said, smiling.

Thus began what islanders would later call The War of the Sexes. Husbands, left standing alone by their wives as the women coalesced, cautiously shuffled their way to the front of the room, nodding and listening as Regan explained his "stochastic, multi-variable family-matching algorithm." It sounded properly organized and scientific, and therefore gained currency among the island's men.

The women, by contrast, applied a different, far older, and arguably more effective problem-solving method: gossip.

"Ben Wilson has had eyes for Rochelle Lavaliere for months," one woman said. "Everyone knows it. And Regan wants to move the Wilsons in with the Lavalieres? Marc Lavaliere will be reaching for his shotgun, sure as the sun rises in the east!"

"Amen, sister," Ginny said. "That just won't work at all. Let's put the Wilsons with the Sanders."

"Ben Wilson gets eyes for me," Tammy Sanders said, "and Joe won't have to find a shotgun. I'll claw Ben's eyes right out of his head."

Given that Tammy Sanders looked like the kind of woman who could and would do exactly that, Hannah didn't think it likely that Ben Wilson would be blinded by that living arrangement.

And so it went for the next three hours. Tom Regan sat at a table, taking data from husbands, crunching his numbers, muttering to himself as he spewed chicken scratch across a yellow legal pad, then announcing solutions as if he were bearing tablets down from Mount Sinai. One or two women, dispatched to "keep an eye on that idiot," reported back to the group. The women then sorted out who couldn't eat garlic and who couldn't cook without it, whose teenage son was making time with whose teenage daughter, which wives were still seething over the last chili cookoff, and which husbands were still holding grudges over the last poker tournament.

"Ahh," Buck said, finally coming to Hannah's side. "Democracy in action. It's a beautiful thing."

"Democracy?" Hannah asked, laughing. "I was thinking more like chaos theory."

"One should never watch sausage or laws being made," he said. "This is the essence of democracy, Sticks. And Tom Regan's learning why I didn't enter that damn mayoral tournament. I know my place, and that ain't it."

They had to stand close to hear each other over the rising and falling din of voices echoing off the concrete floor and cinderblock walls of the hangar. As another marital spat broke out—Connie Estrada explaining in no uncertain terms why her husband

Jose was a fool to listen to Regan—Buck leaned in closer to hear what Hannah was saying.

And that's when she felt his chest brush against hers, and, inexplicably, a tingle shot through her body before landing squarely, emphatically and undeniably in her loins.

"Let's get out of here," she heard herself say, wishing in the moment she could take back the words, praying in the moment that he would say yes.

"Good idea," he said. "It's too damn loud in here, and you need a preflight briefing on the DC-3 before we fly tomorrow."

"Yes," she said. "A preflight briefing. Good idea. Very good idea."

She was tingling head to foot as she slipped out of the hangar with Buck into the balmy Caribbean evening. And as she trotted after him, her inner imp began to emerge.

Oh, was she going to have *fun!*

CHAPTER NINETEEN

BUCK SAW the glint in Hannah's eyes as they climbed into the DC-3. It was a glint he hadn't seen in far, far too many years, a glint that created an instant, insistent throbbing he thought he'd never feel again. Whatever he might have had in mind for a preflight briefing quickly disappeared in a flurry of soft touches, soft kisses, lips and tongues searching along the curves of chins and cheeks and the hollows of throats.

She had an amazing mouth. Astounding. Exhilarating. It was as if she had a map of his most sensitive nerves, and she navigated it with delicate kisses, flicking licks, and firm nipping teeth. His earlobes. The pulse just beneath his ear. The curve where his neck blended into his shoulder. His fingertips. His palms. His wrists.

Never in his life had he been this aroused, and she hadn't yet begun to undress him. Already he wanted to unfasten his jeans and pull them down to release his imprisoned member, but she gave him no chance, holding his hands in hers, arms extended, crucifying him with bliss.

When he looked for opportunities to return the kisses, she simply smiled down at him and shook her head. He would get his turn to lead, but this was not it. She wanted him to follow, to feel, to accept, to savor.

And, my, oh my, oh my, did he ever. He understood the game she was playing, and was only too willing to enter into it. A game like this was every man's dream, and Buck was no different. Who wouldn't want to let a woman like Hannah have her way with him?

She unbuttoned his shirt with only her teeth and lips, her eyes never leaving his as she tugged and manipulated and finally revealed inch after inch of his chest. Still looking at him, she extended her long, pink tongue and just barely touched the tips of his nipples, eliciting a low, shuddering groan that was matched by her growling, teasing laugh.

"Does that feel good, baby?" she cooed.

"Oh, yes, yes, yes, yes, yesssssssss," he said.

"Too bad," she said, withdrawing her tongue and leaning down to bite gently on his chest, capturing the thin tufts of hair in her teeth and pulling.

He was hers…the sexy gardener being taken by the lady of the house. Never mind that this was his island, his airport and his airplane. He was hers.

And he loved it.

Pain and pleasure, carefully measured into doses of incredible arousal and even more incredible frustration, rolled through his senses. He entwined his fingers in hers, allowing her to hold his arms spread, willing himself to relax and give himself totally to her will. For in this moment, her will was his desire.

He could smell her arousal, and saw her stiffened nipples pushing hard through her bra and blouse, but he made no attempt to sate it. She would decide when he was permitted that pleasure. Until then, his longing to give her some measure of the joy he felt would have to languish in the same surrender as that of his own arousal.

He was hers, and oh, man, was he loving it. Never before had anyone in his life made him feel this wanted.

And when her teeth settled onto his pebbled nipples, she left no doubt in his mind. She bit firmly, looking up at him, studying his face for signs of resistance, but he could only gasp out a hoarse, passionate "Yes, ma'am."

Her fingers stroked his reassuringly, matched with the tender moan that rose from her throat, as she began to saw her teeth back and forth over his nipple. It was as if an electric current were running from his nipple to his brain to his throbbing member, which was now growing painful as it tried to expand within the confines of his jeans. Yet he could no longer distinguish pain from pleasure.

Every sensation was pleasure.

Every sensation was pain.

Every sensation was what she wanted him to feel, and bloomed satisfaction in his soul, for that reason alone.

His eyelids fluttered closed as he began to sink into a place he had never before known, then flew open as she bit hard and pain seemed to mushroom through him.

"No, baby," she whispered, low and husky. "Don't close your eyes. Look at me. Share it with me."

She resumed her ministrations, tender suckles replacing biting teeth, soothing him while still pulling firmly at now tender nerve endings. She was taking him on a journey, and she was both pilot and navigator. He was merely a passenger, cherished cargo, the terrain over which she plotted her course of sensation, arousal and need.

He realized that he no longer felt like a partner. He was an object, a toy, and yet…more of a lover than he had ever been in his life.

"What do you need, baby?" she asked, as if sensing his final, complete surrender.

"My pants…. Hurts…."

"Does it really?" she asked, smiling playfully. "Does little Buck need some room to stretch?"

"Yes. Yessssss. Please."

She leaned up and pressed her lips to his, softly, almost too soft to feel, then leaned close to his ear and whispered, "Beg, baby. Beg me."

With any other woman, at any other moment in his life, he would have rebelled. With this woman, in this moment, the thought never entered his mind.

"Please, ma'am, I beg you. Please release me down there. I'll do anything for you. Anything at all."

"Anything," she whispered, kissing the tip of his nose, his cheeks, his eyelids, "is a dangerous word."

"Anything," he repeated.

"Such a good boy you are," she said, looking into his eyes with a smile unlike any he had ever seen before, then pressing her lips to his, searching for his tongue, taking it, sucking it, dancing with it. "Such a good boy."

He hadn't heard those words since childhood, but now they meant something very different than they had then. She was pleased with him, and that thought made his heart well with gratitude and joy.

Joy, pain and pleasure mixed to make him exactly what she wanted: her passion slave. And he was more than willing to give her what she wanted. He groaned the words out. "Thank you, ma'am."

She pressed his hands out gently, silently ordering him to keep them there, then drew her own hands in to tenderly cradle his face as she leaned in to kiss his eyes so gently, as if she sensed his every feeling.

Then, finally, she slowly slid down his body and unfastened his jeans, her fingers moving languidly, as if she had a lifetime to undress him. And, he realized, she did, for he would do nothing to hurry her. To do that would betray what he had given her, what she had drawn out of him, what she had made of him.

His heart cringed at the very thought.

Inch by tantalizing inch, she slid his jeans down his legs, pulling his boxer shorts with them, letting her hair trail over tingling nerve endings as she kissed her way down his thighs, behind his knees, along his calves, and finally down to his ankles. He had never imagined that the simple act of untying and removing his shoes could be this sensual, and yet she turned it into a new adventure, a new waiting, a new leg of this journey of discovery.

Now he lay naked but for his opened shirt, and she pushed his feet apart gently but insistently. He made not the slightest attempt to resist her, for now at least he was permitted the full flowering of his arousal. He felt his testicles roll in delight at their newfound freedom, felt his penis bobbing against his belly as muscles gently pulsed out the signals of his need.

He thought she would undress, but no. Instead, she leaned close, gathered her silky hair in her hands, and began to caress him with it. Fingertips softly probed him, here, there, everywhere, places he had never imagined being touched. His thigh muscles spasmed with need, a need he had no doubt she saw and felt, and yet she paid it only so much attention as would keep him at the edge, not quite able to fall over that precipice into total release.

Her tongue trailed over him, almost aimlessly, and yet as if following every progression of begging nerve endings, until finally finding his purple tip to lap away the oozing pearls of his arousal. When she finally took him into her mouth, the moan that emerged from his mouth seemed to have its roots in his very soul.

"Oh, ma'am. Yes. Thank you."

A soft, approving chuckle was her only answer, for now she drew him deeper, alternating slow, pulsing, swallowing laps of her tongue with sharp sparkles as she dragged her teeth over his rim. Her hands still cupped her hair to his scrotum, fingers pressing rhythmically at that most sensitive flesh of his perineum, fingertips teasing his back gate with whispers of ownership.

He felt his knees slowly rise and spread, and the most profound sense of openness spread through his entire being. He was exposed, in the most vulnerable possible way, with nothing protected, nothing held back.

Not his body.

Not his heart.

Not his soul.

Another soft, soothing, encouraging, approving laugh rose from her throat as her eyes met his, and slowly, so slowly, she nodded.

She was pleased.

His breath was ragged, fingers clenching into fists at the ends of outstretched arms, toes curling, his entire body, his entire spirit, his entire being clenching at the edge of the cliff.

With a warm moan, she nodded and engulfed him completely, the base of her tongue caressing his tip as she swallowed him whole, taking him, claiming him, owning him.

The world exploded. White hot sparks burst from every nerve ending. He heard cries that only later would he know were his own as he tumbled, twitched, spasmed and finally felt himself release.

Her mouth never left him, never paused, as she moaned out her own joy. It was the joy of complete possession, of owning the sexy gardener for whose heart she was willing to gamble.

And he knew in that moment that, no matter what, somehow, he would be hers.

He felt something leathery against one of his outstretched hands, and looked over to see Buster's red eyes in the dim light of the DC-3.

"*Mmmhmm,*" Buster moaned.

MMMHMM? BUCK FROZE. In an instant he returned to his senses, lost his arousal and realized that he had let a woman use him like a toy. *Delilah.*

"Cripes!" Leaving Hannah looking utterly shocked, he sat up, pushed her aside—gently, he didn't want to hurt her—and grabbed his clothes.

Yes, ma'am? Please, ma'am? Had he actually been saying those things? Had he actually been thrilled when she called him a good boy?

"Jesus!" The rare oath escaped him as he yanked on his pants and then his shirt.

"Buck?" Hannah was kneeling on the floor of the cargo space, looking at him with confusion and…and what? Disappointment?

"Cripes!" He started hunting for his shoes and socks.

"Buck?"

What could he say to her? That he'd willingly floated into her fantasy, had willingly become her love slave, had willingly taken a subordinate position to her…and now he was scared shitless by his own response.

He didn't mind kinky. Kinky was great. But this kind of kinky was something he wasn't ready to share with anyone. He was never going to risk himself that way again. It made him too vulnerable. He'd been there once and had lived to seriously regret it.

"Buck?"

"Look, I'm sorry," he said finally. "You're a great lover. Really great. You…really swept me away."

"Then what's wrong?"

"Apart from Buster getting involved?"

"Yeah, apart from Buster. He's just a gator."

"More than a gator if you ask me, but who's asking me, I'm just the dumb gardener."

"Buck!"

"No."

"Buck, dammit, slow down!"

He stopped and looked straight at her.

"Why are you scared?" she asked.

"Scared?" But that was exactly it, he realized. She had made him feel helpless. Willingly helpless. He'd actually *begged* her.

"Scared," she said again. "You need to learn to let go. I was helping you to just let go."

"What are you, a psychologist?" He glared at her. Damn, she was the biggest threat he'd ever faced. He *had* to get her off this island.

"No." She rose to her feet. "But I've been watching you since I got here, and I never in my life met anyone who more desperately needed *not* to be in control at least once in a while. You're *always* in control."

"You're right." He glared at her. "I lost control once before. I gave control to someone else. And you know what? I'm never going to do it again. It's not worth the cost."

"But—"

"No buts. That's it." Scowling, he climbed out of the plane. Let Buster soothe her hurt feelings. He wanted no part of her games. Especially not games that left him as emotionally naked as a child.

AFTER BUCK SCRAMBLED out of the plane, Hannah remained kneeling. Buster edged over to her, and she absently reached out to scratch the side of his head.

She'd come too close to something, she realized. What she had meant as a pleasurable diversion, a chance for him to just let go and be loved, had turned into an emotional crisis for him. And for her. They had moved too deeply into emotional intimacy too fast.

She had played with fire, and they both were singed right now, she realized. She felt rejected on so many levels because she had exposed something of herself to him as well, whether he knew it or not.

Her heart squeezed painfully and she lowered her head, letting the tears come. It was now terribly obvious that she had begun to give herself where she wasn't wanted.

And somehow she had to let go of barely formed fantasies and dreams, and get off this plane and face this town as if nothing at all had happened. As if they wouldn't have all figured it out anyway. Being on Treasure Island was like living under a microscope.

Under the glare of general interest, she felt as transparent as a paramecium.

She had to acknowledge that that hurt only because she had been rejected. Under other circumstances, she wouldn't have cared if they could all read her heart.

But right now that organ was feeling bruised, like a black eye.

Leaning back, Hannah rested her head on Buster, a leathery, lumpy pillow, and waited for the urge to cry to abate. At the very least, she didn't want to climb out of this plane with puffy, reddened eyelids. Then she might just as well wear a sign.

She would have liked to get angry with Buck. Anger would have beaten back the ache in her heart, and replaced it with something far more comfortable. She would have liked to blame him for everything she could think of, just so she wouldn't have to hurt anymore.

But she had been roundly and soundly rejected, and she couldn't forget that. Nor could she get angry about it.

Because, for some terrible reason, her heart persisted in clinging to her hurt. Clinging to the ache as if it might explode without it.

And maybe it would.

Dashing at her eyes again, she sat up and tried to compose herself.

Buster hummed contentedly beside her, and she looked down at him through blurry eyes.

"You know," she said to him, "even for an alligator your timing stinks."

CHAPTER TWENTY

BUCK THREW himself into helping people move back into town into the homes they were going to share. Anything to get away from Hannah. Anything to get away from the memory of his own vulnerability. The few times he glimpsed Hannah as she helped others, he thought she didn't look any better than he felt.

Which only served to kick his sense of guilt into high gear. Damn, he hadn't been the only vulnerable one in the back of that plane. He might have hated his own, well, loss of control, but he'd basically kicked her when she was as exposed as he had been.

Great going, Shanahan.

But business didn't leave him much time to kick himself. The women, over repeated objections from the mayor, were organizing every group as it moved out and refusing to let Tom Regan or any other male modify anything they had decided. Tom looked nearly apoplectic at the way he was being ignored. Buck didn't care. He went where they told him to go and helped who they told him to help, like a good mule.

The gardener and the wealthy lady. Hey, didn't that story play out differently? Yes, the gardener was submissive to the woman's position in life, but hadn't *he* been the one to teach her all the wonders of lovemaking?

Most men, he admittedly sourly to himself, would have been thrilled to be where he had been such a short while ago in the cargo hold. Most men would have been delighted by a woman who took control and asked them to just relax and enjoy.

So maybe he was…crazy? He knew he was emotionally damaged goods, all his grumping about Delilahs to the contrary. He knew he was carrying a scab on his heart that had made him damn near misogynistic.

But that was the point, wasn't it? Emotionally she had been reaching him in places he'd locked away a long time ago because they were too easily hurt.

He couldn't let anyone in there again, but she had almost made it, and in the most primitive way possible.

So get her plane fixed, he told himself. Get it fixed ASAP. Get her off this island before she got any closer. Before he couldn't slam doors at her any longer.

The thought caused him to wander away from the steady flow of people into town and over to her plane. The schematics he'd studied were still clear in his head, and he dragged a ladder over to the starboard wing and climbed up to begin opening a maintenance hatch. If the problem wasn't here or near the engine, then it was on the other wing. While the plane had two fuel tanks, as did most twin engine jobs, it also had fuel load stabilization, which would pass gas from one wing tank to the other to prevent weight imbalances that could affect the plane's control or attitude.

So a leak from one engine would soon empty the tank from the other as well, unless the load stabilizers were turned off.

And maybe she hadn't gotten any kind of cockpit warning. What with her radio going out, he was prepared to believe she'd had an electrical system problem to begin with. One which might have led to this problem becoming severe.

Sticking a fresh cigar between his teeth for the first time in at least a day, he dug into the problem with real pleasure. This was the kind of thing he could deal with.

This was the kind of thing that made him master of his universe, which was exactly how he wanted to keep it.

HANNAH JOINED the trip to town to help unload things on the other end. She hadn't missed Buck's withdrawal into mechanical matters, namely fixing her plane so he could get her the hell out of his life as quickly as possible.

Part of her felt hurt, but part of her acknowledged the wisdom of what he was doing. They would only hurt each other, she told herself. Hadn't they already done so?

Unfortunately, she found herself riding in the back of a truck with the mayor and Ginny. The two proved to be a volatile combination.

"I had everything worked out," Tom Regan was saying. "I could have managed the whole thing and made sure everyone had a place to go and that no one was overburdened."

Ginny sniffed. "Tom, you don't know a thing about people. The way you were going we'd have had a couple of murders before the week was out."

"People here aren't like that."

"Not until you crowd them together and someone you don't like is making eyes at your daughter or wife."

Regan bridled. "We're all adult enough to handle that for a few weeks."

"You think so?" Ginny sniffed again and shook her head. "Even Horace knows better than that."

"Horace isn't the mayor. You had no business ignoring my authority."

"You get your authority from *us,* you dimwit. This isn't a police state."

As raw as she was feeling, Hannah would have happily jumped off the side of the truck if it hadn't been rolling so rapidly down the damaged road. At this point it was all she could do to hang on.

That didn't seem to be bothering Ginny and Tom, however.

"So you want a recall?" Tom demanded. "You want to play out a tournament for who's boss? I'll win, you know. I've won the last four times."

Ginny laughed.

"What's so damn funny?"

She just shook her head. But Tom wasn't going to let it go at that.

"No," he insisted angrily. "I want to know what's so funny? I'm a damn good card player. You might as well listen to me now, because I'll just win the job all over again."

Ginny rolled her eyes.

"You take that back," Tom shouted. "You take it back right now!"

He sounded like an eight-year-old on the playground, Hannah thought. Just like a little kid who didn't know how to handle his problem any other way.

"There's nothing to take back," Ginny said finally, when Tom wouldn't stop pressing her.

"Yes there is. You rolled your eyes at me. You can't do that."

"I can do anything I please," Ginny replied with a shake of her head.

"I won this job!"

Finally Ginny had enough. "I hate to tell you, Tom, but you keep winning the election tournaments because nobody *else* wants to be mayor."

Tom spluttered. Actually spluttered. And turned beet red. "That's not true!"

Ginny shrugged. "I don't care what you believe. But the fact is, Tom Regan, you're a tin-pot dictator at times. Difference from a real dictator, though, is that you don't have an army to back you up. We do what we want on this island. Always have. If you can't live with that, then don't bother entering the tournament at the next election, because *I* will."

Tom squawked. "You think you can beat me?"

"I *know* I can."

"That does it," Tom snapped. "Heads-up, you and me, as soon as we get to town."

Ginny shook her head. "Heads-up, you and me, after we get this mess cleaned up. In the meantime, just shut your mouth and save your energy for rebuilding."

Tom's mouth opened yet again, as if he were preparing to launch another salvo. Then, for some reason known only to him, he snapped his jaws shut and hunkered down.

His timing was excellent, Hannah thought an instant later. Because if his mouth had been open and his tongue flapping when they hit that next pothole, he wouldn't have had a tongue to flap anymore.

God, she thought suddenly, she *loved* this place.

SURPRISINGLY, electrical power returned to the entire town by mid-afternoon. The telephones weren't far behind. The people who looked after both things proved their skill, speed and preparation. By nightfall, every occupiable building was back on the grid, and lights shone cheerily from unboarded windows.

Hannah, her arms and back aching as they seldom had, was only too glad to accept a ride to the airport with Bill Anstin, who was carrying another truckload of gaming equipment up that way.

The problem was, it was Bill Anstin. And he was still making eyes at her. She could tell even in the dark with the only light from the dash lamps.

Lord, he made her skin crawl. It was something about him, about the way he seemed to view her as an object. Like a potential notch on his bedpost. She despised men like that, the more so since her dealings with a certain airline pilot.

Nor did she understand why some men were like that. She supposed it was rooted somewhere in the distant past among ancestors who had still been clinging to trees or something. But whatever it was, there were some men who seemed unable to think in any terms but those of conquest. If she'd been a planet, she had no doubt Anstin would have tried to plant a flag on her. He probably wouldn't have lingered long to admire it, but would have dashed back out among the stars looking for yet another place to put a flag.

If she had to guess, Bill Anstin was used to having his way with women. Any woman. And she supposed that a lot of women would fall for his good looks and apparent success. She knew the type: they wanted a man like a trophy, wanted someone to "take care of them." And since Anstin was looking at women as trophies, she supposed the whole ugliness evened out in the long run.

But she wasn't looking for any trophies, and she didn't want to be a trophy, and she *certainly* didn't like the feeling that he wouldn't have been interested in her at all if she hadn't been a fresh face on the island.

She knew the limitations of her looks. To be honest, she was kind of surprised that Buck had so suddenly been nearly overcome with passion for her. She could understand her attraction to *him.* He had rugged good looks that said he worked for a living, unlike Anstin who had—and here she nearly shuddered—soft, white hands. Pampered hands. She liked men whose hands said they were used on whatever needed doing.

Buck's hands alone would have been enough to attract her, never mind those blue eyes in that tanned face, or the way his dark brown hair kept wanting to tumble onto his forehead. She liked the nicks and dings on his fingers and knuckles, and frankly, she even liked it when a little bit of grease clung to those hardened fingers.

A *man's* hands. If Anstin had ever lifted anything heavier than a deck of cards, it sure didn't show.

She recognized her own bias, because there were lots of important things people could do that mattered that didn't require banging up their hands. Like being a doctor. Or a teacher. Or a minister.

But, maybe because of the way she had been raised, she was attracted to hands that looked like they knew their way around tools and the guts of machinery. And attraction didn't give a darn about bias.

Regardless, she couldn't get back to the airport and away from Anstin soon enough. Even Buster made her feel more comfortable now. At that thought she almost laughed out loud, and her spirits lifted for the first time in hours. Longing for an alligator? Lord, what had she come to? There must be something in the air of this island.

Even with all the craziness on this island, she never would have dreamed what lay just ahead, though. Never would have imagined that Anstin had the absolute gall to attempt what he did next. He pulled off to the side of the road without explanation and switched off the ignition.

At once Hannah tensed. "What are you doing?"

"Look at those stars," he answered, as if he had

actually been glancing upward. Now, however, he made a big point of leaning forward and looking up through his dusty windshield. "That's one of the best parts of living on this island, Hannah. The night sky."

"Really?" She didn't move. If she wanted to look at stars, she could do it from the airport with Buster guarding her. More than ever, she wanted that gator beside her. Or Buck, of course, but she was firmly shoving Buck out of her thoughts, or at least trying to.

"Yeah, really." He looked at her, smiling widely. It sort of reminded her of Buster when he saw those pork hocks at the barbeque before the storm. Predatory.

"Well, I'll look another time," she said. "Right now I need to get back and see how Buck is doing with my plane." Her heart began to pound uncomfortably. She didn't want this, didn't want to have to defend herself as she suspected she might.

"What's the rush? You can't go anywhere before morning. Might as well take time to sniff the daisies."

"There aren't any daisies."

"Don't be so literal." If it were possible, his smile widened even more. "Why don't we get out here and take a look at all those stars?"

"Why don't you just start the ignition and get me to the airport? I didn't sign on for anything else."

"Aww, Hannah, what's the rush? I'd like to get to know you."

"The feeling isn't mutual." She realized she was pressed hard against the door, and that he was moving closer. Damn the bench seat in this truck anyway. Right now she'd have given a great deal for a four-on-the-floor right between them.

"You don't mean that."

She bridled. "Don't tell me what I mean. I *know* what I mean. Now, let's get to the airport."

He chuckled. "I like a little spit and fire in my women."

"I'm not your woman!" Now she was getting mad. *Really* mad. Everything she had disliked about him before didn't hold a candle to the things she disliked about him right then.

"Not yet," he said, too suavely. Then he made a royally stupid move. He leaned over her, touching her cheek with his palm, brushing his chest against her breasts. "Admit it," he said. "That feels good."

She would never remember the next three seconds, but afterward she was certain *he* would never forget them.

The next thing she knew, Anstin was huddled up against his side of the truck, covering vulnerable anatomy parts and groaning. For good measure, she grabbed the keys from the ignition and threw them out the window into the darkness beneath the damaged trees.

Then she was walking up the road by herself

beneath that gorgeous star-studded sky and thinking that that jerk Anstin had been right: The night sky was one of the best things about this island.

CHAPTER TWENTY-ONE

BUCK HAD HEARD more than his fair share of cursing in the navy. Fighter pilots, like many in the military, seem to have a primal need to demonstrate their superior manhood by virtue of searching for ever more inventive ways to combine and juxtapose obscene words. Thus was born the phrase "cursing like a sailor."

But he had never in his life heard anything close to the stream of invective flowing from the red-haired, green-eyed, mud-covered form that stormed onto the apron and into the pool of illumination spread by Buck's work light. He had always thought the phrase "a mouth that would make a sailor blush" was mere hyperbole. He was wrong.

In the manner of males throughout history, his first response was to replay his actions over the past few hours, to see if he had done anything to evoke such anger. There would be time later to figure out what was wrong and what, if anything, he might do to fix it. The first priority was to ensure that he was not in danger of losing body parts.

So, let's see…there was his response after their tryst on the DC-3, but that had been hours and hours ago, and she had at least been civil since, even if she was obviously hurt. That didn't seem likely to have created this Lorena-Bobbit-in-being. They had hardly seen each other in the hours since, except for brief "Excuse me," "Oh, sorry" encounters while they were working. Try as he might, Buck couldn't think of anything he had done which ought to have put him in this kind of mortal peril.

Which meant she was angry at someone else.

While he was normally monotheistic in outlook, this seemed to be an appropriate occasion to thank not only his god, but every other god from every other civilization which had ever existed, or would ever exist. Just to be sure he hadn't overlooked whatever deity had spared him.

She neared the plane uttering a pungent phrase which painted the near impossible image of a gay Oedipus, born of a female dog, engaging in oral intercourse while being reduced to a fecal blob. She finally looked up at the wing, and him upon it, and uttered a single word…an old English verb for sexual intercourse which had, in modern times, become the universal expletive.

He, in an act of foolhardiness bordering on a death wish, seemed unable to prevent himself from saying, "Now?"

Oddly, amazingly, her response was not to look for an implement with which to disembowel him. Instead, she looked up at him, then down at herself, then up at him again, and laughed.

"Sure. I've already had a roll in the mud. A roll in the hay sounds just lovely."

"Bad night?" he asked.

"Bill Anstin," she replied, as if that alone were enough to explain the mysteries of life, the universe, and the feminine mind.

"Care to explain?" he asked.

"Not really."

"Fair enough."

He picked up a wrench and leaned back toward the fuel line that he was reconnecting. As she had already said she didn't want to talk about it, this act guaranteed that she would, in fact, talk about it. He might be a troglodyte, but he'd learned that much about women.

"He made a pass at me," she said.

Congratulating himself on his mastery of male-female interaction, he decided to repeat the performance.

"Oh," he said, and leaned back toward the fuel line.

This time, however, she didn't respond. And while he didn't look up, he was aware that neither had she walked away. Finally, she spoke.

"I liked it."

"Bill Anstin?" he asked, looking up, slack-jawed.

In that moment he realized he had it in him to kill someone, and Bill Anstin's life expectancy could now be measured in hours. The savage thoughts that began to dance across his brain seemed an appropriate accompaniment to vision that had gone red.

"No," she said. "Us. What happened earlier."

"Ah," he said. His vision cleared, and the caveman in him returned to reluctant sleep. Thank God. He figured his chances of getting off with an island jury if he murdered Anstin were pretty good, but then he'd have to live with himself. Buck tried very hard to remain comfortable in his own skin. Anything else cost him too much sleep.

Obviously he had missed the deft segue in her mind. Someday, he promised himself, he would read one of those books that teach men how to notice such things. Not that he expected it would help.

"That's it?" she asked. "Ah?"

He took a moment to weigh his options. Ignoring her while continuing to work on her fuel line, given her mood, risked that she would rethink her decision not to search for an implement with which to disembowel him. On the other hand, engaging the conversation, given her mood, carried the same risk. On the plus side, fixing her fuel line guaranteed that she would get off the island soon. On the plus side, engaging the conversation offered a small chance at something that might be far better...that she would decide to stay.

So, in one column, a guarantee of being rid of her versus the risk of disembowelment. In the other column, the possibility they might find something truly special together…also versus the risk of disembowelment. He was certain that John Nash's beautiful mind might be able to sort through these options and fashion a formula by which Buck could derive the proper game-theory solution.

Alas, John Nash wasn't here.

Alas, Hannah Lamont was.

In the end, it came down to a simple poker concept: outs. In poker, an "out" was a card that would help your hand. If you had four Hearts, with the Ace and King of Hearts in your hand, and nothing higher than a Queen on board, there were nine other Hearts, three other Aces, and three other Kings that would give you either a flush or top pair. That meant you had fifteen outs in forty-six unseen cards, fifteen cards that would help you versus thirty-one that would not. The odds of hitting one of those outs on the next card were 31:15, or about 2:1. If the pot odds—the amount of money in the pot versus the amount of the bet you had to call—were 2:1 or better, and if you were sure that top pair would win the pot, then it was correct to call. Yes, you would still miss twice for every time that you hit, but the one time you hit would more than pay for those two misses.

Continuing to work on the fuel line offered no

outs. Ignoring her while continuing his work would only anger her more, and eliminate any possibility that they might part as friends, let alone anything more. By contrast, while he was equally likely to anger her if he talked, there was at least some chance of reaching some resolution that would leave him feeling like less than a total screw-up of a man.

The risk was the same each way, but only one choice offered any real reward.

He put down the wrench and looked up.

"I did, too, Sticks." He swallowed, and thought: *in for a penny, in for a pound.* "I enjoyed it too much."

She made no move to climb the wing, and he made no move to climb down. Distance seemed the better alternative to both at the moment.

"I don't know what came over me," she began, but he knew what happened wasn't her fault and he wasn't about to let her apologize for it.

"It was wonderful, Hannah. I've…you were great. More than great. You were…amazing. Intoxicating. And I screwed up."

"By having sex with me?"

He shook his head. "No. Not that. After."

"Bad memories," she said.

It wasn't a question. She knew.

"She was…."

He tried to find the words to continue, but nothing seemed to fit. He picked up the wrench again, tightening the bolt he'd been working on. This time, he wasn't trying to avoid the conversation, or goad her into continuing. He was giving himself time to think.

"I gave her every part of me," he finally said. "It wasn't like what you and I shared in the DC-3. That was, wow. But…in every other way, I…she was the stars in my eyes, the moon that lit my path home on the lonely nights at sea. She was…everything. To me."

"And you weren't. To her."

He shook his head. "When I was out of town, she was shacking up with anyone who was interested. Provided they were officers. Ideally officers of higher rank. Steps in her personal quest for promotion, I guess. I was still a lieutenant. Her first, I later found out, was a lieutenant commander. I guess she finally married a captain, who is now an admiral. Maybe she found what she was looking for. Maybe they ended up divorced. I don't know. I just know that my everything, the everything I thought about when I was sitting in the officers' mess after a hairy mission, the everything that kept me from giving in to the utter exhaustion so I could take a few minutes to write a letter home…that everything…was gone."

"I don't want to be your everything, Buck."

"I don't know any other way to love someone."

She paused at that, as if considering how to respond. Finally, she looked up at him. "It wasn't just her fault, Buck. And you can hate me for saying this, but it's true. You weren't in love. You were obsessed. There's a huge difference."

The words stung, even as he realized the truth in them. He slowly nodded.

"No one can or should be anyone's 'everything,' Buck. It's not healthy. I'm not saying you drove her into the arms of another. You didn't. That was her choice, and she was a bitch for making it. She'll get no excuses from me. But how many friends did you have in the Navy? None, I'll bet. No close ones, anyway."

He nodded again. "You're right. There was my weapons officer, but we weren't like you see in the movies. We got along well enough, but I didn't confide in him apart from the ordinary stuff of flying together. Apart from that, I spent my time by myself. Reading, mostly."

"And when you were in port?" she asked.

"If we went out, it was with her friends. If I was invited, which wasn't all the time. Otherwise, yeah, I was a homebody. I cooked. I kept the place up. I figured it was my contribution, since I'd been gone all those months. I worked on the car in my spare time, not because it needed the work, but because I needed the outlet."

Her voice softened. "You put yourself in a position where life could crush you, Buck. And life obliged.

It could have happened a lot of ways, even if she hadn't left you. What if she'd died? You'd still have been crushed, because you'd still have had nothing left. No kids. No family or friends to comfort you. No one to drag you out to the bowling alley for an hour or so, just to get you out of your funk. Nothing. And that's just not healthy. For anyone."

"I'd never thought of it that way."

She smiled. "Who would, after what she did? You were, what, twenty-five?"

"Twenty-six."

"You were still a kid yourself. You might have been flying a multi-million-dollar, state-of-the-art jet at twice the speed of sound, but you were still a kid. It takes a lot of guts to do what you did, but not half as much as to look inside yourself and ask what went wrong. And there's no adrenaline rush there."

"Why is this not making me feel like less of a screw-up?" he asked.

"I'm sorry," she said. "You don't need me to lecture you. I'm sorry."

"No, don't apologize, Sticks. I *do* need you to lecture me. No one else has. And you're right. But it still doesn't excuse how I acted toward you."

"You're right," she said. "It doesn't. But it does explain it. And I forgive you."

She could have chosen a thousand things to say there. A million, maybe. She'd chosen the one thing that cut through him like a buzz saw and left him feeling so raw, so vulnerable and so grateful.

He dropped the wrench.

"Am I messed up or what?" he asked, as much to the universe as to her, as he reached into the wing, fishing around for the wrench. "God*damn* it."

"What?" she asked.

"Well, unless you feel like flying around with a wrench rattling around in your wing, I'm going to have to take some more parts off."

"Let me see if I can reach it," she said, climbing up onto the wing. "I have smaller hands."

"You have amazing hands," he said, reddening as he heard the words come out of his mouth. "Hell, you're just amazing, period."

"Why, thank you, Buck Shanahan," she said, kneeling beside him to thread her hand through the open port in the wing and down to where the wrench rested. She brought it back up and held it out to him with a victorious smile. "You're pretty damn amazing yourself."

"Nah," he said, taking the wrench and returning it to his toolbox. "I'm just a broken down old jet jockey."

She took his chin in her hand and turned it to face her. "I talk too much, Buck. I know that. And most guys I've known, if I'd said what I just said to you… well…they'd have suggested that I engage in airborne intercourse with a rolling donut."

He laughed, not having heard the phrase she alluded to since his Navy days. The girl sure did have a mouth to make a sailor blush. This sailor, at least.

"You didn't," she said. "You heard me out. And I know it hurt to do. That takes a kind of courage that, well, like I said—pretty damn amazing."

When she leaned in to kiss him, it felt like the most natural, most wonderful thing in the entire world. And he kissed her back. Firmly. To thank her, but also, because he needed it. And wanted it.

They embraced, a melding of mud and grease, and it was as wonderful an embrace as he had ever known. He could take her now, right here, on the wing of her jet. In fact, he would. His hands stroked her face, her shoulders, her sides, and finally her breasts. Her breath deepened into a low, aching moan. His loins twitched in anticipation.

And then Edna walked out of the hangar. "What the hell are you two doing?"

CHAPTER TWENTY-TWO

EDNA'S SQUAWK was reminiscent of a pterodactyl in a hunting rage. Buck and Hannah jerked apart, Hannah nearly falling off the wing except that Buck's grip saved her.

"How dare you!" Edna said. "We haven't even played our match for him."

Buck, who had earlier thought it might be funny to see two women play a heads-up game for him suddenly didn't find it quite so funny. What made Edna think she'd have any claim on him just because she beat Hannah at a game?

Didn't *he* have anything to say about this?

Thing was, earlier he'd kept his mouth shut because he hadn't given a damn. Or hadn't wanted to. The ground beneath his feet, however, was shifting as rapidly as sand.

What the hell was he thinking, getting involved with Hannah? Maybe he'd owed her an explanation for his behavior, given what had happened, but he sure as hell shouldn't have fallen straight into her arms again.

He was losing his marbles. For real this time. He was getting waste deep in a pile of no-good really fast.

Facts were facts, and the facts were these: Hannah would fly out of here in the next couple of days. Edna would still be here, hounding him and making his life uncomfortable if not hellish. And hellish looked more likely the way that woman was glaring at him and Hannah right now.

Did he need any of this?

Absolutely not.

He grabbed a rag and descended the ladder, leaving Hannah on the wing. Wiping his hands, he studiously avoided looking at either woman. "I found out what's wrong with your fuel line," he said. "I'll need to get some parts tomorrow to finish the repair. As for the radio…there was an electrical short. That's why you didn't know you were running out of fuel until it was too late, and why you couldn't radio for help."

"Oh," said Hannah.

He didn't like the sound of that "oh." It seemed to suggest a wealth of hidden feelings, all of which probably boded ill for him. Which he deserved, he supposed, because he *had* been acting like a jackass who couldn't make up his mind about anything. Hell, he was *still* acting like a jackass. Hannah might be leaving, but Edna would still be here to chap his hide. In fact, he thought sardonically, the only thing that could protect him from Edna was an eruption of Big Mouth that would take her with it. Unfortunately, he wouldn't wish that on anyone. So where did that leave him?

Standing here with hands reeking of gasoline, clinging to a rag as if it were a lifeline, that's where.

"So she'll be gone in a couple of days?" Edna asked, sounding as if the idea delighted her.

Buck had had enough. He turned to face Edna. "Maybe you can fly out of here with her. It sure would make life easier around here."

She gaped at him. "I'm not leaving my volcano!"

"Then go back to your volcano and stay the hell away from me."

"How dare you talk to me that way!"

"How dare you act like you own me? Nobody owns me. So if the two of you don't mind, I'll just go back to being my happily hermetic, misogynistic self."

With that, he tossed the rag into a bin that he'd brought out by Hannah's plane, and stalked away.

He'd go to his house and lock the door. Anstin could move his own damn equipment into the hangar. Buck was going to shut down his airport and stay away from the entire human race until tomorrow morning when he could fly out of here and solve half his problem by buying parts for Hannah's jet.

It didn't improve his mood at all to realize that he was probably behaving irrationally. But what the hell, had he ever been rational to begin with?

HANNAH GLARED at Edna, then slipped down off the wing, leaving a streak of mud behind her. Her feet hit the concrete, and for a few moments her ankles stung.

"What is it with you, Edna?" she asked. "You don't own the man."

"Neither do you!"

"The difference is that I don't *want* to own him. In fact, I can't wait to get the hell off this island."

"We're still playing heads-up." Edna's chin set.

What the hey, Hannah thought. Why not? At the very least she'd have the pleasure of beating this woman at something before she left. Pin her ears back a little.

"Absolutely. But win or lose, I'm leaving anyway."

"That's just sour grapes talking."

Hannah rolled her eyes. "I haven't lost yet. How can it be sour grapes?"

"Because you know you can't have Buck regardless."

"Nobody has Buck. Buck's a man with his own mind. You can win him in as many poker games as you want, Edna, but he'll still be the one who decides whether he wants to get involved with you. And from what I've seen so far, he doesn't want to get involved with anyone."

Liar, a voice whispered in Hannah's brain. He

wanted to have sex with her. If nothing else, she was sure of that.

She squirmed a little inwardly as she walked into the hangar and headed for the gravity shower in the corner. After she'd left Anstin in her dust, figuratively speaking, she'd managed to slip and fall in the failing light and land in a puddle of mud that probably would have thrilled a pig. It didn't thrill her, though.

She yanked the chain that released the deluge and closed her eyes as it hammered her. One thing was for sure, this shower would clean the mud off fast. And she wanted fast. She wanted to get away from Edna, away from Anstin, away from Buck, who seemed to keep twisting her in knots.

It didn't matter how much she had come to love this island and its quirky inhabitants, she had to get out of here to save her sanity.

A familiar roar caused her to let go of the shower chain. The water stopped immediately and she opened her eyes. Between her and Edna stood Buster, if he could be said to stand. And the way he was looking at Edna boded ill.

Edna apparently thought the same thing. She backed up. "Call off your watchdog."

"I wish. He doesn't listen to me."

"I know differently!" Edna backed up another step.

"*Hmmmm,*" said Buster, moving toward her.

"What's with him?"

Hannah shrugged. She was soaked from head to foot and even her shoes were full of water, but the mud was gone. "Darned if I know. He just seems to feel protective of me."

"I didn't threaten you."

"Really? I guess not. But we *did* raise our voices."

Edna eyed the gator distrustfully. "I don't like the way he's looking at me. Make him stop. He doesn't usually look so mean."

"I can't control how he looks, Edna. Maybe you should just go away."

Edna visibly bridled. Buster apparently sensed the reaction because he took another step toward her and thrummed deep in his throat.

Edna backed up again. "Okay, I'll go, but we're not done yet."

"Sure. I know."

As Edna returned to a distant corner of the hangar, Hannah sighed. "This might be a wonderful island, full of wonderful people," Hannah said to Buster as she came to stand, dripping, beside him, "but there's one or two I just don't think I can put up with."

Buster hummed and twisted so that his head lay on her foot. He seemed to be saying, "You've got me."

Suddenly, very oddly, Hannah was on the edge of tears. Squatting, she scratched Buster's neck just behind the massive jaw. "I'm gonna miss you, guy. I'm gonna really miss you."

Reptilian eyes looked up at her but she couldn't read them at all. Maybe he didn't understand her, or maybe he didn't care.

IF BUSTER HAD had tear ducts, he would have cried. That seemed to mean a lot to the two-legged ones. Alas, he had no tear ducts, so he could only look up at her, and hope against hope that perhaps these two-legged creatures were capable of true understanding.

His plans were already in motion. He had watched as the casino man searched for the keys she had thrown into the woods. If the man had not found them on his own, Buster would have moved them to a more visible place. But the man had persisted, in the process using up his entire inventory of angry words, to the point that he had begun to create new sounds that reminded Buster of the sounds made by an egret he seized once at the water's edge.

The casino man would then have to load all of his stuff back into his car, because while he had been looking for the keys, Buster had taken the opportunity to unload the car. Tails were wonderful tools for such tasks. Just a single swipe had been enough.

If Buster had planned things well—and he usually did—the casino man would be arriving soon, as would most of the others who were still living in the hangar. They would help to set up the casino here.

Buster would also help, in his own way. For he had thought this through carefully, in his own, slow, careful way. He had plans. And he wasn't going to allow the two-legged ones to mess up his plans.

For now, though, he was content to receive the scratches from the woman, then follow her as she left the hangar and climbed into her jet. He stretched out in the narrow cabin, facing the cockpit, his back to her as she changed. Soon she would settle into the bed, and he would find a place on the floor beside it.

Tonight, they would sleep.

Tomorrow, they would go to war.

CHAPTER TWENTY-THREE

BUCK WAS HARDLY surprised when Buster followed Hannah out of her jet the next morning. He stood in the hangar doorway and watched as she tried to explain to Buster that she would, in fact, be back that night. For his part, Buster looked positively dubious.

"You about ready for preflight, Sticks?" Buck asked.

"Sure," she answered. "Just let me grab some coffee and something to eat first."

"No problem," Buck said. "We're only taking a couple of short hops, and I've called the vendors. They'll have the supplies waiting at the airport. Shouldn't be gone more than four or five hours, tops."

"Sounds good," she said.

"Not to me, it doesn't," Edna said, appearing beside them with her hands firmly planted on her hips. "We still have a wager at stake here, and she's not going anywhere with you until the wager is resolved."

"She's got a point," Horace added, joining them. "A wager is a wager. Buck, I know you, and I know you won't take the opportunity to fly off into the wild blue forever with this lovely woman. But still, a wager is a wager."

Buck sighed. He'd been looking forward to these few hours together with Hannah, perhaps to sort things out, or simply to confuse himself more. Regardless, this business of the wager was getting in the way.

"There's still a storm out there, Horace," he said. "I'm going to need another pilot with me."

"Take someone else," Edna snapped.

"And just who should I take? Who else on this island is multi-engine qualified? Hmmm?" Buck paused while Edna searched in vain for an answer. "I thought so. Wager or no wager, she's my copilot for this hop."

"Then I'm coming with you!" Edna said.

Both Hannah and Buck visibly cringed at that prospect. Having to deal with her here, on the island, where they could at least drive to somewhere she *wasn't,* was difficult enough. Being locked up with her inside a steel tube at ten-thousand feet? Hell, he'd crash on purpose, just to be rid of her.

"Count me out," Hannah said. Her face left no doubt as to her determination. "If she's going, I'm not. End. Of. Story."

"I'll go," Horace said. "I need to haggle with those vendors anyway. Buck, I know you try, but you just don't have it in you to be a proper haggler. And I'll keep the two of you out of mischief."

The last was obviously meant for Edna's benefit. Buck knew Horace would do no such thing—probably much to the contrary—but Horace's presence would placate Edna, then at least they could get the supply run done.

"That good enough for you?" he asked.

Edna hmmphed, and was about to protest, when Buster out-hmmphed her. She obviously wasn't happy with the plan, but it was the best she was going to get.

"Fine. If Horace chaperones, fine."

Buck saw fire flare in Hannah's eyes, but she nodded. "It makes sense. Horace needs to stock his store, after all. He knows what he needs. Buster, you'll make sure my jet is safe, right?"

He looked up at her and made a growly moan that left no doubt that no one would get near the Lear while she was gone. Then he looked over at Edna and let out another, as if to emphasize whom he thought the greatest threat might be.

"Exactly," Hannah said, glaring at Edna. Then she looked at Buck and smiled. "Let's get some coffee and discuss the flight plan."

"MUST BE NICE, having a watch-gator," Buck said, as Hannah finished the last link of sausage on her plate.

The hotel staff had moved their serviceable equipment up overnight, and was offering a free breakfast to anyone who was helping with the recovery.

Hannah had taken them up on the offer with glee. The picnic atmosphere during the storm had yielded the roast pork and a hearty potato salad, but in the flurry of activity yesterday, she'd made do with only a couple of packages of cheese and crackers. She'd once made the mistake of taking off on a flight while hungry. Unwilling to risk spilling food on an aircraft she would be selling at her destination, she'd flown the entire way with her stomach rumbling, and sworn she would never do it again.

"Buster is a treasure," she said, after swallowing. "I'd never imagined that an alligator could be so, well, like Buster is."

Buck chuckled. "Like you said. It's a weird place."

"But a nice kind of weird," she said. "You're all a bowl of nuts and flakes, but as bowls go, I could get used to it."

"Don't let Edna hear that," Buck said.

Hannah huffed as she rose from the table. "That woman could make Job turn gray."

Buck exploded in laughter, drawing the attention of everyone around, then put a hand to his mouth to stifle the sound. "Jeez, Sticks. Don't sugarcoat it. Tell us how you really feel."

"There are no words," she said. "Let's grab Horace and saddle up the DC-3. I need to know she's *not* going to be appearing in the middle of something for a few hours."

"Roger that," Buck said. He couldn't have agreed more. However, he didn't say so, nor did he tell her he'd spent a lot of time last night trying to figure out how to get Edna out of his hair short of throwing her off the top of the volcano like a virgin sacrifice. Edna had always been mildly irritating to him, but Hannah's arrival had stepped up her irritant status from mild to outright irksome, and maybe beyond. A day away, even one spent picking up supplies, which was about as boring as it could get except for the flying, was beginning to look like a trip to paradise.

The three of them walked around the old airplane, Buck and Hannah inspecting, Horace trailing along as if he knew what to look for. Hannah spotted a square of duct tape on the fuselage, near the cockpit.

"Oops," she said, pulling it off. "That would've been very bad news."

"Yeah," Buck said. "Craig must've missed it last time he hosed down the old bird."

"What was that?" Horace asked.

"The pitot tube," Buck and Hannah said in unison.

"The what?" Horace asked.

Hannah looked at Buck, but he nodded back to her, indicating that she should answer. "It's the pitot tube. Aircraft altimeters measure ambient air pressure. As you climb, air pressure decreases. The altimeter interprets that into altitude."

"Ah," Horace said, looking at the now exposed

duct in the fuselage, then at the tape in Hannah's hand. "So if it's taped over…."

"Exactly," Buck said. "A mistake like that brought down an airliner off the coast of Chile. A multi-million-dollar airliner, with state-of-the-art avionics, but a six-inch strip of duct tape left them flying blind. It was nighttime, and they were flying through clouds, right up until they spiraled down into the ocean. Like Sticks said, very bad news."

"Good that you spotted it then," Horace said.

"That's why I wanted a copilot," Buck said.

"I'm sure that's all it was," Horace said, winking as he climbed into the aircraft. "Wouldn't have anything at all to do with getting some time alone with your lady."

Hannah swatted Horace's bottom as she climbed up behind him. "Shush, you."

"Better watch yourself, Horace," Buck said. "If she gets in a dominant mood, you may end up hogtied on the deck. Best just be a good boy and say 'yes, ma'am.'"

"Yes, ma'am," Horace said, giving her a face like a cocker spaniel that had lost its last chew bone.

For her part, Hannah simply hoped the redness in her cheeks didn't show in the dim light inside the aircraft. Then she realized that simply was Buck's way of coming to terms with what they'd shared, and that Horace would have no idea what it meant.

As she and Buck settled into the cockpit and Buck started the engines, she felt a familiar thrill. The DC-3 might be an old airframe, but she was sturdy, and Buck had obviously pampered her like a lover. While he'd replaced her avionics, he'd done it in a way that preserved the original layout and feel of the cockpit. The glass in every gauge was polished. The windscreen was spotless. This was truly a museum quality aircraft, and she felt honored to settle into the right hand seat and rest her hands on the control stick.

"Wow" was all she could manage to say.

"She's my baby," Buck said, with obvious and well-earned pride. His eyes scanned the indicators with the confident assurance of an experienced pilot. "And we're good to run up number one."

Hannah didn't need to ask what he meant. She pulled the choke lever and pushed the ignition button for the number one engine. It sputtered, coughed, then let out a low, thrumming roar that Hannah felt more than heard. In an old aircraft like this, "flying by the seat of your pants" really meant something. You could, indeed, feel it respond to every command.

"Run up number two," Buck said.

Within minutes, they were taxiing down the apron, Buck handling the aircraft while Hannah ran through the last of the preflight checks. She was not surprised to find that he had the entire original flight manual, nor that he had carefully updated every stage where new equipment had been installed and that he'd had the updates printed such that the entire manual looked as if it were straight out of the 1940's. This was more than an airplane to him. It was a labor of love, an expression of his love for the sky.

"Flaps thirty," he said as they moved into final takeoff position at the end of the runway.

"Flaps thirty," Hannah answered crisply, her hand settling on the wing-shaped flap control and pushing it two clicks downward. "Flaps at thirty."

"We're good to go, Craig," Buck said into the radio.

"Roger that," Craig answered from the tower. "Clear for takeoff. Have a good hop, Buck. See you for dinner."

"Keep it hot for me," Buck said, then pushed the twin throttle levers forward. "We're rolling."

Hannah knew well that the two most dangerous elements of any flight were takeoff and landing. Her eyes swept up and down, back and forth, from runway to instruments, in a continuous, Z-shaped pattern. She didn't have to look over to know Buck was doing the same thing. The aircraft picked up speed, and soon she felt that familiar tingle as first the tail and then the nose of the plane lifted skyward.

"Gear up," Buck said.

"Gear up," Hannah replied, reaching for the wheel-tipped lever that controlled the landing gear.

She pushed it forward and heard the comforting *clunk* as the wing gear lifted and found their housings. "Gear up."

They climbed in a gentle left-hand turn, giving Hannah a breathtaking view of the island through Buck's side of the windscreen. Soon they were passing through five-thousand feet, on their way to their cruising altitude of ten thousand, on a southeasterly bearing. Buck checked his flight plan, then turned the frequency dial on his radio.

"Curaçao regional, this is November-Charlie-four-six-niner-seven," he said. "We are en route from Treasure Island to Aruba, passing through flight level seven-five-zero to one-zero-zero, bearing two-one-zero, over."

"Copy you at flight level seven-five-zero, bearing one-five-zero, Treasure Island. Designate call sign Treasure One, over?"

"Copy," Buck replied. "Call sign Treasure One."

"Treasure One, climb to flight level one-zero-zero, then intersect and fly Aruba radial three-two-zero until twenty miles out." The regional controller gave Buck the weather and expected traffic data, then added, "Good to see you haven't lost that old bird yet, Treasure One."

"She's still in one piece," Buck said, laughing. "Treasure One out."

"I guess you know him, huh?" Hannah asked.

He laughed and nodded. "He was one of the controllers on my old ship, actually. His wife hit the lottery and he left the Navy and moved her to a beach house she'd picked out in Venezuela, of all places."

"Nice life," she said.

"That's what he says. He quit controlling for a couple of years, then got bored with hanging out on the beach all day every day. So he signed on down there."

Hannah flipped to the second page of Buck's flight plan, then set the VOR navigational radio to the Aruba regional frequency. Their radio would interpret the phased signal from Aruba and show their precise bearing from that station.

The controller had told Buck to intersect and fly radial 320, putting them on a direct, south-southeasterly bearing, until they were twenty miles from Aruba. The regional controller would then hand them off to the local approach controller. "Flying the radial" allowed the regional controllers to predict where Buck would be at any time, allowing them to fit him into the traffic pattern.

"Aruba VOR three-zero-five," Hannah said.

Buck nodded and began a slow, right-hand turn, allowing the aircraft to drift over to the prescribed radial just as he brought it onto the correct bearing.

"Aruba VOR three-two-zero," Buck said. "Bearing one-four-zero. Confirm."

Hannah checked the bearing and VOR indicators. "Bearing one-four-zero on Aruba VOR three-two-zero. We're on the radial and on course."

Buck keyed the radio. "Curaçao regional, this is Treasure One. We are on Aruba radial three-two-zero, at flight level one-zero-zero."

"Copy that, Treasure One. You are clear of traffic to twenty miles out."

"Thanks, Jay," Buck said. "Treasure One out."

Buck set the autopilot to keep them on their present course, then unfastened his seat belt and turned to look at Horace. Hannah looked back and saw Horace sitting in the jump seat, his face faintly green.

"I still hate flying," Horace said.

"We haven't even done any loops yet," Buck said.

"Don't even think about it," Horace replied. "Just keep the airsick bags coming."

"You should've brought a lime with you," Hannah said. "It's an old sailor's trick. Lie back, put an ice pack behind your neck, and suck on a lime. Guaranteed to settle motion sickness."

"I'll drink a few margaritas in Aruba," Horace said, laughing weakly. "They have ice and lime. And alcohol."

Hannah laughed. "That might work, too."

"So," Horace said, "now that I've got the two of you alone, what's your master plan, Sticks?"

"Master plan?" she asked.

"He wants to know why you have him shorting the odds on your match with Edna," Buck said. "Come to think of it, so do I."

"Oh, *that,*" Hannah said, laughing. "Well, you two, how would you like to own Anstin's casino?"

CHAPTER TWENTY-FOUR

"OH THAT IS *wicked,*" Horace said, grinning as Hannah finished explaining what she had in mind. "Buck?"

"You are one devious creature," Buck said to her. He rolled the idea around in his mind. "The scary thing is, it could work."

"Damn right it could," Horace said. "Bill would dive into that feet first, face first, and every other body part first. So he made a pass at you, in his Jeep?"

"Sure did," Hannah said. "I was too mad to think straight at the moment, but I knew I had to find a way to fix his little red wagon. Everything came together last night as I was falling asleep. It's perfect."

She was truly a scary woman, Buck thought. She was willing to bet her future, and Buck's, on a heads-up poker game. And, given the proposition she was planning to offer, she was deadly serious about it. Whatever Bill Anstin had done to her, he was in a far deeper hole than he could possibly imagine. And Hannah was planning to cover the hole with concrete.

The problem is, did Buck really *want* to own a casino? Sure, he was going to all but own one for a while anyway, since it would be running out of his hangar. But what she proposed was far more than that. What she proposed would cut Bill Anstin off at the knees, leave his investors out of the loop, and put Buck and Horace squarely in charge of the island's future.

And maybe that was what bothered him. What Hannah had in mind would saddle him with a lot of responsibility. And unlike Bill Anstin, Buck wouldn't manipulate that for his own enrichment. He'd want to do right by the people of Treasure Island. They'd become his family over these past years, and he wondered if he were up to the challenge of making sure they had a secure future.

"You sure know how to put a guy in a vise, Sticks," he said. "And I don't just mean Bill Anstin."

"Oh, c'mon," Horace said. "It'll be great, Buck. You run the airport and glad-hand the guests. I run the shops and concessions. We can even leave Anstin in charge of the casino floor, if he wants to do it."

"He will," Hannah said. "He'll be our Bobby Baldwin."

Buck nodded. Bobby Baldwin was a former World Series of Poker champion who now managed the gaming at one of the largest casinos in Las Vegas. While Bill Anstin lacked Baldwin's class, elegance and expertise, he did at least have the bracelet. And he'd jump at the opportunity to be likened to one of the most respected men in the industry.

"Okay, Sticks," Buck said. "Count me in. But you'd better damn well win."

"I will," she said, her voice firm. "For all of us."

HANNAH WISHED she felt as confident as she sounded. Sure, she was a better poker player than Edna. She had not the slightest doubt of that. But poker was a fickle game. Indeed, that's how professional poker players earned their living. If the cards always fell according to the odds, the amateurs would never win, and they'd quickly quit. Over the course of a single evening, the greenest newbie could take down a world champion, or at least leave the table ahead. Those fickle blessings of fate would keep him coming back, only to lose his money over the long haul as the cards inevitably evened out. The pros were playing the odds, and sooner or later the odds came through.

So yes, she was a stronger player than Edna. She would play the odds. But would they come through for her, often enough, tonight? That was a question only time could answer. And worrying about it wouldn't make her play any better. She tried to put it out of her mind.

"So what are we getting in Aruba?" she asked.

"You want the whole list?" Horace asked. "Or just the most important items?"

"The latter," Hannah said. "Or all of it. Anything to keep me from thinking too much."

"I know that feeling," Buck said. "Yeah, Horace. Read us the whole list."

Hannah spent the next half-hour listening, watching the instruments, and wondering what Buck was trying to avoid thinking about. When the Curaçao controller's voice came on the radio, telling Buck that they were twenty miles out and passing into Aruba approach control, Hannah let out a sigh of relief. Now, at least, she could concentrate on helping Buck bring the old bird down safely.

"You want to land her, Sticks?" Buck asked.

"Are you sure?" she asked, feigning a light-hearted smile. "You saw my last landing."

"I saw an ace pilot bring down a wounded bird as skillfully as it could be done," he replied. He took his hands off of the control yoke. "So yes, I'm sure. She's yours to fly."

"Copy that," Hannah said, instantly falling into the feel of the aircraft as her hands gently grasped the yoke. "I have control."

"Beatrix approach, this is Treasure One," Buck said. "Passing the outer marker at flight level five-zero, over."

"Copy you at the outer marker at flight level five-zero," the controller replied. "Descend and maintain flight level two-zero and execute standard left visual approach for runway two-niner."

Hannah pulled back the throttles slightly as she nudged the yoke forward, putting the plane into a gentle descent.

"Runway elevation is five-niner feet," Buck said, checking the airport data on his flight plan, even though he had long since committed it to memory. Aruba was his most common hop.

Hannah nodded. The old bird was a dream to fly. Every touch of the controls seemed to flow through the aircraft and back into her body, the throb of the engines, the gentle shifts of attitude. Aruba spread out in the windscreen, green and beckoning. She should have been here four days ago, at the controls of her Learjet. And she would be back here soon, with that sleek, modern aircraft. But somehow, it would never be like this.

"I can see why you love her," Hannah said. "It's as if she whispers back everything you tell her."

"She sure does," Buck said. "They don't make 'em like this anymore. She's a grande dame."

"Flaps thirty," Hannah said. After he had set the flaps and confirmed, she watched the runway grow from a thin gray slit to a beckoning path. "Gear down."

"Gear down," Buck answered.

She heard and felt the landing gear extend and

lock in place. Now it was all a matter of feel. The crosswind was so slight that she could almost keep the runway centered in the windscreen, with only the tiniest hint of rudder. As they passed one hundred feet, she eased back on the yoke a fraction more, pulled back the throttle, and let them bleed off airspeed with a slightly nose-up attitude.

One gentle squeak of the wing landing gear, as the tires spun up to speed, and she felt the tail gear settle as gently as a butterfly landing on a leaf.

"Brakes on," she said, almost to herself.

"Brakes on," Buck answered. "Great job, Sticks."

"Yeah," Horace agreed. "Better than Buck does. I didn't throw up."

AN HOUR LATER, Horace was still haggling with the vendors whose trucks were parked and waiting on the apron. It was, Buck thought, like watching an Olympic competition between used car salesmen. Unlike in America where prices on most items were fixed, in much of the rest of the world haggling was not only common, but expected. The listed price was merely a starting point for negotiations, and Horace was a master of the art.

"The lumber's wet," Horace said, shaking his head firmly. "I'm not paying a dime a foot for wet lumber."

"It doesn't expand," the vendor replied. "And it's not like you're buying it by the pound."

"No," Horace replied, "but I do have to fly it out of here, and I have to think about weight limits. An extra fifty pounds of water in this lumber is fifty pounds of other supplies I can't haul back on this trip. That's a half-pallet of baby food I can't bring back with me."

"Oh, be reasonable," the vendor said. "Eight cents a foot."

"Five," Horace said. "I have to cover the costs of an extra trip."

"Seven."

"Six."

"Six-and-a-half."

"Six," Horace said, shaking his head. "No more."

"Fine," the vendor said, feigning disgust. "Six."

And so the process went, on item after item, with vendor after vendor. Buck knew the extra fifty pounds of water in the lumber would be insignificant. He never loaded the DC-3 that close to the maximum. He also knew Horace knew that. And still, Horace made it sound as if that fifty pounds were the difference between loading or not loading a case of baby food for the infants of Treasure Island. It was a compelling appeal, if not exactly a truthful one.

On the other hand, it was obvious the vendor didn't believe it. The added weight wasn't a reason for Horace to argue for a lower price. It was merely an excuse. Buck knew Horace would have haggled just as hard if the lumber had been bone dry. It was a game to Horace, and to the vendors. Horace never walked away having paid less than the vendors were willing to accept, and they still made their profit. But he did manage to pay rock bottom prices, and for that Buck was grateful. Despite his run-in with Hannah, Horace passed those savings along to those who came to his shop, and that meant a few extra dollars in the hands of the people of Treasure Island.

Buck left Horace to his haggling and wandered over to the charter terminal, where he found Hannah at the pilots' lunch counter, sipping a coffee and nibbling at a sandwich.

"Hey, Sticks," he said, settling into a stool beside hers. "You did a nice job landing her."

"Thanks," she said. "She's a beautiful airplane. Horace still doing his *Green Acres* routine out there?"

Buck laughed. "Oh, yeah. Honest to God, that man should have been born in Cairo."

"They haggle a lot there, too?" she asked.

"Oh, my yes," Buck said. "You would not believe. We had shore leave in Alexandria once, and a few of us took a bus tour down. Saw the pyramids—which are very big—and hit Cairo just as the markets were winding down. People descended on the markets like vultures then, because the vendors didn't want to have to pack up any more wares than they had to, so they were willing to bargain lower. I stood there watching it, trying to take in the sounds. The word 'cacophony' definitely applied."

"I'll bet," Hannah said, smiling.

"Why the smile?" Buck asked.

"Well," she said, "for most people, that story would have been all about the pyramids. One of the seven wonders of the ancient world, et cetera, blah, blah, blah. But you talked about the people, haggling as the street markets closed. It was touching."

Buck shrugged. "We were talking about Horace. One thing led to the next."

"No," she said. "Don't dismiss yourself that way. You like to think of yourself as a loner, but I see the way you relate to the people of Treasure Island. You're a born people person, Buck. People are important to you."

"Don't burst my bubble here, Sticks," he said. "I have a self-image to maintain."

"But not a very accurate one," she said.

"So what were you thinking about as I walked in?" he asked, anxious to change the subject. "You looked, well, positively pensive."

It was Hannah's turn to shrug. "Just thinking about the match tonight."

"Nervous?" he asked.

She seemed to consider the question for a moment. "Yeah, I guess I am. It's an important match. Not just for me—for us—but for everyone on Treasure Island."

"Don't do that," Buck said, shaking his head. "Don't think of it that way, or you're dead before you start."

"I know," she said. "But it's hard not to."

"So don't raise the stakes," Buck said. "You don't have to pull this double-reverse, Newman-and-Redford sting. It's a slick idea, and I have to admit, when you explained it I got a quiver in my belly, like I was watching a true gambler's mind at work. But it's not necessary, Hannah. We can struggle by on our own. We always have."

"No," she said. "Don't you see? Someone has to teach Bill Anstin a lesson. Yes, you could beat him at the poker table, but he'd just write that off to bad cards. Someone has to show him just where he fits in the pecking order of life. And this is a prime opportunity to do it. And after what he did to me...I want to be the one to do it."

"Fine," Buck said. "But you can't think about that while you're at the table. I don't have to tell you that, Sticks. You know what emotion does to you in poker. You have to keep focused."

"You're right," she said, nodding. "I just hope I'm as good as my bruised ego told me I was last night."

Buck laughed. "You know the joke about the two men being chased by a bear? One took off running, and the other asked, 'Do you really think you can outrun a bear?' The guy who's running looks back and yells, 'I don't have to outrun the bear. I just have to outrun *you.*' You don't have to be the best poker player in history tonight. You just have to be better than Edna."

"And lucky," Hannah said. "Don't forget that part."

"So minimize the luck factor," Buck said with a shrug. "Play small-ball with her."

She gave him a questioning look.

"Don't tell me you don't know what small-ball poker is," Buck said.

She shook her head. "I've heard the phrase, but no."

"Ahh," he said. "Well, it's simple. Keep the pots small. Avoid the all-in, coin-flip pots, your big cards versus her smaller pairs, and vice versa. Force the play deeper into the pot, to the turn and river, where you'll have more information about where you stand. Make her make a big hand to win a big pot."

"In short, play it like it's a limit game," she said.

He nodded. "Exactly. Or pot-limit. Don't give her odds to chase you, but don't build huge pots on the early streets either."

She studied him for a moment, then nodded dubiously.

"Look," Buck said, "your advantage is that you're the stronger player. You make better decisions, on average, than she does."

"Right," Hannah said.

"So the more decisions you force her to make...."

"The more likely she is to make a mistake," Hannah said. "And then I make her pay for it."

"You got it," Buck said. "And not all at once, either. Don't make a bet that she'll only call if you've miscalculated and she has you beat. Force her to make a dozen good decisions for every one mistake. I guarantee you, Edna's not that good."

"But she could still get lucky," Hannah said.

Buck nodded. "That's true. But this way, she has to get even luckier, because you're not going to let her hit one lucky pot to beat you."

"Makes sense," Hannah said. "It's not my usual style, but it makes sense."

"It's not your usual style because you're not used to thinking you're the best player at the table," Buck said. "But I'll bet you have been, a lot more often than you've thought."

"I guess we'll find out tonight," Hannah said. She pushed her sandwich aside. "C'mon, let's see if Horace is done hornswoggling them yet."

Buck laughed. "That's a word I haven't heard in a long time."

Hannah smiled and shrugged. "Hey, I'm from Texas."

CHAPTER TWENTY-FIVE

BUCK WAS AS CAREFUL a pilot as Hannah had ever seen. He oversaw the loading operation with an almost fetishistic eye for detail, checking every load, plotting them both on his manifest and his load plan, ensuring the DC-3 was as balanced full as she had been empty. Perhaps it was because she was his airplane, or perhaps it was simply his nature to ensure that every detail was handled correctly.

The more she thought about it, the more she concluded that it was simply his nature. She remembered how pin-neat his office was, and his home. While Hannah also liked to be confident about details, she didn't take it nearly as far as Buck did. She wondered if that would be one of those lifelong irritants that drove a couple crazy, then shook her head at the mere notion. They weren't a couple. They might well not become one. Fretting over hypothetical issues that might trouble a hypothetical union was like counting the feathers in the wings of angels dancing on the head of a pin.

It was, she thought, a "Buck thing."

The idea that she could imagine "Buck things" brought a smile to her face. She'd known him only a few days, and yet it felt as if she'd known him for years. She wanted to win tonight's match, as much for her own future as for that of the residents of Treasure Island. There was no doubt about it. She wanted Buck. Badly.

And, she realized, he was right. She had to put those concerns out of her mind. Emotional motivation wouldn't help her win tonight. She would have to rely on her skill, and make cool, calculated choices. Thinking about Buck, or the rest of it, would not help her to do that. Maybe she'd ask him not to watch the tournament. Out of sight, out of mind. But she rejected the notion as quickly as it came. He would need to be there, if for no other reason than to distract Edna.

Once the plane was satisfactorily loaded, Horace joined the two of them. "I don't want to fly back just yet."

Buck arched a brow in his direction. "We said four or five hours."

"You think your momma is waiting for you, boy?"

Buck scowled at him.

"We can take all the time we want," Horace said. "And considering where my money's going to be riding tonight, I'd mightily appreciate it if you'd take

Sticks here for a walk or something and calm her down. She's wound up tighter than a drum." He waggled his eyebrows at Buck in a way that made Hannah redden.

"Meanwhile," Horace continued, "this old goat needs to fortify himself with a few margaritas before getting on that crate again. And I know just the place to do it." He strode off, leaving Hannah and Buck standing uncomfortably beside the plane.

"I guess we could take a walk," Hannah said finally.

"Yeah. A walk." Something in his face suggested that walking wasn't on the top of his mind.

Nor was it on hers, she realized as they left the airport behind. There was this nice, big, convenient hotel right nearby, and somehow she wasn't even a little surprised when Buck steered her toward it. This time, she promised herself, she'd let Buck run the show. This time…oh, heck, she didn't want to scare him away again. It was as simple as that.

"You're being a good sport," she remarked through a tightening throat as the front doors of the hotel came closer. "About this wager with Edna, I mean."

He shrugged. "She's gonna lose, so I have nothing to lose."

That warmed her a little. His confidence in her, far from panicking her even more, seemed to shore her up.

When they entered the lobby and walked to the desk, he took her hand in hers and squeezed quickly before letting go. Then he booked a room, a double, and didn't even offer an explanation. She liked that about him. He didn't try to pretend. Not even to a stranger.

Because regardless of what he might have said, regardless of the clerk's stated assumption they were two pilots who needed a few rack hours before heading out again…she knew, felt it deliciously in her stomach, exactly what was coming.

The room wasn't the best the hotel had to offer, but it might have been a palace for all Hannah cared. And after the last few days, the luxury was incredible.

"Why don't you go enjoy a hot shower," Buck suggested. "They're going to be in short supply back at the island for a while."

She nodded slowly, uncertain how to take the suggestion. Had he indeed merely brought them here to freshen up and rest? Then she remembered her plane.

"Oh, God, I should call the guy who's waiting for his plane."

Buck reached out and touched her upper arm. "Do me a favor and think about business later. Please."

His eyes caught hers and held them, and what she saw there made a delightful shiver run through her. "Okay. Okay…."

Stripping off her flight suit felt good. She only wished she could launder it. Then she stepped under the shower spray, reveling in the heat of it. It felt like heaven, and as it washed the dust and dirt from her, she felt as if it washed away all her nervousness. Between shampoo and soap, she didn't miss an inch of her body. Then she stood under the spray, letting the heat steal the last trace of tension from her body.

She was leaning against the tiled wall resting on her elbows, the hot water running over her head and down her body when she felt a slight draft. At once her heart quickened, then arms slipped around her from behind, and large, work-worn hands cupped her breasts gently. At once a shiver ran through her, and a murmur of pleasure escaped her. "Ahh…."

Lips found her nape, kissing her gently there, as his hands caressed her breasts, bringing her nipples to taut, aching peaks that he then gently twisted.

He might as well have twisted her insides. Every cell responded, and heavy heat settled in her core, an ache that could be answered only one way.

"Don't move," he murmured, as he continued to play with her breasts. She doubted she could have moved even if she had wanted to. His kisses and his hands imprisoned her as surely as any jail.

Then the kisses moved, trailing across her wet shoulders and down her back. She vowed to remain still, to let him have his way with her as the heat built in her to near-scorching levels. She didn't want to frighten him away again.

But then she realized he was kneeling behind her, his hands slipping from her breasts to her hips, his kisses sprinkling themselves across her rounded rump.

And in that instant she realized something. Everything would end right here if she gave him control. She needed to break through that wall....

And even more, she needed to have him her way. Now.

She turned swiftly. He looked up, surprised, but then she captured his face between her hands and kissed him soundly on the mouth. The water ran over them in sheets, the air was filling with steam, and the rest of the world fled.

Then she pressed his face to her mons and leaned back against the shower wall, gasping with delight as his tongue darted out and found that most sensitive nub. He had given her control, and when she pressed her hand to the back of his head, he leaned in harder, taking her to heights she had only dreamed of.

Moments later she exploded in a starburst of delight, but when she felt him start to pull back, she pressed him close again.

"More," she said throatily, and he obeyed, taking her soaring over the mountaintops again, and yet again.

At last the convulsions eased, and her legs felt like rubber. She could have collapsed, but she wasn't done with him yet. Pulling him to his feet, she rotated their positions, pressing him against the wall beneath the shower head. Leaning into him, waiting for her strength to return, she began to taunt and tease him with her mouth and fingers. He was already hard, but she was determined to make him harder yet. When a groan escaped him, she chuckled deep in her throat.

"All mine," she murmured.

"Oh, yeah…."

She laughed, feeling her energy return, and she proceeded to take him on a journey that left him helpless, choosing to ignore the hints his body gave her, the gentle nudges of his hands as he tried to tell her what he needed until finally he groaned, "Please…"

That was the word she had wanted to hear. Taking his hand, she pulled him from the shower. Without toweling off, they pulled back the bedspread and fell wet on the sheets.

Hannah mounted him then, throwing her head back and taking him deep within her, riding him as if he was hers to ride. When she opened her eyes to narrow slits, she saw utter surrender combined with heavy passion on his face.

Just as it should be, she thought…and carried them both away to the stars.

DESPITE A NAP after their lovemaking, Hannah was surprised to find herself sleepy on the flight back. Buck seemed not to mind, although he kept looking at her as if she were as dangerous as a pit viper. Well, let him worry, she thought hazily. Whether he knew it or not, they'd *both* let their guard down in that hotel room. But oddly, she felt safe rather than frightened.

At last she let her eyes drift closed, feeling the soothing rumble of the DC-3's engines through her seat as if the old bird were rocking her, singing a lullaby. She dreamt of poker hands, impossible combinations of real and fictitious cards, puzzling out the correct way to play Ace-Pi of Grapes.

When Buck nudged her to let her know they were on approach to Treasure Island, she didn't feel as if she had slept deeply, and yet she felt rested, more relaxed. She opened her eyes and saw the speck of land in the teal blue of the Caribbean, with the familiar brown cone of Big Mouth protruding from the carpet of green. She would never have imagined, even forty-eight hours ago, that she would feel what she felt as she saw the island. It looked like home.

"Welcome back, Buck," Craig said over the radio. "We are CAVU. Five-knot crosswind at two hundred feet."

CAVU stood for *ceiling and visibility unlimited,* and Craig needn't have said so, Hannah thought. It was as beautiful an evening as she had ever seen, as if the storm had scrubbed the air clean and clear.

"Thanks, Craig," Buck said. "You ordered up perfect weather for me, I see."

Thirty minutes later, Buck had set the plane down every bit as gently as Hannah had on Aruba, although Horace still grumbled at him. Craig and Horace oversaw the off-loading as Buck and Hannah went to the office to complete their flight logs.

"Good flight?" Bill Anstin asked, walking in as if he owned the place.

"Smooth as silk," Buck said. "Sticks here is one hell of a copilot."

Hannah shrugged off the compliment. "It's easy to fly a beautiful bird like that."

"Beautiful?" Anstin asked. "It's a dinosaur! If we're going to run a proper business here, people need to see we're up to date. First thing we need to do is get you a better plane, Buck. One like Sticks has. *That* would impress tourists." He held his hands up as if framing the words on a sign. "Treasure Island Airline, where every flight finds the end of the rainbow."

Buck looked up. "You just don't get it, do you, Bill? Sure, that Lear is slim and sexy, but she's also a high-maintenance bird. The least little thing—a microscopic crack in the fuel regulator—and you're looking for any spot of green to set her down on. That's how Sticks ended up here. That DC-3 may be old and fat, but she'll fly in any weather, and on half a wing at that.

"Newer and flashier isn't always better," Buck continued, obviously warming to the task of dressing down Anstin. "Sometimes what you need is solid and reliable. So, no, thank you. I'll keep what I've got, because I trust her, and she's never let me down. Just like this island."

Anstin seemed about to answer, then closed his mouth and walked out. Buck sat back down, and Hannah smiled.

"Never come between you and your favorite aircraft?" she asked.

He shook his head. "Anstin just doesn't get it. He's all about flash and glitz. He wants this place to be the Las Vegas of the Caribbean. I bet he'd cover Big Mouth with neon lights and tinsel if he could."

"Careful," she said. "You're starting to sound suspiciously like a leader."

He looked at her for a moment, impassive, and finally nodded. "Yeah, I guess I am."

"Good," Hannah said. "Because you're going to need to be, after tonight."

He smiled and winked. "Yes, ma'am."

Hannah winked back. "Good boy."

BUSTER WAS THRILLED to see Hannah step off the plane, and even more thrilled when he heard the discussion in the office. Things were coming together quite nicely. He had only a couple of pieces to move into place.

One of them was a poker table.

Buster could sense the anxiety in Buck, even if the man tried hard to hide it from Hannah. By the time the game started, Buck would be as edgy as a chicken watching Buster walk past. And like the chicken, Buck would want to be on familiar ground, most likely the room he was in now.

Of course, this would not do. Buck needed to be where the other woman could see him. The other woman, the one who spent far too much time up on the mountain, lost all sense of reason when Buck was in sight. This, Buster knew, was important to his plans. While Buster did not pretend to understand the game that kept these people so enthralled into the wee hours of the morning, he had learned a bit about the people who played it, and why some seemed to come away pleased while others left disappointed.

The ones who came away pleased reminded Buster of himself. They were willing to wait, almost motionless, for hours at a time, as if lying in the reeds at the edge of a pond, waiting for a careless bird to wander nearby. Then, like Buster, they pounced fast and deadly. They were, Buster realized, as coldly calculating as he was.

The ones who left disappointed, by contrast, seemed more like the small dogs that some of the two-legged ones kept with them. Always yapping, always sniffing, never still, announcing their presence to anyone who came nearby, as if their incessant noise were a deterrent to the Busters of the world. In fact, all it did was let him know where a meal could be found, if he happened to be hungry, and if one of the two-legged ones were so careless as to leave a gate open. They rarely did, of course, and he was rarely that hungry. But he could still dream....

Buster wanted the mountain woman to be like a yapping dog, and that meant she had to be able to see Buck. That would keep her sniffing around, noisily, while his woman lay in the reeds, ready to strike.

Thus, Buck could not hide in his office. It was as simple as that. And that meant he would want to go to the other place that made him most comfortable, his big, silver bird. There wasn't room for the bird in the hangar, now that it was full of people, not to mention the garishly bright machines that seemed to constantly beep and ding and, less often, spit out the little shiny disks that the people seemed to think were so important. So the big silver bird would have to stay outside.

And if the bird was to be outside, then the poker table would have to be there as well. What's more, it would have to be under the wing of the big, silver bird. Buck would be comfortable there, and there he would stay, squarely in the mountain woman's line of sight.

Of course, getting the two-legged ones to move the table outside would be a challenge. They seemed to think they knew how things ought to be, especially the one man who had gone in to confront Buck. That man—the one who had tried to fondle Buster's woman in the Jeep—wanted the poker table in the center of the hangar, surrounded by rows of chairs.

This, Buster knew, would not do.

Fortunately, like most of the two-legged ones, that man was afraid of Buster. So Buster decided to place himself squarely where the man wanted the table.

"Move, Buster!" the man yelled.

Buster simply looked at him.

"I said move!" the man repeated, shaking a fist.

Buster now allowed himself to wonder what the man might taste like, and whether there was enough meat on his bones to make a satisfactory meal. The man seemed to sense this change in Buster's attitude, lowering his fist and backing away.

"Well damn," the man said. "How are we supposed to set up the table with this stupid alligator in the way?"

Stupid? Buster asked himself. Would Buster have survived as long as he had by being stupid? Hardly. He was sure this two-legged one would not survive as long in the wild, nor if he had to rely on the generosity of others, as Buster had come to do. Buster might not think as fast as the two-legged ones, but he had managed quite nicely, thank you, with the intellect he had.

Having reasoned through why the man's word

upset him, Buster responded with what he thought was a restrained yet emphatic *Grrrrrrr.*

This, he was pleased to note, caused the two-legged one to wet himself. If Buster could have laughed—and that was one thing he envied in the two-legged ones—he would have let out one of their deep, belly laughs of glee. Fortunately, other two-legged ones did that for him, and the man stormed away, red-faced.

"What's going on?" Buck asked, coming out of the office to check on the commotion.

"Bill Anstin wanted to put the poker table here," one of the women said. "Buster wouldn't move. Bill got feisty and Buster got feistier. Then Bill had…an accident…and stormed off."

Buck laughed and looked at Buster. "Good boy."

Mmmhmmm, Buster replied contentedly.

"I guess you don't want the table here?" Buck asked.

Uhmmmuhmm.

"I'll take that as a no," Buck said, which Buster found encouraging. It was nice to know that some of the two-legged ones could understand simple things. "Okay, so where do you want it?"

Buster turned his head toward the hangar door and let out a low grunt.

"Outside?" Buck asked. "What if it rains?"

Uhmmmuhmm.

"It's not going to rain?"

Uhmmmuhmm.

"I won't even ask how you know that," Buck said. "Okay, show me where you want it."

"Now wait a minute," the mountain-woman said, walking up to Buck as if her opinion mattered. "Are you seriously going to let an *alligator* decide where we play this match?"

Buck looked at her calmly. "Are *you* going to argue with Buster?"

The mountain-woman looked at Buster.

Buster looked at the mountain-woman.

"Umm, no," she said. "Outside is fine."

"That okay with you, Sticks?" the man asked.

Buster's woman looked at him silently for a moment, as if trying to read his thoughts. For his part, Buster tried his best to convey thoughts of *Please? Trust me?*

"Sure," she said, finally. "Outside is good."

"Then it's settled," Buck said. "Buster, you lead the way."

As Buster led them out to the wing of the big silver bird, he grumbled in delight. When the two-legged ones listened, they could be very pleasant to be with. He could get used to leading them.

He could get very used to it, very easily.

CHAPTER TWENTY-SIX

"AND TONIGHT'S FEATURE event," Bill Anstin intoned as if calling the faithful to prayer, "is a heads-up match between Hannah Lamont of Houston, Texas, and our very own Edna Harkin. The prize is nothing less than mating rights to our airport owner, Buck Shanahan."

Anstin paused to let the applause die, then continued. "The game is No-Limit Hold 'em. The format is best two-of-three games. Each player receives twenty-five hundred dollars in tournament chips. Blinds begin at twenty-five and fifty dollars, with half-hour rounds. By prior agreement, as the home player, Edna begins with the button. Our dealer is Ginny Devaneau. Good luck, ladies. Ginny, please *shuffle up and deal!*"

Anstin had pitched it as if it were the World Series of Poker, and in truth, Hannah felt as if it were. While there would be no diamond-studded bracelet to the winner, the stakes were even higher than that. She fought down the butterflies in her stomach as she tossed out one chip for the small blind and watched Ginny wash and riffle the deck.

Surprisingly, though, when the first two cards landed in front of her, Hannah felt a deep calm. She peeled up the corners of the cards and saw a dismal but potentially useful Jack and Three of Diamonds. She was tempted to raise, as was her customary strategy in heads-up play, but remembered Buck's advice to keep the pots small, and simply tossed in another chip, calling the big blind.

Edna rapped the table to signal her decision to check rather than bet, and Ginny deftly slipped the top card off to the side and peeled off the next three cards, spreading them face up. The Ace of Spades, Jack of Spades, and Six of Clubs.

Because Edna had the dealer button for this hand, Hannah had to act first. She'd paired her Jack, and the poker books said that when playing heads-up, she should ignore the top card and play as if her Jacks were the top pair. However, with two Spades on board, and a weak Three kicker, Hannah had no desire to get deeply involved. She simply tapped the table, checking to Edna.

"Let's make it one hundred," Edna said, counting out a stack of four chips.

Ordinarily, Hannah would have raised at this point, both to push Edna off of a possible flush draw and to gain information. If Edna simply called her raise, Hannah would read her for having a pair of sixes, or perhaps an inside straight draw like King-

Queen. If Edna reraised, Hannah would assume she had a strong flush draw, two pair, or a Jack with a better kicker. Hannah's usual aggressive style entailed higher risk, but she usually knew where she stood in the hand.

You're the better player, she told herself. *Keep the pots small. Force Edna to get lucky, often, to win.*

"I'll call," Hannah said.

"Three-hundred dollar pot," Anstin announced. "Let's see the turn card please, Ginny."

Once again, Ginny slid off the top card and put it facedown in the muck, then turned up the next card. The Three of Spades.

It was, Hannah thought, the ugliest card in the deck. It gave Hannah two pair, but if Edna had two Spades in her hand, the three Spades on the table gave her a flush. And worse, Edna had position; she could act after Hannah. If Hannah checked, Edna would surely bet strong, and Hannah could not call. If Hannah bet and Edna raised, again Hannah could not call. She mentally cursed herself for playing the hand so weakly at the flop, and tapped the table to check.

"I'll check, too," Edna said casually, leaning her chin into her hand and looking off toward the setting sun.

"Possible flush," Anstin said. "Let's see what the river brings."

Ginny again "burned" the top card and turned up the final community card. The Six of Hearts. Now

Hannah knew her hand was dead. If Edna had bet a pair of Sixes at the flop, the river had given Edna three of a kind. If she had bet a flush draw, the turn had given her a flush. Either way, Hannah's two pair were not good enough.

"Two hundred," Hannah said, counting eight green chips into the table in two stacks of four.

Edna paused for only a second, then said, "I'll raise." She counted out two stacks of four chips to call Hannah's bet, then added four more stacks. "Four hundred more."

There was now eleven hundred dollars in the pot, with Hannah needing to commit four hundred to call. The pot was offering Hannah nearly three-to-one, yet she knew it didn't matter. Her hand was beaten.

"I'll call," she said, turning up her two pair.

"Ha!" Edna exclaimed. She turned up the Queen and Ten of Spades. "Flush!"

Buster let out a growl, but Hannah silenced him by rubbing her foot over his head, and patted the table. "Nice hand, Edna."

The sting was on.

IT WAS, BUCK THOUGHT, as masterful a performance as he had ever watched. If he hadn't known what she was doing, he would have thought Hannah was just getting unlucky, or was off on her game. In fact, she was playing beautifully. For the next hour, again and again, in critical pots, Hannah had a good hand that wasn't quite good enough. And while she never made an obviously bad call, she managed to manipulate Edna into betting small enough that Hannah's call seemed reasonable.

He'd heard about players dumping chips to confederates in tournaments, and doing it so skillfully that even the security experts found it difficult to detect. Without a doubt, Hannah's dumping to Edna would have gone unnoticed. Even playing heads-up, with no other distractions at the table, no one seemed to suspect that Hannah was losing intentionally. The groans of disappointment from the crowd were too real.

Buck forced himself to give Edna a smile and a wink as she scooped in another pile of chips. Hannah was down to nine hundred in chips now, and the blinds were up to one and two hundred.

Buster let out another vaguely threatening groan, and Hannah reached down to scratch behind his jaw. "It's okay, big guy. Sometimes the cards just go that way. We'll be fine. Just relax."

The groaning stopped, though Buster looked no more relaxed to Buck. This was something Hannah hadn't counted on when she'd cooked up her scheme. An angry gator making Edna uneasy was not part of the plan. Or perhaps it was. Buck wondered just how devious Hannah could be, and found himself hoping she had indeed included Buster's reactions in her calculations.

He could love a woman like that. Oh yes, he most definitely could.

Ginny dealt out another hand, and for just an instant, Buck saw tension in the muscles of Hannah's shoulders. Edna looked at her cards and raised, setting Hannah all-in. Hannah paused for a long moment, as if trying to decide what to do.

"This isn't the hand I'm going to go broke on," Hannah said, flipping her cards facedown to Ginny. "Could I have something better next hand?"

She'd caught the rockets, Buck thought. Hannah had just folded pocket Aces. He would bet his plane on it. He glanced over at Horace. Horace met his eyes and gave a tiny, fleeting nod. It was time.

"I guess these stakes just aren't enough to keep you interested, Sticks," Buck said.

"I'm busy," Hannah replied tartly.

"Busy losing," Buck said. "Maybe you don't think I'm worth playing for?"

"Maybe not," Hannah said.

"Well fine, then," Buck said. "But on Treasure Island, we take our gambling seriously. If I'm not worth playing for, what would be?"

"Are we changing the stakes?" Edna asked. "Look, I'm playing for Buck here, and I'm winning him fair and square. I don't want any funny business."

"No," Buck said. "That part of the stake stays. I've never been fought over before, and I'm kind of enjoying it. But obviously we need to motivate Sticks here."

"So what are you suggesting, Mr. Ignore-Me-In-Aruba-Like-I'm-Not-Even-There?" Hannah asked, the fire in her eyes so convincing that Buck almost believed her.

"Oh, did we have a spat?" Edna asked, grinning cruelly. "He didn't fawn all over you like the princess you so obviously believe you are?"

"You stay out of this," Hannah said. "Or I'll sic Buster on you."

Buster punctuated the sentence with a growl that nearly lifted Edna out of her seat.

"Fine," she said. "You guys figure out what stakes you want. But I'm playing for Buck!"

"So what stakes sound good to you, Sticks?" Buck asked. "What would it take to keep your interest? Maybe you need a stick to go with the carrot. Loser has to marry Bill Anstin?"

"Whoa!" Anstin said. "Let's hold on here."

"Sure," Hannah said, looking at Anstin. "I'd do damn near anything to avoid *him.*"

She had set it up perfectly, Buck realized. Anstin's ego could not survive rejection.

"Oh, you'd get to like me, Sticks," Anstin said with a smile that would make flowers wilt and die. "Since we're playing for love, why not?"

"Just deal the damn cards," Hannah said. "Let's play some poker."

"I NEED A BREAK," Hannah said as she pushed the last of her chips across to Edna.

While she'd hoped to come back and win the first game, Edna had found pocket Kings on the next hand, and they'd held up against Hannah's pocket Fours. Hannah had expected to be down a game, and knew she was strong enough to beat Edna in the final two games to take the match. But still, the pressure of the new bets seemed to sit on her shoulders like an elephant.

"You okay, Sticks?" Buck said as she rose.

"Don't talk to me," she said, hating herself for saying it, hoping he would know she didn't mean it. "I need to take a walk."

She strolled across the tarmac, Buster at her side, rolling her shoulders and arching her back against the tension of sitting at the table. While poker wasn't an athletic event in the usual sense of the word, it did call for an extraordinary amount of mental stamina. In large tournaments, players commonly put in sixteen-hour days, with only brief, hourly breaks.

The stress of forcing oneself to concentrate on

every breath, every twitch, every gesture, every change in posture, from every player at the table—even when the player had already folded his hand—wore heavier as the hours mounted. Poker commentators often said that it had become a young man's game, yet some of the older players still had the stamina to grind away, hour after hour, and keep their focus at its peak.

But they had several advantages over Hannah. First, this was their livelihood, and they were accustomed to the long hours. More importantly, the best poker players had what Doyle Brunson called "a casual disregard for money." You couldn't play at their level if you thought of a two-thousand-dollar chip as a mortgage payment. To the top pros, they were just chips, tokens in a game, and a way of keeping score.

Hannah wasn't playing for "just chips." Even now, if things were going to plan, Horace was buttonholing Anstin, saying the money on Hannah was too long. That is, despite the odds, that too many people were betting on Hannah to win the tournament. Given what had happened so far, and Hannah's rejection of Anstin earlier, Anstin would jump at the chance to cover any bets placed on Hannah to win. He would think he was putting himself in a position to own most of the island, thinking the islanders were mortgaging their futures on Hannah's comeback.

In fact, no one was betting on Hannah in any significant amount. Not yet. But once Anstin agreed to cover the bets on her, Buck would place his bet. And what a bet it would be. If Hannah should happen to lose, Buck would have to mortgage the airport, and probably everything else he owned, to cover it. But if she won…

…if she won, Anstin would not have enough cash in his bank accounts to cover the loss. Like Buck, Horace knew the combination to Anstin's vault, and earlier that evening Horace had used that to access Anstin's financial reports. Horace and Buck knew, to the penny, exactly how much cash and equity Anstin had. He would have to sign over his interest in the casino in order to pay off the bet.

They weren't doing this to get rich. In fact, they'd give Anstin almost everything back. Everything *except* the casino. That they would keep, and with that they could guarantee the kind of future the residents of Treasure Island hoped for.

These people deserved more than to become cogs in the wheel of another Caribbean tourist trap. They'd come here looking for a casual lifestyle, where friendship and the bonds of community mattered more than a corporate bottom line. They'd made a time machine, stepping back into the days when barn-raisings and pot-luck dinners were the norm, and neighbors took care of each other. As the hurricane had clearly shown, they had come to depend on each other.

And now they had come to depend on Hannah.

She owed all of them the best that she had.

Mmmhmm, Buster moaned, as if reading her mind.

"I can still win this, Buster."

Mmmhmm.

"You knew it was going to come down to this, didn't you? If I didn't know better, I'd suspect that was why you'd wandered into Buck's kitchen to begin with. To set up this very situation."

Mmmhmm.

She squatted down and looked into his eyes. "I ought to bonk your scaly head for that, but it was too good of an idea. But don't be thinking you're free to keep plotting like this, kiddo. Buck and I will need to find our own way together."

Buster seemed hurt by that statement, but then he did something Hannah could never have believed if she hadn't seen it for herself.

Mmmeeee?

She had to be hearing things. Buster hadn't just spoken an English word. Alligator throats weren't built for speech. It was not possible.

Mmmeeee? he repeated.

There was no doubt. He had. Hannah's heart squeezed.

"Yes, honey. We'll keep you, too. I promise."

Slowly, ever so gently, Buster rubbed the side of his snout up and down her calf. She reached down and gave him another affectionate scratch under his chin. "You're welcome, Buster. And thank you. For everything."

She saw eyes that almost smiled. *Mmmhmm.*

"You know they're waiting for us."

Mmmhmm.

"So let's go kick Edna's butt."

Buster's eyes seemed to harden. *Mmmhmm.*

CHAPTER TWENTY-SEVEN

MANY PROFESSIONALS believe that heads-up poker is the purest form of the game. More than in any other format, in heads-up poker, the game is all about the players. Even a lowly pair of Deuces, in the hands of a player who senses weakness in an opponent, can play as if they were a royal flush.

While Edna had won the first three pots of the second game, they had been small pots. Hannah had to work hard not to let her demeanor change, to maintain a faint air of overconfidence, mixed with disappointment at Edna's good fortune in winning the first game. But that was only part of the puzzle.

The other part was continuing to file every subtle move Edna made, every tone of voice, into an ever-growing database that was Hannah's most powerful weapon. She'd begun building that database when she'd played Edna in the hurricane tournament, and she'd added to it during the first game of the match. Slowly, increasingly, the clues fell into place.

Hannah looked down at an Ace and Ten of Spades,

a very powerful hand in heads-up poker. Edna had already raised, and Hannah knew the book play was to reraise, and reraise big. But the only book Hannah was playing by was the book she'd written in her mind, the book of how to beat Edna Harkin.

"I'll call," she said.

Ginny dealt out the flop, the Eight and Ten of Clubs with the Five of Hearts. Without a second's hesitation, Edna pushed out a stack of twenty chips, a five-hundred-dollar bet. Hannah paused for a few seconds, not because she didn't know what Edna had—a Ten and an Eight, for two pair—but because she wanted to think about how to bluff Edna off of those two pair later in the pot. Edna was not a strong player, but she was careful. Hannah would use that caution against her.

"Sure, why not?" Hannah said, pushing a stack of her own chips out to call the bet. "I feel like gambling."

Edna seemed to flinch when Hannah said that. In most cases, when a player says *I feel like gambling,* it means *Oh, please keep betting because I have a huge hand.* Edna knew that, and Hannah knew Edna knew that.

Ginny dealt out the turn card, the Nine of Diamonds.

"Let's make it another five hundred," Edna said.

Hannah made as if to think for a moment, then nodded. "Five hundred it is."

The river card was the Four of Clubs. Hannah smiled inwardly. Edna had her two pair, but she couldn't be happy. The turn card had made a possible straight and the river a possible flush. Edna recognized that, and after a long moment, tapped her fingertips on the table.

"Check," she said.

She may as well have said, *I surrender,* Hannah thought. While Edna had tried to feign confidence, the slightest quiver gave it all away.

"So how much is in the pot right now?" Hannah asked, looking at Ginny.

"Twenty-five hundred," Ginny said.

"Well," Hannah said, "I've only got a thousand left. I'll bet it all."

"Damn it," Edna said, almost under her breath. Her brow furrowed as she puzzled through the situation. After a long moment, she sighed and threw in her cards. "Take it. You got lucky."

Hannah turned up her cards. "Yup. I did."

"Why you little…."

"What, Edna?" Hannah asked, smiling as she scooped in the chips. "Bitch? I've been called worse, and by better. But you can show me your two pair, if it will make you feel any better."

Edna gave her an icy glare that bordered on homicidal. Hannah simply smiled in return. She didn't normally show her cards, but this time she'd done it with a purpose. Edna was rattled now, and that was precisely where Hannah wanted her to be. If Edna was thinking about revenge, she wasn't thinking about the hand she was playing.

As if realizing Hannah's strategy, Buster chose that moment to emit a low, grumbling growl, and twitch his tail.

"Oh, shut up, Buster," Edna said.

Buster growled again.

"Look," Edna said. "I can't play with that damn alligator sitting there. He's upsetting my concentration."

"So tell him to leave," Hannah said, calmly. "Who knows, he might even listen to you."

"Billlllll," Edna said, looking at Anstin. "Make him leave!"

"No way," Anstin said, obviously remembering his last encounter with Buster. "I'm not getting near him."

"Then tell *her* to make him leave!"

"Say one word," Hannah said, looking up at Anstin, "and I'll make your night of romance into your worst nightmare."

"She's not joking," Buck added. "Trust me."

Hannah had to stifle the laugh that grew within her. It was not yet time to let Bill Anstin know he'd been had. Instead, she turned to Buck. "A gentleman wouldn't kiss and tell."

Buck gave her a leering grin. "Whoever said I was a gentleman?"

Horace held up a stopwatch. "That was the last hand at fifty and one hundred. Five minute break."

"How lucky for you," Hannah said to Edna. "Maybe you can walk it off."

"And maybe you can go to hell!" Edna said, storming away into the hangar.

"DON'T GET HER too riled," Buck said quietly as they stood in the darkness at the tail of his plane. The others had gone into the hangar to partake in the buffet, leaving Buck and Hannah alone. "You don't want her playing for blood."

Hannah nodded. "Yes, I know."

Buck knew why she'd showed Edna the bluff. He also knew that such mind games could easily backfire. If Edna started betting in anger, she was likely to bet big, and that would void Hannah's strategy of playing small pots. On the other hand, it was Hannah's game to play, and he'd come to respect her Machiavellian mind. If Edna had a weakness, Hannah was determined to exploit it.

"Did Horace get Anstin on the hook?" Hannah asked.

Buck nodded. "During the break after the first game. If you hadn't asked for one, Horace was going to announce one anyway. Good fake out with the 'I don't want to talk to you,' though. I almost believed you."

"I felt awful about saying that, Buck. I'm usually an honest person." She winked at him. "I guess being around you brings out the worst in me."

"So now it's my fault?" he asked, mock consternation in his voice. "I wasn't the one who dreamt up this little sting, Sticks. That's all you."

"Yes, but I didn't think of it until after I met you!"

"Well, duh," Buck said, laughing. "You hadn't heard of Treasure Island, Bill Anstin, or any of the rest of it before you met me!"

"My point remains," she said, giving him a playful punch to the shoulder. "And as for getting Edna riled, I know what I'm doing. She's down to fifteen hundred in this game. I can give up a lot of blinds before she'll catch up to me. I want her gunning for me, every pot. I'll keep on folding, folding, until I catch the hand to take her out."

"Sounds like a plan," Buck said. He paused for a moment, searching for the right way to say what he had to say next. "You took a hell of a risk on that last pot. If she'd called...."

"I know," Hannah said. "If she calls, she busts me and wins the match. And you'd have lost your airport."

"No," Buck said. "I hadn't set the hook that deep yet. Anstin's only on the line for fifty thousand. Now, with you having nearly evened things up, it will make sense for the money to go deeper. Horace is probably pushing it to a hundred thousand right now. So let Edna come back some. I want it up to a half-million by the end of this game. All told, we need to get it up to a million-six."

"Gotcha," Hannah said. "And Horace is sure he'll bite for the whole amount?"

Buck nodded. "He told Anstin he couldn't take any more action on the match unless someone covered the bets on you. According to Horace, Anstin said, 'I'll take as much of their money as they're willing to give me.'"

It wasn't a contract that would stand up in a court of law, Buck knew, but this was no court of law. This was a wager, on Treasure Island, where betting was nigh unto sacrosanct. Anstin had to know he'd be run off the island on a raft if word got out that he'd welshed on the deal.

"So long as we don't bet too much too fast," Buck said, "Anstin will come along like a lamb to slaughter."

"So all I have to do is win," Hannah said.

"Well, yeah," Buck replied. "But you know you can."

"Big difference between 'can' and 'will,' though," she said. "There's still the little matter of the cards."

"I have every faith in you," Buck said.

Hannah gave him a half-smile. "That makes one of us."

EDNA WAS STILL in a simmering fury when the match continued, and Hannah folded the next six hands to all-in bets. Edna pushed all-in again, and Hannah looked down at her hole cards and saw a pair of Tens.

Hannah figured to be at best a seven-to-three favorite, putting Edna on at least one overcard, a Jack or higher. If Edna had two overcards, it was roughly a six-to-five coin flip. And if by chance Edna had an overpair—a pair of Jacks or better—Hannah was a five-to-one underdog.

"Take it," Hannah said, flipping her Tens into the muck.

"Thanks," Edna said, turning up a pair of Kings before raking in the two-hundred-twenty-five-dollar pot. "I think I will."

Edna had won seven straight pots at two-twenty-five apiece, so they were about even again. Hannah glanced up and saw Buck nod to Horace. As Ginny dealt out the cards, Horace pulled Anstin aside. They were doubling the action, Hannah knew, probably to an even quarter-million. It was setting up nicely.

Hannah looked down to find the Ace and King of Spades. Ace-King-suited, otherwise known as "Big Slick," was widely considered the third best starting hand in Hold 'em, behind only pocket Aces and pocket Kings. It was only a slight underdog against a pair of Queens or less, and a favorite against any non-pair hand. But it was called "Big Slick" for a reason. Many a player's hopes and dreams had slid down the tubes when Ace-King missed, or was misplayed.

In a full ring game, with eight or nine opponents, Hannah would have to make a large raise. Ace-King was not a hand that performed well against three or more opponents, so she would have to raise in order to make her opponents fold mediocre hands. But this was a heads-up match, and moreover, Hannah still wanted to play small-ball poker.

"I'll call," Hannah said, pushing three chips out to match the big blind.

Edna looked at her cards. Perhaps it was the way her fingertips turned white for an instant as she squeezed the cards, or the subtle shift to a more upright posture. She had a hand, Hannah knew. The question was, what hand?

"Raise," Edna said. She counted out six chips. "Three hundred more."

"Three hundred," Hannah said. "Okay. I'll call."

Ginny dealt the flop. Ace of Diamonds, King of Hearts, and Jack of Clubs. It was a good flop for Hannah, giving her top two pair. It was also a dangerous flop. If Edna held a Queen-Ten, she'd made a straight. If she held pocket Jacks, she'd made three of a kind. On the other hand, if Edna held Ace-Jack or King-Jack, she'd made two pair, but a lower two pair than Hannah's Aces and Kings.

In short, it was exactly the kind of flop that could make Hannah's Ace-King very good, or very bad.

"Check," Hannah said.

Edna paused for a long moment, then counted out six chips. "One-fifty."

Compared to the nine-hundred dollars already in the pot, it was a small bet. There was a chance that Edna was betting a middle pair, Nines or Tens, but Hannah didn't think so. It looked like "a bet that wanted a call," the play of someone with a strong hand who hoped to get paid off for it. The question was, did Edna have a weaker two pair, three Jacks, or the straight?

Hannah ran through the probabilities in her mind. There were two other Aces, two other Kings, and three other Jacks in the deck. That left six ways that Edna could have Ace-Jack, and six ways that she could have King-Jack, a total of twelve ways for Edna to have a weaker two pair, and three ways to have pocket Jacks for three of a kind. There were four Queens and four Tens in the deck, and thus sixteen ways that Edna could have the straight.

Ignoring the possibility that Edna was betting a weaker Ace, or a lower pair, that meant there were thirty-one possible combinations for her hole cards. Nineteen of those thirty-one holdings put Edna ahead with either three Jacks or an Ace-high straight.

So Hannah had to assume she was behind in the hand. However, if she did hit another Ace or King on the turn, making her a winning full house, it was very likely that she could get all of Edna's chips. With a thousand-fifty dollars in the pot right now, and the sixteen-hundred in chips Edna had left in her stack, and the forty percent chance that Edna was betting a weaker two pair rather than three Jacks or the straight, Hannah was certain she had the right odds to call.

"One-fifty works for me," she said. "Call."

"Four of Clubs," Ginny said, turning up the next card.

Hannah tapped the table. "Check."

"Three hundred," Edna said immediately.

Hannah did the math in less than a second. Fifteen hundred in the pot. Three hundred to call. Five-to-one pot odds. Plus another thirteen-hundred in Edna's stack, if Hannah hit an Ace or King at the river. Almost nine-to-one implied odds. Plus the probability that Hannah's two pair were already good. It was close, but she thought the odds were still right.

"Call," Hannah said.

Ginny turned up the river card. "Six of Diamonds."

Hannah had missed her draw. If Hannah bet now, she knew Edna would not call unless she had a better hand. She tapped the table. "Check."

Edna counted her remaining chips. "I'm all-in, Sticks. Another thirteen hundred."

Now Hannah was in a bad spot. There was thirty-one-hundred dollars in the pot, and thirteen-hundred for Hannah to call. Right around three-to-two odds. If Edna had her straight, or three Jacks, Hannah was beaten. If she had two pair, Hannah could even the match.

"Time," Hannah said.

"Sticks has three minutes of extra time," Anstin said, clicking a stopwatch. "Starting now."

It was so close. Too close. But if Hannah's hand was good, she would even the match right here. Twelve chances in thirty-one that Hannah's two pair would win this pot, and the game. The pot odds weren't quite there. But if Hannah folded, she would be left with only fourteen hundred in chips, and the blinds were about to increase to one and two hundred. Hannah knew she would have to get very lucky to come back from that.

"Oh, just call already!" Edna said. "Let's get this over with."

It was the worst thing she could have said. *Strong means weak.* She didn't have the three Jacks or the straight. She had two pair. The wrong two pair.

"I call," Hannah said, turning up her cards. "Aces and Kings."

"Shit!" Edna muttered, throwing her cards at Ginny.

As they spun in the air before landing on the table, Hannah smiled. Kings and Jacks.

They were even.

CHAPTER TWENTY-EIGHT

"THAT WAS ONE HELL of a call, Sticks," Horace said during the break before the final game. "Hell of a call."

They were in the hangar, where Hannah had dashed to relieve her bladder before refilling her coffee mug. She was feeling the length of the day. She needed the coffee to keep her mind sharp for the final game.

"She should've kept her mouth shut," Hannah said. "The odds were so close, and my match equity if I folded was pretty grim. I might have called anyway. But once she said that, I knew."

"You figured either she had the straight or a lower two pair," Joyce Fenster said.

Hannah nodded and explained her calculations. Joyce listened intently. By the time Hannah had finished, some of the other women had come over to join the conversation.

"Classic Bayesian analysis," one said.

"But if Edna hadn't said anything, she didn't have the odds to call," another interjected.

"Not in terms of pot equity," Joyce said. "But for overall tournament equity, I still think she had to call."

"Only with her read from what Edna said," the second woman insisted. "Her tournament equity was slim if she folded, yes, but if she called and was wrong, she's done! That's *zero* equity."

Hannah slowly eased out of the coffee klatch and began to walk toward the door. Horace joined her, chuckling.

"What?" Hannah asked.

"It reminds me of a Web site that was the talk of the island for awhile," he said. "Same thing. Did this player play this hand right? Should that player have folded in this spot. On and on, round and round."

Hannah glanced back at the women, who were still deep in their discussion. "They know their poker."

"Sure they do," he said. "When they're talking about it over coffee. It's a whole different thing at the table, when it's your money out there on the green felt, and you don't have a half-hour to sweat each decision. Then it's all instinct and feel."

"Not really," Hannah said. "I did actually work out the math on that hand."

"You're making me wonder how I beat you for all of those supplies," Horace said, with a sly wink.

"You're a stud player," Hannah said. "Different game, different feel."

Horace shrugged. "Maybe, but I think if it'd

been a real game, you'd have ended up owning my store."

She shook her head. "Not likely. Unlike Anstin, you wouldn't have risked your business on a game of cards with an unknown player."

"True enough. Speaking of that, we've got Anstin for a half-million right now," Horace said. "I hate to ask this, but if you could keep it tight in the last game…."

"No pressure or anything," Hannah said with a smirk. "Win, but don't win too fast?"

"Exactly."

She laughed. "Well, at least you don't ask for much."

"So," Horace said, his voice dropping, "what's the real deal here, Sticks?"

"You and Buck get control of the casino," she said, unsure if that was exactly what he was asking.

"I don't mean that. Look, I know you and Buck have hit it off. A blind man could see that. So we're back to the original bet. What happens when you win?"

"Why, Horace," she said, "are you asking me if I have honorable intentions?"

He paused for a moment, and Hannah realized that he was like a father asking a daughter's boyfriend whether he was going to do the right thing.

Horace nodded. "Yeah, I guess I am. I mean… look, we like Buck around here. He's been a solid contributor to the community, and people respect that. You've seen how we're all like family here. I don't want to see his heart get set on something he can't have."

She studied his face for a moment. This was a kind of straight-from-the-heart honesty she wasn't accustomed to seeing in Horace. Apparently not everything in Horace's life was an angle to be played. He really cared for Buck.

And so did she.

What's more, she could easily imagine herself living here. It would make the business operations a tad more complex, but not unreasonably so. Most of her business involved travel, and she could fly to and from Treasure Island as easily as she could to and from Houston. And, she had to admit, the people here—if a collection of nuts and flakes—were mostly appetizing nuts and flakes.

"I like Buck a lot," she finally said. "I like this place. I like not being the only odd egg in the carton."

Horace let out a belly laugh. "You are one odd egg, Hannah Lamont. But just the kind we collect."

"So we'll just have to see," she said. "First, I have to win this match. Then Buck and I can talk about happily-ever-afters."

"Fair enough," he said. "Like I said, just don't win too fast. We need to snag ol' Anstin for another million before we're ready to reel him in."

"A million-one," Hannah said. "We want it all."

"HOW MUCH OF THIS have you been planning?" Buck asked, still wondering why he was talking to an alligator as he strolled along the moonlit tarmac. "Why do I think you've been pulling more strings than anyone of us would believe?"

Mmmhmm. If an alligator could look coy, Buster did.

"You know it's still going to come down to how the cards play out," Buck said. "We can't predict that part. And God help us if Edna hits a lucky streak."

Grrrrr.

"Believe me, I know," Buck said. "I'm just as worried as you are."

Mmmhmm.

"I want her, Buster. She's…wow."

Buster looked up. *Mmmmmmmmhmmmmmmmmm.*

Was that a smile? Buck wondered. Regardless, there was no doubt what Buster meant.

"You would know what I mean, big guy. You've been here for, jeez, sixty years? With no mate. So you know what it's like to be lonely."

Mmmhmm. More plaintive this time.

"And you think of Hannah as that mate you've been waiting for?"

Urmmmmm.

"No, of course not," Buck said, shaking his head. "You'd want a girl gator, not a girl human."

Urmmmm.

"You don't know?"

Uhmmuhmm.

"She really does have you twisted up in knots," Buck said with a laugh. "Just like me."

Mmmhmm.

"And you're afraid if we got you a girl gator, Hannah wouldn't want you around anymore."

Buster paused for a long time, as if having to process each of the moving parts of that thought independently, and then reassemble them. Finally he looked up.

Mmmhmm.

Buck stooped down and, for the first time, gave Buster an affectionate scratch beneath his chin, right where he'd seen Hannah scratch him. "Buster, you worry too much."

Hmmmmm?

"Yes, you're right. I worry too much, too."

Mmmhmm.

"I guess we both just have to trust her," Buck said. "We have to trust her to win this last game, and we have to trust her for what happens after."

Buster didn't seem happy with that thought, but he did seem resigned to it. *Mmmhmm.*

Buck knew that feeling exactly. Could he trust Hannah to do the right thing after she won the match? What was the right thing? Could this work? Did he want it to work?

Yes, he did. That was the simple truth of the matter. He was ready to let someone into his life again, if that someone were Hannah Lamont. But he couldn't make that happen, any more than he could make the cards shake out the right way in this last match. Hannah would do what she thought was best, and the chips would fall where they fell.

Buck just hoped that some of them landed in his lap.

"Well, kiddo, let's go watch her work her magic."

Mmmhmm.

Buck made his way back down the tarmac, Buster at his side. "And maybe there's enough magic for all of us."

"I GUESS everyone's talking to the alligator now," Craig said, approaching out of the darkness.

Buck tamped down his startle instinct, then nodded. "Buster's a lot cheaper than a shrink, that's for sure."

"This whole island's going to need a shrink if Hannah loses," Craig said. "This is turning into a dangerous game of poker."

Buck studied Craig for a moment. No one was supposed to know about the side action with Bill Anstin. Had word leaked out?

"What are you hearing?" Buck asked.

"Just that Anstin has three assistants poring over the island's property records, and another two on the casino's balance sheet. Someone said they heard Anstin talking with Horace about shortening the odds on Hannah. Something's in the wind here, Buck, and it smells like Anstin is trying to take over the whole damn island."

Oh shit, Buck thought. If the word was indeed "in the wind," as Craig so aptly put it, it was only a matter of time before the individual "are you betting on Hannah?" conversations turned into a collective "so if we're not, then who is?" And if *that* word reached Anstin's ears, the whole sting might come crashing down around them.

There was no doubt that Buck could trust Craig. It was time to enlist another ally. "Craig, I need you to do some damage control here."

"What's going on?" Craig asked, a conspiratorial glint in his eyes.

"No one else is betting on Sticks. It's a set-up. Her idea, actually."

"Oh, this sounds good," Craig said, smiling.

"It will be if we can pull it off. The deal is that Horace told Anstin there was too much money going down on Sticks to win. Anstin said he'd cover all of that action, and we've been pulling him deeper into it ever since. If I read Horace's body language right, he's committed for half-a-million right now."

Craig let out a low whistle. "Ohhhh-kay. So who's betting on Sticks?"

"I am," Buck said.

"Buck, you can't afford that bet," Craig said. "If

she loses, you lose the airport. You lose your house. You lose…everything."

Buck nodded. "I suppose I should be worried about that, shouldn't I?"

Craig looked at him for a moment, slack-jawed, then broke into a wide grin. "Sticks dumped that first game, didn't she?"

Buck nodded.

"Wow," Craig said. Then, again, "Wow. Okay, Buck. So…what do you need me to do?"

"Anstin thinks he's making a play to own most of the property on the island," Buck said. "If he finds out there's only one bettor against him, he's going to put two and two together, and figure out he's been set up. He'll back out of the bet."

"Gotcha," Craig said. "You need me to make sure it sounds like a lot of people are betting."

"Without saying anything too directly," Buck said. "Anstin does have some friends here, after all. So pick your people carefully."

"Will do," Craig said. "But you'd better be damn sure Sticks is going to win."

"I'm betting the farm on it," Buck said. "And I don't make stupid bets."

CHAPTER TWENTY-NINE

HANNAH SAT at the table and sipped her coffee. This was it. For all of the marbles.

She'd been aware for the last ten minutes or so of Craig moving slowly through the crowd and murmuring things in the occasional ear. A couple of times she'd gotten a serious jolt when she heard someone say, "I've got the house riding on Sticks...I hope she knows what she's doing."

But after a number of other people had muttered similar things about their businesses or boats or whatever, a feeling of calm had come over her. It was part of the sting. Craig was encouraging people to make it sound as if the entire island was riding on the outcome of this match. It was important to keep Anstin slavering until he was fully committed. Probably Buck's idea. So she didn't have the homes and livelihoods of most of the island riding on her shoulders.

Just Buck's.

For an instant she tensed, scared half to death.

God, what would she do if her crazy idea cost Buck his airport? How could she ever make it up to him?

Then, with a second jolt worse than the first, she realized she might be on the edge of losing Buck as well. Yes, they'd had a fine time making love in Aruba, but no promises had been made, no words of love had been spoken. Oh, man, if she lost this game, she'd lose him, too. Never mind the wager that Edna *thought* was the stakes in this game. Buck would find his way around "being won" some way or another. Of that she had no doubt. Win or lose, he wasn't going to belong to any woman he didn't want to.

But if he lost his airport, she'd never stand a chance. How could he ever forgive her for betraying his faith in her?

What a time, of all times, to realize she was tumbling head over heels for a guy who...well, he'd never promised anything, had he?

Suddenly strong hands were kneading her shoulders. She jumped and looked around to see Horace standing there with his worst cockeyed grin, and behind her stood one of the island women who was working hard at the tension in Hannah's shoulders.

"May-Lou here is a mass-soose at the casino," Horace said. "Ain't you, May-Lou."

"Sure enough."

Horace squatted down. "It's like this, Sticks. You

need to relax. Looking like a deer in the headlights will only give your opponent an advantage."

Edna laughed, a distinctly annoying sound. "Massage her all you want, May-Lou. That girl's going down."

At that point, Anstin caught sight of what was going on. He yelled at them to stop it, and pushed someone out of the way to reach the tape that designated the rail beyond which no one could approach the players.

"Hey, Horace," he bawled. "You taking sides? You can't make book if you take sides!"

Horace gave Hannah a wink. "I ain't taking sides," he said, straightening and glaring at Anstin. "Bets are in the book, and I write 'em down just like people tell me. But if it'll make you feel better, I'll buy Edna a massage, too."

"No way," Edna said, smiling with obvious pleasure. "*I'm* doing just fine."

"You better be," Anstin said. "I got a bundle riding on you."

Edna glared at him. "Shut up. I know how to play poker, and I could care less about your bundle."

Anstin turned red. For an instant it looked as if he would jump over the tape, but Buster chose that moment to let out a warning growl. Anstin paled and backed up a step.

"Idiot," Edna said, then returned her attention to Hannah. "What's the matter, Sticks? Lost your nerve?"

No, Hannah realized. She hadn't. She shrugged off the massaging hands, saying, "No thanks, May-Lou. I don't want to be distracted."

Then, with a deliberation her father had taught her at the negotiating table in business, she tamped down the fear and forced herself to become as calm as the eye of a storm. Allowing fear to rule her would give Edna an edge Hannah couldn't afford to spare.

"Edna and Hannah are tied at one game each," Bill Anstin said, still sounding as if he wanted to strangle someone. "This is the third and deciding game of the match. Shuffle up and deal!"

At Edna's request, Hannah had asked Buster to sit behind rather than beside her. Predictably, Buster had declined. Hannah simply threw up her hands. "What can I do? He's bigger than me, and he has a mind of his own."

Hannah would have preferred Buster to accommodate Edna, at least for the time being. She didn't want Edna playing angry, aggressive poker. Horace needed more time to draw Anstin deeper into the side betting. If Edna was in the mood to gamble it up, the game could end too fast.

Hannah looked down at her first hand, the Queen of Clubs and Eight of Diamonds. The computer hand, so named because computer simulations showed that it was the median starting hand in Hold 'em poker. It was not a hand that Hannah would have played at a full table, but in a heads-up match, it was worth a call.

Edna seemed content to see a free flop, and Ginny dealt out the Eight of Clubs, Seven of Hearts, and Deuce of Hearts. Hannah had top pair with her Eights, but something in Edna's posture gave her pause.

"I'll check," she said.

Edna flipped out two chips. "Fifty."

It was the minimum bet, but not suspiciously small for a one-hundred-dollar pot. *Seven-Deuce.* The idea began as a faint niggle, but loomed larger and larger as Hannah weighed the situation. Edna was angry; that was obvious in her posture. And her tendency was to play aggressively when she was angry. But she hadn't raised pre-flop. That said she had a weak starting hand. Very weak. And Seven-Deuce was the weakest hand in Hold 'em.

Until a Seven and a Deuce fell on the flop.

If Edna had that hand, Hannah had only five outs, the three remaining Queens and the two remaining Eights. Five outs was nowhere near enough to call a half-pot bet unless Hannah were playing for implied odds, hoping to take all of Edna's chips if a Queen or Nine fell. She couldn't do that, because it wouldn't give Horace time to draw Anstin in deeper.

"You hit your hand," Hannah said, turning up her cards. "And I'm folding top pair."

"Dammit," Edna muttered. She flashed her cards,

the Seven and Deuce of Diamonds. "You call when you should fold, and fold when you should call."

"I suppose you could see it that way," Hannah said calmly. "I see it differently."

"Whatever," Edna said.

Edna bet hard on the next six pots, and each time Hannah folded before the flop. The pots were small, and it was only costing Hannah seventy-five dollars a round, but soon the blinds would double. The small-ball strategy that Buck suggested required a player to have enough chips in reserve to get to the later betting rounds. Horace would need to reel Anstin in soon, or Hannah would find herself without much maneuvering room.

Hannah pried up the corners of her next hand, and found a pair of Queens. It was a big hand, even at a full table. In a heads-up match, it was a monster. She counted out six chips.

"Raise," she said. "One-fifty."

"One-fifty more," Edna replied, doubling Hannah's bet.

Hannah considered pushing all-in, to shut Edna out of the pot, but then paused. As more than one poker expert had written, pushing all-in with pocket Queens turned that very good hand into Seven-Deuce. That is, she would only be called by Aces, Kings, or Ace-King. If Edna held one of those hands, Hannah was either badly beaten, or at best a slight favorite. Otherwise, Edna would fold, and Hannah would pick up only the chips that were currently in the pot…a move Hannah could have made with any hand, even the lowly Seven-Deuce.

"I'll call," Hannah said.

Ginny dealt out the Ace and Ten of Spades, and the Six of Hearts. Hannah felt both a sinking feeling and a wave of relief. The sinking feeling owed to the Ace on the table. If Edna were playing an Ace, and she would be right to reraise with an Ace in a heads-up match, then she'd made a pair of Aces, and Hannah's Queens were all but dead. The wave of relief was that she had only called Edna's reraise, rather than pushing all-in.

"Check," Hannah said.

"Three hundred," Edna announced.

There was no doubt in Hannah's mind. Edna's voice had none of the tiny wavers that it had when Edna had stated her bets with the King-Jack in the last game. She had an Ace. Absolutely.

"Fold," Hannah said. "It's yours."

Hannah was now down five-hundred dollars, and Edna held a three-to-two chip lead. She wasn't desperate yet, but she'd have to turn things around soon. Still, when she glanced up, Horace gave a tiny shake of the head.

Not yet.

"You're getting the best of me here," Hannah said

to Edna. She hoped the subtext of the message, intended for Horace, came through loud and clear: *I'm going to have to start moving soon.*

"So I am," Edna replied. "So I am."

IF HORACE HADN'T picked up on Hannah's message, Buck certainly had. He slowly worked his way closer to Horace, and tugged at his arm. Together, they edged back out of the crowd.

"You've got to get Anstin in now," Buck whispered. "Sticks is good, but this is getting too dicey. Edna's betting like she has a cab waiting, and now she has the chip lead. We can't keep Hannah on a leash much longer."

Horace nodded. "You're right, Buck. Let me get Anstin into the deep end of the pond, and then we'll turn Sticks loose."

"Quickly, please," Buck said.

Horace nodded again, then turned and began to work through the crowd. Buck stayed behind, looking up at the Caribbean night sky, as if the answers to his life might lie in the pinpoints of brilliance light-years away. He wouldn't be this anxious if he were at the table. But was that a matter of not having full confidence in Hannah, or simply the anxiety of not being in control?

Intellectually, he considered Hannah his equal at the poker table. Indeed, she might well be his better. He had no idea whether he could have made that call with Ace-King, for all of his chips, with the entire match on the line, on that dangerous board. But Hannah had not simply made that call. She'd made it with confidence...as if there were no doubt that her two pair were good.

Indeed, for much of the match, it was as if she could see Edna's cards. Her reads had been flawless so far, and that had enabled her both to dump the first game without anyone suspecting, and to come back in the second without making it seem as if she'd been sandbagging.

As a dispassionate observer, he recognized her skill. But he was not a dispassionate observer. He was a pilot, and like most pilots, he was most comfortable when he was at the controls. Hannah's scheme had cast him into the role of passenger, a role he found very uncomfortable.

But when he thought about it, she had cast him in the role of passenger in many ways. She hadn't asked for his opinion before making the original bet with Edna. And while she had run the greater scheme past Horace and him on the flight to Aruba, it was clear that his only decision was to join in or opt out. After that, it was up to Horace to get Anstin locked into the bets, and Hannah to bring off the sting. Just as she'd taken control of their sex, both on the DC-3 and in Aruba, she'd taken control of the showdown with Edna, and the duel with Anstin.

The simple fact was that Hannah Lamont was a force of nature, every bit as much as the hurricane that had swept through. Could he deal with that?

His ex had been a force of nature, too, but a cruel and destructive force. She had cut him off from his support network, and he had let her do it. Then, when he was alone and vulnerable, she had kicked his heart with such force that he had gone into a shell, vowing never again to put himself in such a situation.

He'd moved here to Treasure Island, a place with no real government to speak of, and he'd worked to keep it that way. He didn't live in town, where he would have to deal with the day to day jockeying of life with others. His life was clean, crisp, orderly, and most of all, his own to manage.

If he and Hannah did join lives, she would be in the pilot's seat far more often than he was. He would once again be at the mercy of a force beyond his control. Even now, Horace was laying a bet which placed everything Buck owned at risk, his destiny in the hands of a woman and the fate of the cards.

But she *had* explained her plan beforehand, and he *had* been given the choice to decline that risk.

What's more, she hadn't done it out of sheer pique. Yes, Anstin had made a pass at her, and apparently a very clumsy one at that. But she could have wrought vengeance in any number of ways. Instead, she'd chosen to use that opportunity for the betterment of the people of Treasure Island, to ensure that their future lay in their own hands, in the hands of people she knew would look out for the interests of the island as a whole.

This wasn't a grudge bet. She'd seen and seized an opportunity to do something good for these people. His people. In fact, he realized, she stood to gain nothing from the match apart from the "right" to Buck himself, and she obviously understood that matters of the heart could not be dictated by the turn of a card.

A force of nature, yes, but a benevolent force.

And while she had been equally a force of nature in their lovemaking, there had been no selfishness in her dominance. He had not felt used. He had felt nurtured. Cherished. Precious. Protected. Carried away, yes, but to a place of beauty and peace and total sharing.

And how much of herself had she put at risk in those encounters? All of her, he realized. She'd known, at some level, where his emotional minefields lay. Yet she'd gone into them, revealing herself in ways that he might easily have rejected so totally as to leave her crushed.

Just as she would be crushed if she lost this match. He'd seen the tension in her face. Not for what she might lose, but for what *he* might lose. And for what the island might lose.

Hannah was in the pilot's seat, but she did not fly recklessly. If anyone could be trusted with his heart, surely she was that woman. And in that realization came another.

He had already given her his heart.

Win or lose, he had hitched his star to a force of nature. Now he had to trust her.

It was at that moment, about twenty feet away, that Horace cackled into the face of Bill Anstin and said, "Too bad you didn't bet more on Edna, huh?"

He might as well have waved a red flag in front of a bull.

CHAPTER THIRTY

HANNAH HAD chipped away at Edna's lead, picking up small pots when they were there to be had, but she still had only twenty-one hundred dollars to Edna's twenty-nine hundred. But with the big blind now at one-hundred-fifty dollars, she now had very little room to maneuver. With the standard opening raise now at four-hundred-fifty—nearly one quarter of Hannah's total chips—any contested pot was likely to be an all-in coup.

Thus, she had to fight the urge to let out a sigh of relief when Horace gave her a quick nod. Anstin was in for all of his assets. She could finally stop hustling, and simply play to win. But she would have to get the cards to do it.

She looked down at the Ace and Ten of Diamonds. It was a start. She counted out nine chips.

"Four-fifty."

"Call," Edna announced quickly.

This would be a battle, Hannah knew. She hadn't been raising often before the flop, trying to keep the pot size down while Horace was maneuvering with Anstin. Edna had folded to Hannah's few previous opening raises, obviously giving Hannah credit for a strong hand. This time, Edna's voice left no doubt that she was ready to make a stand.

But Edna had only called. If Edna had held an Ace with a Jack, Queen, or King, or a strong pair, she would have reraised. Hannah mentally ran through the hands that Edna was likely to simply call with. Hannah was a significant favorite against most of those hands, and only a slight underdog to the others. But all of that might change with the flop.

Ginny turned up the Ace of Clubs and the Eight and Nine of Diamonds. This gave Hannah a pair of Aces, as well as four Diamonds. Discounting the possibility that Edna had simply called with a stronger Ace than Hannah's, the only hands Hannah had to fear were Ace-Nine or Ace-Eight, giving Edna two pair, and pocket Nines or Eights, giving Edna three of a kind. Even if Edna had one of those hands, Hannah was hardly dead. Any of the nine remaining Diamonds would give Hannah a flush.

And weren't Diamonds a girl's best friend?

Yes, this was a hand Hannah was willing to play for all of her chips—for Buck and his airport, for Anstin's casino, for the people of Treasure Island.

"Check," Hannah said.

"Five hundred," Edna said.

"I'm all-in," Hannah replied before Edna had even finished counting out the chips.

"Damn," Edna muttered.

She studied Hannah as if trying to divine the secrets of the cosmos. And the longer she studied Hannah, the more Hannah became convinced that she wanted Edna to call. If Edna had three of a kind, two pair, or a big Ace, her chips would have flown into the pot. At best, Edna had a weaker Ace. More likely a smaller pocket pair, or a straight draw such as Seven-Six. Regardless, Hannah knew she was now a prohibitive favorite.

And her face must have reflected that confidence. Hannah mentally cursed herself as Edna finally folded. Edna had picked up on a tell. But what?

Even as Hannah scooped in the chips, she replayed the last two minutes in her mind. How had she spoken when she announced she was all-in? Had she adjusted her posture, moved her hands, drawn a deeper or shallower breath? Had she looked at Edna's stack, or her own? Or had Edna simply not had a hand that could call an all-in bet? Edna's play made sense, somewhat, if she held a small pair like Fives.

Hannah realized she could torment herself until the end of time looking for the answer to that question. She had won the pot, taking the chip lead in the process. Whatever else had happened was done and over with. It was one of the keys to success in poker: play *this* pot, not the last pot, and not the next pot. In poker, as in life, it paid to keep one's focus in the here and now.

Fifteen minutes later, Edna was on the ropes. She had gone into a shell, defeat staring her in the face, and Hannah was taking full advantage with aggressive raises on every pot. But Hannah knew Edna could not afford to sit around waiting for a big hand. At two-hundred-twenty-five dollars every two hands, the blinds were eating away Edna's stack. Now the shoe was on the other foot. Now Edna would have to pick a hand and go with it.

But the match was not over. If Edna won two big pots in succession, Hannah would be back in the corner, hoping to catch the right cards at the right time. Such was the nature of no-limit poker, and Hannah knew this was no time to relax.

"Four-fifty," Hannah said, lifting the corners of her cards. The Seven and Eight of Clubs.

"All-in," Edna said, without a moment's hesitation. "Another nine hundred."

Thirteen-fifty in the pot, Hannah thought. *Nine to call.* The odds were close, but not quite good enough. Not with only Eight-high. With two overcards, Edna was at least a two-to-one favorite. The pot was laying Hannah only three-to-two. And if Hannah called and lost, they would be nearly even in chips.

"Take it," Hannah said, pushing her cards out to Ginny. "Nice hand."

"Thanks," Edna said. "I needed one."

"That was the last hand at one-fifty," Bill Anstin said, his voice full of barely contained glee. "We'll take a five-minute break, and then resume at one and two hundred."

"YOU'VE GOT HER," Buck said, standing beside Hannah as she sat on the steps of the Lear.

Hannah nodded. "This is way too close, Buck. Why did it take Horace so long to get Anstin?"

"Horace knew how hard he could push, Sticks. Him getting you that massage was a stroke of genius. That must have been what pushed Anstin into believing you were the weaker player."

Hannah nodded wearily. "Maybe. Horace *did* wink at me."

"That man knows what he's doing. And so do you. If I didn't think so, I wouldn't still be in on this. Now stop worrying. You have thirty-five-hundred, right? That's not exactly what I call 'close.'"

"And she has fifteen-hundred," Hannah said. "What if she wakes up to pocket Queens on the next pot, and I have a hand like pocket Tens? With the blinds this big, all the money's going in. And if she wins that pot, she's back in the lead. There's no room left to play *poker,* Buck. It's down to push-and-pray, and in a game like that, Edna stands as good a shot as I do."

Buck studied her face. It had been a long day, and

the fatigue was etched on her features. The luminous dial on his watch said it was nearly midnight. Exhaustion, he knew, could drain the confidence of the hardiest soul. And it was draining Hannah's now.

"Maybe you're right, Sticks," he said. "Maybe Edna's as good in a shootout as you are. She probably is. But you know that's not all there is to it. You have the chip lead. *She* has to get lucky to win. You just have to not get *unlucky.*"

"There was a lot of L-U-C-K in that speech, Buck," she said. "That's the part that worries me."

"That's poker," Buck said.

"Railbird," Hannah said with a smirk.

He held up his hands. "Yeah, I know. Easy for me to say, right?"

She shook her head. "No, not really. You have more riding on this than I do. I'd be going nuts if I were in your place."

He laughed. "I've been doing some of that, too. But it is what it is, and I like our prospects. I like them a damn sight better than I would if Edna held the lead now."

"True," she said. "I'd just be happier if she hadn't hit that last pot. I'd be asking if you had the champagne ready, instead of chewing my nails."

Buck shook his head, chuckling. "That's one thing I've never seen you do. And I'm willing to bet you haven't done it in years."

"Clear nail polish," she said. "It tastes awful."

"And I suppose your point is that you would be chewing your nails, if you hadn't discovered that little trick?"

She nodded. "Yup. I did it for years."

"And thus you have good grounds for your anxiety?"

She cocked her head. "Huh?"

"I gave you a compliment," Buck said. "That I doubted you'd chewed your nails in years. You brushed it off, as if it were only the nail polish that solved the problem. I'm no psychiatrist, but it sounds like you're looking for reasons to put yourself down, at a time when you need to be building yourself up. Reinforcing your self-doubts is not a recipe for success, Sticks."

"Maybe not."

"Look at it this way," he said. "That nail polish didn't paint itself on your fingernails, did it?"

"Of course not," she said.

"*You* painted it on."

"Right."

"It wasn't the nail polish that solved the problem, Sticks. It was you. The nail polish was just a tool you used to do that."

"And therefore I'll win this match?" she asked, frustration apparent in her voice.

"Maybe you will and maybe you won't," Buck

said. "But you've given yourself the best chance you could. Yes, from here on it's mostly who catches the cards. But like I said before, Edna has to get lucky now, not you. You've played your way into a spot where your opponent will have to get lucky to beat you. That's all you can hope for in poker."

"So that's my pep talk, coach?" she asked.

For a moment he was taken aback by the sarcasm that seemed to drip with her words, but then she cracked just the tiniest smile and gave him a wink. He could get very used to that smile, that wink.

"That's right," he said. "That's the pep talk. Now go out there and win one for the Blipper."

"The Blipper?" she asked.

"Hey, if you lose this, I'll have to move in with my air traffic control buddy in Venezuela. He'd hate that."

"The Blipper." Hannah shook her head. "Don't quit your day job."

He leaned in and kissed her. "Just make sure I don't have to."

THE TRUTH WAS that she'd needed the pep talk. It had been a long time since her alarm had rung that morning, and her body was feeling it. But as she returned to her seat, adrenaline and residual caffeine combined to sharpen her senses. She could hear the faint calls of the night birds in the trees, the soft sigh of the sea breeze, the shuffles of feet and murmured words as people returned to watch the final act of this little drama. A drama whose full import they wouldn't know until the match was over.

Edna took her seat and smiled. "It's nitty-gritty time, I guess."

"Looks that way," Hannah said.

Edna extended a hand across the table. "Good luck, Sticks. For what it's worth, I think you're a stronger player than I am."

Hannah took the proffered hand. "Thanks, Edna. And good luck to you, too."

"If it were a money match," Edna said, "I'd offer a deal here. But I guess we can't split Buck between us."

"You get him from the knees down and I get the rest?" Hannah asked, laughing.

"Oh, you can have the knees," Edna said. "Give me his crotch and take the rest."

Buster growled.

"Well, at least we know what you want," Hannah said with a wink and a chuckle, reaching down to scratch Buster's neck. "But somehow I doubt Buck would like it that way. And I know Buster doesn't like the idea."

"Apparently not," Edna said, still smiling. "So, like I said, it's nitty-gritty time."

"That it is," Hannah said. "That it is."

And that really sucked, Hannah thought. All along she'd been trying to defeat a woman whom she'd come to think of as an arrogant, near-sociopathic stalker. And then, right at the point where Hannah was ready to pummel her, to utterly destroy and humiliate her, Edna shows some grace? Even good humor?

Yes, the old poker adage still applied: Hannah would bust her own mother if she could. But somehow, Edna's words took some of that particular fire away. On the other hand, there was still Bill Anstin, whose offenses were far more grievous than anything Edna had done.

And who stood to lose far more than the hypothetical rights to Buck Shanahan.

"Blinds are now one- and two-hundred," Anstin said. "It's money time, ladies."

Oh, yes, Hannah thought, suppressing a smile. And it's *your* money.

CHAPTER THIRTY-ONE

"SIX HUNDRED," Edna said, opening the first pot.

Hannah looked down at her cards. Pocket Fours. Any pocket pair was a strong hand in heads-up poker, but did Hannah want to risk doubling Edna's chip stack with only a tiny pair of Fours? Edna had only nine hundred dollars left in her stack, and she would certainly put the rest in on the flop, no matter what cards fell. The likelihood that Hannah would see a third Four on the flop was only one-in-eight. And she couldn't call Edna's all-in bet at the flop with anything less.

No, this wasn't the right time.

"Take it," Hannah said.

It was a tiny pot, and Hannah still had thirty-three hundred dollars against Edna's seventeen-hundred. But with only five more such pots, the match would be even. Then Buck's pep talk echoed in Hannah's mind. *Edna* has to get lucky to win. Hannah could afford to lay down a marginal hand. Edna couldn't afford to play one.

And that's what it came down to, Hannah realized. The pressure was on Edna to catch good cards. All Hannah had to do was not misplay bad cards, and trust that the luck of the deal would be at least close to even. She couldn't control the luck of the deal, but she could make the right decisions. As she'd done with the Fours.

Hannah folded a miserable Six-Deuce the next hand, not even contesting Edna's big blind. And the hand after, she mucked a Jack-Three to another opening raise. She now had three thousand to Edna's two thousand. Still a three-to-two lead. Edna's good cards would dry up. Hannah simply had to be patient.

Like an alligator lying in the reeds beside a pond.

Buster certainly hadn't spoken the words, but Hannah had no doubt whence the thought had come. She reached out with a foot and nudged his chin. *Yes,* she thought. *Just like you, Buster.*

Mmmhmm.

Edna flinched. "What was that?"

Hannah smiled. "Just Buster giving me a pep talk."

"One player to a hand," Edna said, shaking a finger in mock rebuke. "No fair getting help from an alligator."

Grrrrrr.

"Relax, Buster," Hannah said. "She's just joking."

"Yeah," Edna agreed. "I'm just joking, Buster."

Mmmhmm.

"That alligator has more sense than all of us humans put together," Ginny said. "And to think Sticks nearly jumped out of her skin when they met."

"Silly me," Hannah said.

Mmmhmm.

"Are you ladies going to play poker?" Anstin asked. "Or sit there discussing the local fauna?"

"You never learned, did you?" Hannah asked, looking up at him as she folded another abysmal hand.

Twenty-nine- to twenty-one-hundred.

"Never learned what?" Anstin asked.

"My dad used to tell a story," Hannah said, peeking at her next hand. The Jack and Eight of Hearts. Edna pushed in four chips, calling Hannah's big blind. Hannah tapped the table. "I'll check."

"What story is that?" Anstin asked.

"He was sitting in a game with T. J. Cloutier," Hannah said, barely watching as Ginny dealt out the flop. The Jack of Clubs, Three of Spades, and Nine of Diamonds. "This was back in the day, long before poker went big-time on television. It was illegal back then. The game was in a smoky room over a pool hall. Dad might have been worried about it, but the sheriff played every Tuesday and Thursday night, and he made more playing poker than the county paid him, so he was hardly going to bust the game."

"Four hundred," Edna said.

"Call," Hannah said, counting out the chips as she

spoke. "Now, Dad didn't know who T.J. was. Like I said, this was back in the day. But T.J.'s the new guy at the table, and he seemed to have some moves, so Dad's playing it careful, not getting too frisky."

Ginny dealt out the turn card, the Ten of Hearts. Hannah had top pair with her Jacks, but with Nine-Ten-Jack on the table, she was already drawing dead if Edna had a Queen and King in the hole. But King-Queen was a strong heads-up hand, and Hannah knew Edna would have raised with it before the flop.

"Another four hundred," Edna said.

Another teaser bet. A pair of Tens, perhaps? Two pair? If Edna had Nine-Eight, she had a made straight, but Hannah could split the pot if another Nine fell. There was now two thousand dollars in the pot, and it was only four hundred for Hannah to call. Was there a one-in-five chance that her Jacks were good, or that she would hit a Nine to split the pot? She decided there was.

"I'll call," she said. "So Dad's doing pretty well, up about two thousand, which was big money for him in those days. He's thinking maybe it's time to cash out and take his winnings. But then he gets pocket Kings."

Ginny dealt the river card, the Jack of Spades. It wasn't the Nine that Hannah had hoped for, but still it gave her three Jacks.

"I'm all-in," Edna said, pushing in her last nine-hundred chips.

"Now," Hannah said, "Dad looks at his stack, and then at T.J.'s stack. They have about the same amount of money in front of them, maybe three grand. And Dad's thinking to himself, if he takes it all here, he's going home that night with a five-thousand-dollar profit. That would have paid off his mortgage on the house, and the loan he'd taken to start his business. They're playing five-ten no-limit, so Dad makes it forty, and T.J. makes it a hundred more. Now Dad knows T.J.'s on a hand, and he can get all of the money in. But he just calls."

"Speaking of calling," Edna said, pointing to her bet, but Hannah ignored her.

"The sheriff's dealing, and he puts up an Ace, a King, and a Three," Hannah said. "Dad has a set of Kings, and he checks it, knowing T.J. will have to bet an Ace. And sure enough, T.J. bets two-fifty. Dad makes it seven-fifty, and T.J. gives him that steely-eyed look we've all seen on TV, and calls him."

Anstin nodded impatiently. "Like Edna said, *'speaking of calling.'*"

Hannah waved a hand and continued. "So the turn card is another Three, and Dad has Kings-full. He's thinking he can get Mom that new washer she's been wanting, and spruce up the house a bit. He checks, and T.J. checks back. Now he's sure T.J.'s on that Ace, maybe Ace-Queen or Ace-Jack, hoping to make his straight on the river. And damned if the dealer doesn't put a big, fat Queen of Spades up there on the last card."

"It's a nice story," Edna said. "But we're still in a pot here. It's nine-hundred to you."

Hannah nodded, but made no move toward her chips. "Dad checks, and T.J. puts in the rest of his money. Dad's sure T.J. has made his Ace-high straight, and just about beats him into the pot. Dad flips up his Kings, showing his full house. 'Now ain't that a sad thing,' T.J. says to him, 'cuz I only have these.'"

Hannah paused, letting the moment linger. "Then T.J. turns up a pair of Aces. And Dad goes home broke. That's when Dad learned the lesson you never learned, Bill."

"What's that?" Anstin asked.

Hannah turned to Edna. "I'll call. And your Ten-Three is no good, Edna. I've got three Jacks."

Hannah turned up her cards. Anstin looked as if he'd been kicked in the stomach.

"And that's about how Dad looked," Hannah said. "That's your lesson, Bill. Don't gamble with an unknown."

"Tell me you have that straight," Anstin said, his voice tight. "Edna, *tell* me you have that straight."

Edna's face was frozen. She turned up her cards. "No, she's right. Tens and Threes. She's won."

"Noooo!" Anstin shouted, looking stricken as the crowd erupted in applause. He waved his hands in a futile attempt to silence them. "You have to have the straight, Edna! You have to have the straight!"

"I don't," Edna said, the pain of defeat now displaced by a look of confusion. "She won, Bill. She gets Buck."

"But I've—you're supposed to have the straight," Anstin pleaded. "I'm supposed to…I've…."

"You've lost everything," Horace said, opening his betting book. "A million-six, if my numbers are right. That's your house, and your shares in the casino. But we'll let you keep the house."

"Of course," Hannah said, a tired smile on her face. "I'm sure Buck won't mind, would you, dearest?"

Buck shook his head. "A man needs a place to live. He can keep the house."

Now it was on Anstin's face that defeat turned to confusion. "What the hell…. But…why?"

Hannah's gaze was unflinching. "You shouldn't have pawed me that night in your Jeep, Anstin. If you'd only acted like a gentleman, I'd have kept to the bet with Edna. After that…well…someone had to stand up to you. For the way you treated me. For the way you've treated everyone on this island. They came here to get away from the very things you want to bring down on them, but you wouldn't listen. You had your bracelet and your dreams, and you were going to have things your way. Someone had to stand up to you. And we did."

"You sandbagged that first game," Edna said, the realization dawning as tears formed in her eyes. "You set him up. You set *me* up! You let me think there was hope!"

"No," Buck said, softly, touching her chin. "There was never hope. Not for us, Edna. You knew that. You always knew that, even if you didn't want to believe it. You can't win love on a game of cards."

She nodded, twisting her fingers together. She nodded toward Hannah. "And what about her?"

"She makes me feel safe again, Edna," Buck said. "She makes me feel whole again."

Edna scrubbed a tear from her cheek, forcing a smile. "So she's good for you?"

"Yes," Buck said. "She's good for me."

Edna paused a moment, then reached up to take Buck's hand from her chin and place it in Hannah's hand. "Then she's good for me, too."

"But what about *me?*" Anstin almost wailed.

Horace grinned. "If I remember the bet right, you've won a night with Edna."

"But I have *nothing!*"

"That's not true," Hannah said, pointing to his wrist. "You still have that bracelet. You're still a former world champion. Seems to me that ought to be worth a good job at a casino somewhere. Maybe even this one. But of course, I'm not the owner."

Buck smiled. "I'll be busy running an airport. And

Horace has his store. I'm going to deed the casino to the island, but someone will have to keep an eye on things, and make sure their casino is run well."

"I'll be an…employee?" Anstin asked.

Buck shook his head. "You'll be a part owner, just like everyone else. If they do well, you do well."

Anstin nodded. "I guess."

"Don't be an ass, Bill," Edna said. "They're giving you a lot more than they have to."

"You're right," he said. "I wonder why?"

"Because you're family," Horace said. "Every family has its jackass. You're ours."

"Gee, thanks," Anstin said.

"Eee-orrr," Edna said, playfully poking his ribs.

Eeeeohhhh, Buster echoed.

"Even Buster likes you," Hannah said. "After all, he hasn't eaten you yet."

Anstin scowled at Buster. "Thanks for small favors."

Buster replied with a yawn big enough to remind them *all* that he didn't have to be such a nice guy. But it was getting cold on the pavement, and the cold made him drowsy, so finally he gave in and settled his head down and closed his eyes, knowing the morning sun would reinvigorate him.

An alligator sigh of pure contentment escaped him as he felt a familiar hand scratch him gently. The two-legged woman would stay. Of that he was now sure.

CHAPTER THIRTY-TWO

A MONTH LATER, under blue Caribbean skies with balmy temperatures, a crowd once again gathered outside Buck's hangar. Buck and Anstin were facing each other down, the two last players standing in the island's most recent referendum on whether to replace the tiki hut casino with something sturdier.

Buck rather liked the tiki hut operation. Far below, on sparkling waters, a cruise ship lay at anchor and tourists gambled merrily, many of them playing between dips in the calm blue-green waters. The tiki huts had been easy to replace after the hurricane, and many islanders felt it ought to stay that way. Anstin was still dreaming of a bigger operation, even though he was only one of many shareholders now.

Déjà vu. Buck stared at a pair of sevens in his hand. The flop came with another seven and two queens. He was about to look at Anstin and grin, fairly certain his full house would beat anything Bill held.

But at that moment a corporate jet chose to swoop

in low, scattering cards everywhere. Hundreds of pairs of eyes looked up.

"Damn it, Sticks!" Buck let go of his now useless sevens. Anstin, in considerably better spirits these days since he'd begun dating Edna on a regular basis, started laughing until he was holding his sides.

A minute later, the jet touched down, a precision landing followed by a deafening roar as reverse thrust kicked in. Everyone covered their ears tightly.

Hannah powered the engines down at the far end of the runway, sparing everyone the racket they would have endured if she'd taxied back to the hangar.

A short while later, her trim figure appeared in the hatch. She descended the stairs and walked back toward them.

With the game over, or perhaps showing unusual sensitivity, the crowd began to melt away. Even Anstin took his leave. Cars began to roar down the still-damaged mountain road.

Buck waited for Hannah, hands on his hips. When she got close enough, he said, "You did it again. Sevens full."

She laughed.

He tried to maintain his glare, but simply could not. Laughing, too, he lifted her from her feet and whirled her around until the entire world seemed to spin with them.

"I missed you, Hannah," he said gruffly. "I missed you like hell."

"I've only been gone a week."

"A week too long."

Her smile softened and she caught his face between her hands, kissing him soundly. The greeting rapidly turned into something deeper, something more hungry. She was gasping for air when she pulled her head back.

"I've only got tonight. But after I deliver the plane tomorrow, I've got a whole week to spend here."

"You need to spend more time here, period." There was no laughter left on his face, simply a look of yearning. He was deadly serious.

"I can arrange that," she answered, still breathless. "I've been working things out in Houston."

"Good."

He swept her up, one arm beneath her knees, one beneath her shoulders and carried her toward his office and house. "'Cuz it's time to get serious."

"Serious? About what?"

He didn't answer until they entered the cool, quiet confines of his house. Then he lowered her feet to the floor, letting her slide against the entire length of his body. Her nearness was a touch of heaven.

"Serious about everything," he said gruffly. "I want to marry you. I want to make a family with you. Kids, and all. I want to have all those dreams I thought I'd lost forever. Hannah, I love you."

She gave him a crooked grin. "Boy, you *have* missed me." But her grin faded as she studied his face. "You're serious."

"I've never been more serious in my life."

For long moments he thought she was going to refuse. He watched every twitch of every little muscle in her face, trying to read her expression, and failing. For agonizing moments he felt as if he hung suspended over the pits of hell.

But then a soft sigh escaped her. Her eyes closed and she leaned into him, suddenly as soft and cuddly as a kitten.

"Yes," she said. "Yes. I love you, too, Buck. I want to be your wife."

"Wait a minute," he said huskily.

"Why?"

"Because we'll be partners. Real partners. I don't want to possess you. I want to be part of you."

She was silent for a moment, hugging him tightly around the waist. Then she gave a little giggle. "Two control freaks. I guess there's no other way."

He laughed then, too, as joy filled him. "Yeah, but in the end you'll always be the boss."

Another giggle escaped her. Then she grabbed his hand and began dragging him toward the bedroom.

"I'll be the boss in one place at least," she told him.

"Yes, ma'am," he said, desire thick in his voice.

Essssammm.

"Buster!" Hannah shouted. "Get those handcuffs out of your mouth!"

AUTHOR NOTE

No alligators were harmed in the writing of this book. No humans were harmed by alligators in the writing of this book.

Poker is not advocated as a way to settle disputes or make money, except on Treasure Island.

Flights to Treasure Island depart regularly. Return flights are unpredictable.

Buster will meet you at the airport. Bring a chicken.